ASHLEY LYNN EAST

The Nemesis Pact

To Vinny
May you always shine bright and go after your dreams!

Preface

THE NEMESIS PACT
PLAYLIST

I Forgot That You Existed
Taylor Swift

Bad Idea Right?
Olivia Rodrigo

Anyone
Demi Lovato

Don't Start Now
Dua Lipa

The 1
Taylor Swift

Blinding Lights
The Weeknd

Shut Up And Let Me Go
The Ting Tings

The Man
Taylor Swift

That's The Way It Is
Céline Dion

Some Nights
fun.

Lost In My Mind
The Head And The Heart

Electric Love
BORNS

Maggie May
Rod Stewart

Talk Dirty
Jason Derulo

Can't Fight This Feeling
REO Speedwagon

Electric Feel
Oracular Spectacular

Good 4 U
Olivia Rodrigo

Illicit Affairs

Taylor Swift

No One Knows
Queens of the Stone Age

Take Me To Church
Hozier

Kiss Me
Sixpence None The Richer

l'Il Be Around
CeeLo Green

Lover
Taylor Swift

I Know The End
Phoebe Bridgers

Vampire
Olivia Rodrigo

I Hate Myself For Loving You
Joan Jett & The Blackhearts

Cigarette Daydreams
Cage The Elephant

Hard Place
H.E.R.

Acknowledgments

To my parents, my sisters, and my sweet nieces—thank you for always cheering me on, no matter how chaotic the dream. And to my son, my biggest fan and brightest light—you are the reason I keep going. Your love means everything.

To my incredible book coach, amazingly patient editor, my generous beta readers, and every ARC reader who took a chance on this book—thank you for your time, your feedback, and your unwavering support.

And to every single person who purchased this book: you helped make a lifelong dream come true. I'm endlessly grateful. If you enjoyed the story, please consider leaving a review on Amazon or Goodreads—it truly makes a world of difference. Your support on social media is also so appreciated, and I'd love to hear from you!

Email me at ashleylynneast@gmail.com or DM me on Instagram at @ashleylynneastauthor

xo Ashley

1

Abby

It's like my brain short-circuits at the thought of standing here alone, vulnerable, painfully single in front of my past love, Marcus and his almond-munching, yoga-bodied girlfriend. I don't even know if my hair's doing that weird cowlick thing it does in the summer and I didn't even check before leaving the office if the mascara I've been rocking since yesterday was still pulling off that fresh-and-flirty thing or if it had already surrendered to full-blown exhausted raccoon energy.

And just like that, the absolute last person I want seeing me frozen like a deer caught in headlights shows up: *Jonathan Slack.*

Some kind of survival instinct kicks in, fight or flight, as he strolls over, probably ready to give me a hard time about my marketing pitch from this morning, even though we both know I crushed it.

"Hey, AJ..." he calls out, like we're best friends and not mortal workplace enemies who've spent the last six years secretly sabotaging each other's projects.

My ex looks surprised as Jonathan joins me and all I can think is… I wish Jonathan was someone else. Anyone else. *Literally anyone.* But the universe has a sick sense of humor, so of course it's my work nemesis making his way over at the exact worst moment. Because why not pour lighter fluid on my already flaming humiliation?

Without thinking, because thinking would've stopped me, I blurt, "This is my boyfriend, Jonathan," and yank him into me. My palms are sweating, my stomach's doing that awful swirly thing it does when anxiety throws a party and I'm dangerously close to blacking out from pure secondhand embarrassment.

Then I kiss him. I don't mean for it to become a mild make-out session, but… it sort of does. The second our lips touch, mine part like I haven't kissed another human in, oh, I don't know… years? Decades? What even *is* intimacy anymore? It's truly pathetic.

In spite of the suddenness, his lips part too and suddenly our tongues are colliding like they've been planning this rendezvous all along.

He tastes like bourbon and trouble and his hand slips to my lower back like it has every right to be there. I massage his tongue with mine. Yes, that's a sentence I never thought I'd narrate. And for a solid five seconds, we're locked in each other's arms. Well… more like *he's* in *my* arms.

I finally pull back and Jonathan looks stunned. Like, actually stunned. It's not every day you see the human embodiment of arrogance, dressed in an expensive, tailored three-piece suit, look like he just got hit with a glitter bomb of feelings. His whole face is frozen in disbelief. And honestly, I can't blame him. We've hated each other for six years. If anything, he should've expected a punch to the face, not a kiss so electric, it could set off a citywide blackout.

But then it happens. His face does that thing. That overly smug transformation where his cockiness starts to leak out like an oil spill. It's Grinch-esque. Just like the scene where the Grinch decides to steal Christmas and his mouth curls into that wicked, slow-motion smirk. Yeah. That's the exact look Jonathan Slack is wearing right now. And all I want to do is slap it off his face. How someone with an objectively attractive face can also look like a creature you instinctively want to run from is beyond me.

"Say *hello*, honey," I chirp, turning my body toward the ghost of my past and his long-legged goddess of a partner. Who even wants to be over 5'10" and genetically flawless anyway?

Jonathan shifts smoothly to my side like we're a well-oiled, completely stable couple who totally didn't just make out for the first time thirty seconds ago.

"Yesss…" he starts, dragging the word out like he's stalling for time. "I'm Jonathan. Abby's… boyfriend?"

Boyfriend? Of course he says it like a confused *Jeopardy* contestant. Why can't he just commit to the lie smoothly, like a normal deranged person? He's so infuriating. So deeply, cosmically pretentious.

Jonathan reaches out to shake the hand of my walking, talking, ill-fated failure of a relationship. Well, technically, engagement.

"Hey, buddy. I'm Marcus. Nice to meet you," my ex says, all plastered charm and high-end douchebag energy. He looks exactly how heartbreak should not look: relaxed, glowing, freshly moisturized. And the girlfriend? The woman radiates effortless glamour like she was born on a runway and raised on retinol.

"Oh shit," Jonathan says, loud enough to make me wince. "You're Abby's ex-fiancé?"

Marcus clears his throat. "Yes. Yes, I am. That was a long time ago." He straightens his posture like he's posing for a stock photo called *Man Pretending Not to Be Uncomfortable.*

Jonathan flashes a smile. The kind that makes you want to slap him *and* maybe kiss him again, which is severely unfortunate. "Is the AC okay in here, or are your feet still cold?" he quips.

God, he's such an ass. Mildly funny, though. If anyone can get under your skin and then poke around with the sharpest emotional needle he can find, it's Jonathan.

Marcus's handshake freezes, then drops.

"Whoa, it's all good, buddy," Jonathan continues, clearly enjoying himself. "If you hadn't left this little teapot at the altar, I'd never have had the chance to scoop her up. So… thanks." He winks. *Winks.* Then he turns to Marcus's girlfriend and extends his hand like a polite sociopath. "And you must be his girlfriend," he says. "I loved you on page twenty-three of the *Victoria's Secret* catalog."

The girlfriend gives him the world's most reluctant handshake before dropping his hand like it's contagious. She shoots Marcus a look, equal parts *why did you bring me here* and *is this your ex?*

"This is Jasmine," Marcus says, as if the rest of us aren't painfully aware that she's one of the *actual* Angels from the runway.

Who cares?… Okay, *I* care. I panicked when I saw Marcus and his airbrushed arm candy and did what any emotionally stable woman would do, I grabbed the first warm body next to me. And of course, it had to be *Jonathan Freaking Slack;*

hazelnut-colored hair so styled it looked like he rolled out of a cologne ad and just enough scruff to make him look like part rugged cowboy, part slick playboy bachelor. He must've been walking over to say something crude and soul-crushing, like always. That's basically his love language.

Admittedly, it could've been Dolores from accounting in her fuzzy cat sweater, oversized glasses and eternal scent of canned tuna standing next to me and I still would've declared her my new lover. That's how powerfully unhinged I became the second Marcus showed up.

Grabbing Jonathan into my already spiraling disaster of an evening? Possibly the lousiest decision of my adult life, stacked up against my failed engagement and the time I accidentally sent a meme of a dumpster fire to our boss during a team Zoom. Now Jonathan will never let this go and make me suffer with the memory of this night every time we run into each other in the break room.

I nervously chuckle. *What is wrong with me?*

"Well, this is great," I say brightly, trying to save face. I gesture to Marcus. "You're happy." Then I point to Jonathan, who's giving me the *wrap it up, Abby* look like I'm an awards speech running long. "I'm happy. This is… great."

"You said that already, *hun*," Jonathan says as he casually grabs my hand, like we hold hands all the time and I didn't just panic-kiss him into this mess.

"Have a pleasant evening," he adds with a perfect smirk, turning to Marcus and his baby giraffe of a girlfriend. "And try the goat cheese balls. They're amazing."

Then, without waiting for a response, he pulls me toward the other side of the bar. We weave past tables full of post-work happy hour regulars, dodging a server carrying a tower of martini glasses and someone loudly trying to Venmo-split mozzarella sticks. I should protest the fast exit. But, he saved me from saying *great* one more time and I'm pretty sure that would've been the end of me. The air shifts the further we get to the back of the bar. Less clinking glasses and flirtatious laughter, more buzzing tension and the scent of aged whiskey clinging to dark wood.

Jonathan backs me up against the side of the bar and gives me a look like he's about to read me the riot act. His expression screams *Are you insane?* But then something changes across his face. Maybe he sees the tears collecting at the corners of my eyes, even though I'm trying my absolute hardest not to let them spill.

"Listen, I know what you're going to say," I start, already bracing for impact.

"That you're a good kisser, AJ," he interjects, with that annoyingly conceited lift of his eyebrow.

He always calls me AJ. My name is Abigail Jean and while everyone calls me Abby, he refuses to. Jonathan calls me AJ because he knows it gets under my skin. And it does, mostly because when he says it, it's laced with egotism. He says it like it's a joke. Like I'm a joke. Though the truth is, I've never told him to stop. Because every time he says it, I get this flash of my grandpa in his recliner, yelling for me to come watch the Yankees with him. He used to call me AJ, too. Only when he said it, it sounded like love. Like home. He was obsessed with baseball and somehow made me a fan, too. I haven't been to a game in years, but I think about him every time I pass Yankee Stadium. Or, agonizingly, when Jonathan, of all people, calls me AJ. My grandpa would have hated Jonathan. And if he saw me standing here, talking to him like this, he'd be shaking his head and muttering that I was making a *rookie mistake*.

"No! Gross." I wrinkle my nose. "I mean…yes. Okay. Thank you. But I know you're probably confused."

"Oh, I'm not confused," he says, with maddening ease.

"You're not?" I shoot back.

"Duh. I've seen enough rom-coms to know exactly what your play was." He smirks, then grabs both my arms. "And I gotta say"—he gives them a little shake—"I didn't think you had it in you."

"Alright! Ease up on the shaking or I'll give you something to really remember me by," I snap, jerking my arms free. "Okay, so now that you know how pathetic I really am… what are they doing now?" I ask, trying to sound nonchalant and failing so hard.

Jonathan stays facing the direction they were standing while I stay pressed against the bar, my back to the crowd, eyes locked on his. Behind him is a wall covered in old Yankees memorabilia: photos, jerseys, autographs. All perfectly curated. Which makes sense, because we're at *The Yank*. One of New York City's most thriving, slightly-too-trendy bars. Yankee-themed, but in that high-end, exposed-brick, $18-cocktail kind of way. Every booth has cracked leather seats and the walls are lined with vintage Yankee pennants, like someone's grandpa created a Pinterest board titled *Baseball But Make It Sexy*. The drinks are legendary, with baseball pun names like *The Babe*, *Bronx Cheer*, and *Bleacher Creatures*. And yes, the goat cheese balls are elite. That's not even me being dramatic. I come here a lot. Unfortunately… so does Jonathan.

"They're just talking and sipping their drinks," he says, glancing in their direction. Then his tone shifts. "Oh, he's looking this way." He meets my eyes, like he's waiting for me to make the next move.

"What should I do?" I ask, already bracing for another bad decision.

"I think we should kiss," he says smoothly, cupping my face. "Make him jealous again."

His hands are warm and soft. Way softer than I ever would've expected from the King of Narcissism.

I nod before I can overthink it.

He leans in and kisses me again. This time, it's more relaxed—he's not caught off guard like he was when I panic-grabbed him earlier. His lips melt against mine and then his tongue slides into my mouth and... *oh okay.* It's kind of a great kiss. Not shocking, I guess, he *is* a Man-Whore. I'm sure he's an expert in all forms of intimacy: casual, passionate and apparently performative, public jealousy kisses.

I try not to overthink it and I kiss him back. Because this is for show. *Obviously.*

After what feels like a very long kiss for a totally-random-bar-moment fake-out, Jonathan finally pulls away. I awkwardly twist my neck to glance over my shoulder, trying to see if Marcus is still watching and to my shocking surprise, he's not looking this way. As in, he's *gone.* Full-on *Elvis has left the building* level of vanished. I snap my eyes back to Jonathan, who's wearing the world's brassiest grin.

"I thought you said he was looking!" I hiss.

"Oh, he was," Jonathan says innocently. "But then they left." He smiles wider.

"Then why didn't you stop kissing me?!" I shout, throwing my hands in the air.

He shrugs, totally unfazed. "Figured it was my payment for

playing the role of hot new boyfriend."

Hot. New. Boyfriend. My heart does this little skip in my chest, not because I like what he said, but because I'm livid.

"You are positively the worst," I snap, shoving him off of me. "And you're not even hot!"

He just waves his hand like I'm a gnat buzzing too close.

"Listen," he says, suddenly more serious, "why do you even care what that dumb fuck thinks, anyway?" His facial features harden and he looks me right in the eye. "He left you at the altar, AJ. Fuck 'em."

Then he raises a middle finger Marcus's way, not a care in the world. Only... Marcus is already gone, so now Jonathan's just flipping off the bartender Carl, who raises an eyebrow but doesn't say anything. Pretty sure this bar has seen worse.

I press my hand to my forehead. The bar lights suddenly feel too bright, the buzz of conversation too loud, like everything's turned up just enough to be unbearable and I can feel the early stages of a migraine already starting to tap-dance behind my eyes.

"I mean... technically, he left me at the bridal suite. Not the altar," I mutter.

"Whatever. Dude's still an ass," Jonathan replies without missing a beat. He reaches over me and flags down the bartender. "Hey Carl, pour me another one."

Of course, it's bourbon on the rocks. It's always bourbon on the rocks. And yeah, I hate that I know his drink order. But if I'm being brutally honest with myself? I know a lot about Jonathan Slack. More than I'd care to admit. More than I should, considering how much I hate him. I've picked up on way too many of his little details over the years. The way he rolls his sleeves before a pitch. How he smirks when someone compliments him. That exasperating self-satisfied nod he does when he thinks he's right, which, tragically, is often. He's tall, like over six feet, because the universe evidently has a type. He works out, has an obnoxiously good body, which he generously shares on social media like it's his civic duty. He drives a car so fast and expensive it surely has its own stock portfolio. From what I've gathered, not that I've looked into it, he's also wealthy, along with being obviously handsome and more than aware of all of the above. Basically, if self-satisfaction put on designer clothes and walked around with perfect bone structure, it'd be him.

But he's right. As much as it kills me to say it, I shouldn't care what Marcus thinks. Or who he's with. Or whether his supermodel girlfriend exfoliates with unicorn tears and sleeps on a cloud. My life is thriving. Give or take a few minor breakdowns and an ex-fiancé sighting. It's definitely better to be left before the marriage than during it. Right? Maybe I should get T-shirts made that say that. *Now that's depressing.*

2

Jonathan

Kissing Abigail Jean Madison was *not* on my 2025 to-do list. Actually, it wasn't on *any* list for *any* year in *any* universe. I've never looked at AJ as someone I wanted to hook up with. I mean, sure she's cute. But she's also a pill. A jagged little pill that gets lodged in your throat and takes three bottles of water to swallow.

I can't stand her. She's too perfect. Like, painfully perfect. No one is ever good enough for her and let me tell you that kind of energy? It kills the mood real fast. I don't care how desperate a guy might be, perfectionism is the ultimate boner killer.

Not that I'd know anything about desperation. Sex comes easy to me. Women come easy to me. I'm good-looking, fit, healthy, charming and did I mention I'm funny? Everyone says so. Even the people who don't like me, which admittedly is rare, struggle to explain why they don't like me.

But AJ? Oh, she has no problem telling me exactly why I annoy the hell out of her. I do it intentionally. It's fun. We butt heads more than ramming bulls. We've worked together for the past six years at *Vivid,* one of the top-rated marketing agencies in New York City. Technically, we're on the same team. But in reality? We're constantly locked in battle. Fighting for clients. Competing for campaigns and one-upping each other every chance we get. And man, when one of us wins? We gloat. Big time.

I've always been the more ostentatious one in our dynamic. Like the time we were both assigned to represent competing celebrity-endorsed seltzer brands. My team's seltzer campaign outperformed hers, by a lot, and naturally, I made sure she felt it. I filled her office with congratulatory balloons. Dozens of them actually. Floor to ceiling. She couldn't even reach her desk when she walked in. Then I paid Tim from the cleaning crew twenty bucks to come in, pop a few and say, "Oops, sorry. These were meant for Jonathan."

Wow, was she pissed. She's surprisingly kind of adorable when she's pissed. Not so much right now, though. Not as I look at her and notice the shimmer of unshed tears pooling at the corners of her eyes.

We all heard what happened. Left at the altar. Damn that's brutal. I wasn't invited to the wedding, obviously, she hates my guts. But most of the office was there and the stories spread fast. They said you could hear her crying from outside the venue. That she never even came out to face anyone. Apparently, her ex didn't even have the balls to tell her himself. He called his best man then bailed, leaving the poor bastard to deliver the news to AJ. I mean… what a fucking prick.

So yeah… seeing her tear up after running into that guy at the bar? It kind of makes me want to deck him. Not because I'm some knight in shining armor or anything. *Please.* Nevertheless, landing a solid punch on that asshole's face would arguably make me feel better and let's be honest, AJ would enjoy it too. If I wasn't wearing my Tom Ford three-piece suit, I probably would've. I'm not about to risk bloodstains on custom tailoring, let's be serious.

I'm not a metro guy or anything, I just have taste. *Expensive* taste. Designer clothes, a ridiculously fast sports car and an upscale apartment with a view. Thanks to my high-paying job and a very generous trust fund, I can afford the finer things in life. Why not? You only live once.

I know I shouldn't have messed with AJ or tricked her into kissing me again, even so... *wow*. That kiss was sensational. Who knew AJ could kiss like that? Certainly not me. Look, I'm a man, so undeniably, I'm attracted to all walking, talking women. But with AJ, it never even crossed my mind. Mostly because she hates me with the fire of a thousand suns. Trying anything with her would've been like reaching for a cactus and expecting roses. But then she kissed me and I kissed her back.

So, sure, sue me for wanting to plant one on her again. Well... I guess she *actually* could sue me. Though now that I'm reviewing facts, it wasn't against her will. She could've pulled away at any time. So why didn't she?

The fact that I'm sitting here thinking about this after she left is unsettling. I don't like when I don't have my shit together. And that kiss, *those* kisses, have me completely flabbergasted. I can't even join in on the usual shit-talking my coworkers are doing because all I can think about is whether she made it home okay.

What if she walked into traffic because she was depressed? *Fuck.* Why do I even care? She's made my work life miserable from the moment we met. Things got even worse after she became the jilted bride. It was like she developed a hatred for any man who so much as breathed in her direction. Which, okay *fair*, however… ease up, we didn't all leave you at the altar, AJ.

Maybe I should call her? *No, stop it.* She probably has my number blocked. I'm sure of it.

I *do* know where she lives from the annual Christmas party she throws every year. My invitation somehow always gets *misplaced*, regardless I show up anyway. Mostly to piss her off. Partly to see if any of the perky interns want to make a bad decision before the ball drops and they swear off terrible men like me for good.

Enough, I huff. She's fine. Drink your drink. Pick up the random hottie at the bar and go have fun. Put the kibosh on obsessing over AJ and her feelings.

I shift on the bar-stool, suddenly too aware of how loud everything around me is. The clink of glasses, the low buzz of conversation, the sound of Jerry from the office lying through his teeth to two new interns about once being on a commercial shoot with Jennifer Aniston. I glance at the door, next at my drink, then at the girl at the end of the bar giving me the kind of look I usually don't ignore. Yet I can't stop picturing AJ's face and that flicker of hurt in her eyes.

"Carl, cash me out."

Screw it! I'm going to check on her.

* * *

When I pull into AJ's picturesque little neighborhood, it hits me like a scene straight out of *Leave It to Beaver*. Not that I ever actually watched that show. I'm not ancient, but even I know it's the go-to reference for overly wholesome, squeaky-clean suburbia. Of course she would live somewhere like this. In a city that never sleeps, where the best kind of chaos happens at 2 a.m., AJ somehow found the one pocket of New York that feels like it should come with white picket fences and fresh-baked muffins. It's so *her*. Frustratingly neat. Frighteningly calm. Annoying in that specific AJ way that makes you want to understand it more, even as you swear you never would.

I slide my car into a spot lined up evenly with the freshly power-washed sidewalks and step out, starting my walk toward her door. There are maybe ten little cottages in this neighborhood and I would bet good money AJ bakes cookies for all of them and offers to watch their dogs when they go on vacation. She's such a damn Goody Two-shoes.

Just as I hit the lock button on my key fob, AJ walks out of her house with a trash bag in hand, sniffling like she's been crying for the last hour. Which, she probably has.

"Jesus Christ!" she yells, nearly dropping the bag. "Jonathan! I almost threw this trash bag full of photo frames at you!"

"It wouldn't be the first time you tried to hurt me, AJ," I shoot back with a laugh.

Even though I'm, in reality, being serious. One time, during a team meeting, I stood up to give some insight about a new client. As I went to sit back down, *boom*. Chair gone and I hit the floor like a sack of bricks. Not to my surprise, who was sitting across from me with the most innocent face on Earth? *AJ*. I know she slid her scrawny legs under the table and kicked my chair out from under me. No one else would've risked it. She's bold like that from time to time. In the moment, I was furious. Mortified even. But looking back? Okay, yeah, it was kind of funny and honestly... well played.

"What are you doing here?" she demands, tightening her grip on the trash bag like she's ready to use it as a weapon. "Please don't tell me you're hooking up with the new neighbor, Isabella."

Isabella? Now *that's* interesting. I shake it off. Focus, Jonathan, one woman at a time.

"As exciting as that sounds," I say, "I'm here to make sure you didn't jump off your one-story roof."

She glares.

I keep going. "You know you'd only break a leg and then I'd spend the next six weeks making fun of your bulky cast and refusing to move out of the way when you tried to hobble around with crutches."

"Ha. Ha. You're *so* funny," she says, totally unamused

"I try," I shoot back with a bow of my head.

"No, I'm fine. You can go now," she says, waving me off like a fly and heading toward the dumpster.

"You said picture frames," I say, eyeing the trash bag. It's lumpy and suspiciously bulky. I reach over, yanking it from her grip.

"Hey! Give me that back!" she snaps.

"What's in this?" I ask, already half-knowing.

She huffs. "If you must know everything about my life, it's old pictures of me and Marcus."

I squint at her, confused and maybe pitying her just a little. "And you're just now throwing them out? Didn't he leave you like… three years ago?"

"Almost four," she says, equal parts sarcastic and tragic.

"My God, AJ. Yeah, okay here, get rid of them," I say, holding out the bag like it's radioactive.

She snatches it back, turns to walk away, then stops. She

turns again and starts walking toward me.

"Why are you *reallllly* here, Jonathan?" she asks, her voice suspiciously sweet as she steps closer like a predator circling prey.

Suddenly, I get the unsettling feeling that this may be how I die. Hell hath no fury like a woman scorned or a woman who's also your work nemesis and has spent six years low-key plotting your demise.

"I told you. I wanted to see if you were okay," I say, instantly regretting ever thinking showing up at her place was a solid gesture.

"There's always some ulterior motive with you, Slack," she says, eyes narrowing.

Ah. There it is. She only calls me *Slack* when she's about to unleash hell.

I put my hands up in mock surrender. "I swear." Now realizing I'm starting to sweat under my jacket, despite it being a breezy seventy degrees and unseasonably cool for summer in the city, I clear my throat. "I'm only making sure my favorite sparring partner is okay and will be at work tomorrow to bask in the glory of my marketing genius." I'm clearly talking about the fact that we have a new partner joining the firm. Silent partner, technically. I've already put together a short but highly impactful presentation to impress them.

"Trust me, Slack," she says, staring deep into my soul like she's trying to melt me from the inside. "I would never miss an opportunity to blow you away with *my* presentation for the new partner." She smirks.

Yes, there she is. Okay, so no jumping off a building tonight.

"You know," I say, grinning, "after that kiss tonight, when you say *'blow'* you get me—"

"Gross! *Stop!*" she shrieks, swinging the shiny black trash bag toward me like it's a weaponized piñata. It nearly clips my shoulder. "Now leave me alone so I can finish *Love Island* and drink my wine in peace."

She stomps off to the dumpster, flips the lid open and a wave of New York City smelly garbage hits me square in the face. She doesn't even flinch. She slams it shut with the kind of energy that says she's imagining it's my face.

From across the street, a voice calls out. "You okay, my dear?" It's her neighbor, some angelic older woman yelling from her front window like it's a sitcom.

"Yes, Shirley! I'm okay. Thank you!" AJ waves, like she didn't just threaten me with a literal bag of broken memories.

As much as everyone loves me, they love AJ just as much. Which is wild, considering we are walking, talking opposites. I stare at her for a few more seconds, then turn to head back to my car.

"See you tomorrow, AJ," I call out over my shoulder.

Then I feel it while walking to my car, that skinny, Oura-wearing middle finger of hers slicing through the air, sheer heat shooting straight into my back. *God, she really is the sweetest.*

3

Abby

Everyone told me not to go back to work so soon. My parents. Even my sister, who secretly hates me. They all insisted I take more time off, to reset, to heal, to "process what happened," whatever that means. But I didn't want to sit around in my wedding dress, surrounded by snot-filled tissues, watching *Sex and the City: The Movie* on repeat while Carrie gets left at the altar. At least Big realized he was an idiot and turned the car around. Mine didn't even show up to the venue. No, mine waited all day, *all damn day,* until we were about to walk down the aisle, then called his best man to tell him he wasn't coming.

I remember it like it was yesterday. Well, yesterday plus almost four years. I was in the bridal suite with my bridesmaids, all of us laughing and giggling. I was trying not to drink more champagne even though I desperately wanted to. What I wouldn't give for a *Back to the Future* moment. To time travel back to that exact second, before Mike, the infamous best man, walked in and dropped the worst news I've ever received.

Second worst, technically. Losing my grandpa still holds the crown.

I was so happy in that luxury suite, perching there in my foolish little bubble, moments away from becoming Mrs. Abigail Jean Taylor. Wife of the uber-wealthy Marcus Taylor. Handsome, kind, practically perfect Marcus Taylor. God, I was an idiot. What's comical is when Mike walked into the bridal suite and started talking, I laughed. I genuinely thought he was playing a joke on me. Mike was always the funny guy in Marcus's group, the king of one-liners, bad puns and awkwardly timed dad jokes. But not this time. This time, Mike looked pale and clammy. Like he already knew the news he was about to deliver wasn't going to go down easy, definitely not like a cold glass of lemonade on a hot day.

I remember sitting there, completely still, for what felt like hours, but was probably just a few seconds, after he told me Marcus wouldn't be coming. My breathing started to change. My chest got tight. My sister, who was never particularly kind to me growing up, immediately grabbed my hand. She must've known I was about to either pass out or puke. I did both. Puked, then passed out. Real classy.

When I came to, Lila was fanning me, my sister was holding my curls off my neck and my mom was crying. Yes. *Crying.* Like... Mom. For once, could I be the center of attention?

I repeated Mike's words as a question, my voice shaking. "He's not coming?"

The girls around me all nodded *yes* and that's all it took. I broke down. Like full-blown, 1920s silent film actress sobbing. Gasping, hiccuping, shaking. Pretty sure half the guests waiting outside could hear me.

Eventually, my mom told Lila to sneak me out the back

and take me to her place. The limo was already waiting, the one that was supposed to whisk Marcus and me away to our dream honeymoon in Turks and Caicos. Instead, it carried a shell-shocked, dumped bride and her best friend, who held my hand the whole way and swore she could feel every ounce of my pain.

Lila and I grew up together in the city, which feels like a rare thing nowadays. We went to Trinity School from kindergarten through twelfth grade, side by side the whole way. She's always been my rock. Long, straight black hair and a smile that could light up any room. She was the Veronica to my Betty. The guys loved that growing up. We never fought over anyone. Even when we met Marcus at the same time, she could tell I was smitten. I still remember her grinning and saying, "Go get 'em, Betty," with a wink.

Thank God she was there for me that day, the day I got left at the altar. She was the one who grabbed my shoes and my dignity, snuck me out the back of the venue and climbed into the getaway limo with me like we were making a dramatic escape. She didn't try to fix it. She didn't say the wrong things. She just showed up. And in the worst moment of my life, that was everything. She even supported me when I insisted on going back to work just three days later. She walked me to the office every morning that week, holding my hand like it was nothing. Tourists probably thought we were a couple, however honestly? I didn't care. They weren't entirely wrong, either; Lila *is* into women. Well… more bi, I guess. She doesn't see gender, as she likes to say. I've always admired her for that, for being so confident and unapologetic about what she wants.

Sometimes I wonder what it would be like to be that bold. Just walk up to a cute guy at a bar and hand him my number.

Or not hold the door open at Starbucks so I could unusually be first in line for once. Yep. Total rebellion fever over here.

My first day back at work was just three days after the disaster Marcus left in his wake. My eyes were still a little puffy, but Lila said it made me look youthful, hid the wrinkles around the corners of my eyes. Silver lining, I guess. Most of my coworkers had been at the wedding, so of course they already knew. The ones who hadn't been? They definitely heard about it by lunch. Everyone treated me like I was made of glass. Like if they said the wrong thing, I'd shatter into a million mascara-stained pieces.

Everyone *except* Jonathan Slack. I already hated his entire existence, but between wedding planning and keeping up with my workload, we'd gone several months without one of our signature knock-down, drag-out workplace feuds. Which, truthfully, was personal growth for the both of us. There was never a question of whether to invite him to the wedding. He wasn't my friend. He wasn't even friendly. And I once overheard him say Marcus must be a "complete pussy" if he was willing to marry a "ball buster like Abby." So yeah. No invitation was ever given to him.

My first morning back at the office actually started off shockingly well. Someone left the good bagels in the kitchen and no one had touched the everything one yet and my boss, Victoria, tall, cold, vein-covered Victoria; unexpectedly hugged me. *Hugged me.* It was almost unsettling. She hadn't come to the wedding. Claimed "weddings aren't her scene," which was rich coming from someone I'm pretty sure has been married three times before. But hey, I wasn't mad. I didn't exactly picture her slow-dancing under fairy lights with the open bar crowd.

Things stayed quiet and respectful for the first few hours…
until Jonathan strolled in, late, dragging his suitcase behind
him and still tan from whatever luxury vacation he'd been on.
Apparently, he'd skipped town the weekend of my wedding.
Of course he did. While I was busy getting publicly humiliated,
he was probably on a yacht somewhere, sipping a Mai Tai,
blissfully unaware that my life was imploding and off living
his best tan-lined, responsibility-free life.

Jonathan appeared in my office, airy, cocky and far too
pompous for someone who hadn't even bothered to show up
on time that morning. He placed a large box of chocolate on
my desk.

"Congrats on your wedding, AJ," he said, smirking. "Even
though I still can't believe he actually married you."

I opened my mouth to respond, but without fail he cut me
off.

"Don't thank me. This is *the* viral chocolate from Dubai.
Luxurious and delicious." He gestured proudly toward the
gold-trimmed brown box like he was offering up a treasure.
"Figured I'd bring your husband something to snack on while
he tries to drown out that high-pitched voice of yours."

I was speechless. Clearly, no one had told him I didn't get
married. That I'd been left at the altar. And while he's a world-
class prick… even *he* wouldn't mock me for that. *Would he?*

"You know what?" I said, uncrossing my arms and shoving
the box back across the desk. "I don't want it."

He blinked, stunned, like the idea that someone might reject
him or famous chocolate had never once occurred to him.

"I was attempting to be nice," he muttered, snatching the
box and turning toward the door.

Then, like he couldn't help himself, he tossed out one last

jab over his shoulder.

"You better have handcuffed that husband of yours to the bed, or he'll leave you the second he realizes how annoying you really are." He chuckled and slammed the door shut behind him.

Tears rushed to my eyes before I could stop them. My chest tightened, panic bubbling to the surface faster than I could blink. Jackie, my next-door office neighbor, must've heard the whole thing. She rushed in without knocking, knelt beside me and wrapped her arms around my shaking shoulders. She rocked me gently, the way I imagined she did with her four kids at home.

"It's okay, love," she whispered. "Breathe. Breathe. Let it out." Her hands were soft, her voice even softer and somehow, in that moment, her kindness held me together better than any piece of chocolate ever could.

Word of my panic attack must've spread quickly, because for the rest of the day, people kept stopping by to check on me. I didn't mind the sympathy, but I wasn't exactly an attention whore like Jonathan. Or my mother, for that matter. Still, it was nice to know I worked with good people. Well... *mostly* good people.

During lunch, I was walking back from the break room when I spotted Jonathan sitting in my office. Glass walls, great for letting in natural light. Also great for watching your nemesis make himself at home uninvited.

For fuck's sake. I mumbled under my breath, then whipped the door open so fast I nearly took it off the hinges.

"Get out of my office," I snapped.

He looked startled but didn't move.

"Listen, AJ... I didn't know about—" He paused. "I didn't

know that—"

"Oh, you didn't know my life blew up while you were tanning on some fancy yacht, eating grapes off a wannabe Gigi Hadid's belly button or whatever the hell you were doing?" I cut in.

"Yes. Okay. I didn't know you were... dumped." He cringed. "I mean, left. Shit. I don't know what to say, but I just... I didn't know."

"How about you just say, *I'm sorry, Abby. I'm sorry this happened to you.* Then take your selfish, stuck-up, arrogant, cocky face out of my office and don't talk to me again."

Was that harsh? Maybe. Okay, yes. I might've let out everything I'd been wanting to scream at Marcus and accidentally aimed it at the second-worst man I know.

Jonathan's expression dropped. Not quite sad, because that would require him to have emotions. But maybe... somber. Like defeat, covered in fancy cologne.

"I'm sorry, Abby," he said quietly.

Then he placed the box of chocolate, still in his hands, I hadn't even noticed, on my desk and walked out. As cruel as it may have been, it felt so good to finally tell him off.

For a few weeks, Jonathan avoided me. I didn't care. Heck, I barely noticed. Eventually, he started talking to me again, but only when absolutely necessary. Just the basics, limited to mutual ads and shared clients. No jabs. No jokes. No chocolate bribes. Over time, things went back to normal.

I went back to normal. No more sobbing myself to sleep. No more skipping dinner or rewatching breakup montages on TV. I started going out again, with Lila, coworkers, the occasional blind date I wasn't emotionally ready for.

Life moved on and like clockwork so did the feud between

me and Jonathan. Which, weirdly, made me feel… better. Like if I wasn't butting heads with him at work, everything felt too simple. Too normal. It's probably unhealthy, but fighting with Jonathan? Kind of keeps things interesting.

4

Jonathan

I couldn't sleep last night. Not even a little. I tossed around like a rotisserie chicken in the overpriced sheets I splurged on. Too hot, too cold, brain doing backflips. The city lights leaked through my blinds like they were personally offended I was trying to rest. I'm usually not someone who lies awake obsessing about other people's problems or even my own, to be honest. I'm a firm believer in the "what happens, happens" mindset. Control what you can, accept what you can't, move the fuck on. It's a simple yet efficient psyche.

I've carried that mentality ever since I was nine and getting bullied for my lisp and crooked teeth. My younger brother was four; cute as hell, no awkward phase in sight and I was the *weird* kid who couldn't say his S's and looked like his teeth were trying to flee his face.

Eventually, I grew out of the lisp. My parents got me braces I had to wear for three years, which sucked, but they worked. I didn't let the bullying wreck me. And once I went from ugly duckling to, well, the stud I am today, I figured I'd be okay.

Everyone gets bullied. It happens.

Except maybe my brother. He somehow skipped the entire awkward stage. Life's always just... worked for him. Now he's in med school, working his ass off to become a surgeon. Which is, I'll admit, insanely impressive. I'm proud of him. Always have been. He doesn't really need me anymore as *the big brother* and that's okay. I've gotten used to standing on my own. Not a loner, per se. I like people. I like going out, hanging with friends, being the wildly charming, sex-positive man that I am. However, even that gets old faster than you'd think.

Still, none of that mattered this morning. I couldn't take a day off today, even though I gravely considered it. Our boss was bringing in the new silent partner, the one who bought a majority stake in the company and they were planning to spend the week with us, learning what we do and how we help hundreds of companies sell their products to the masses.

Technically, Victoria is my boss, though she doesn't own the company. The place was founded by four original partners like some kind of marketing Mount Rushmore and over the years, they slowly retired and sold off their shares. Charles, the last of them, ended up as the sole owner.

Nonetheless, good ole Charles is pushing eighty and apparently decided it was time to bring in someone young, fresh and most importantly... loaded. So he sold fifty-one percent of the company to some mystery millionaire, which basically makes them the new head honcho.

No one knows anything about them. No name. No face. No idea if they're a man, a woman, or a magician with an MBA.

Victoria's been tight-lipped about the whole thing, then suddenly, surprise, our "silent partner" decided they want to be a hands-on silent partner. Which kind of defeats the point, I'd imagine. Victoria didn't get a say in the matter. None of us did.

So now it's the big day and I've prepared a fancy, mind-blowing *welcome* presentation to highlight the office's success. Okay, more *my* success.

I'm not one to kiss the ring, however I'm also not stupid. I know how to rub shoulders with the right people and that typically gets me exactly where I want to go.

After I manage to survive the Starbucks line, I head toward the office. Outside, the usual Manhattan street circus is in full swing; someone yelling at a parking meter, a guy in a suit pacing with a Bluetooth in his ear like he's closing a shady Wall Street deal and a woman walking three poodles dressed better than I am.

That's all white noise compared to running into AJ just outside the building. She's wearing beige slacks, Tory Burch flats and a long-sleeve silk top that's… off-white? Ivory? Some sort of expensive neutral. Her hair is styled like it always is; mostly straight, parted to the side, with a little wave at the ends. I hate that I know her hairstyle *that* well. She spots me and immediately speeds up, like my presence physically offends her.

I try to hold the door open for her and flash my best smirk, but shocker, she's not buying it. She lets out a tiny huff and pushes the door open herself. Then she speed-walks across the atrium toward the golden elevator doors like she's gunning for an Olympic medal.

Unfortunately for her, she doesn't make it in time. The elevator's still closed, which gives me just enough time to catch up and pull up beside her. Close enough that our arms almost touch. God, I love annoying this woman.

She mumbles something under her breath I don't catch, so I lean a little closer.

"Well, good morning, AJ," I say, turning to hit her with my signature smile.

"Fine. Hi. Good morning," she mutters back, like she just lost an arm-wrestling match.

Naturally, I decide to start messing with her early today.

"I had the craziest dream last night," I say casually. "I was sucked into a vortex."

She doesn't look at me.

I wait a beat. "And the vortex… was *your* lips."

Her eyes roll so hard I'm surprised they don't fall out of her head.

"I am *literally* going to knock that coffee out of your hands," she snaps.

"Wanna share it?" I ask, taking a sip for dramatic effect. "My lips have been on it, but I assume that's not an issue for you." I wink.

Just then, Victoria walks up and we both immediately straighten up. Not that I'm scared of her, still there's this little thing called a promotion to *Vice President of Marketing* happening soon, once Allen finally retires, and I'd love to snag his sweet office. Be the one calling the final shots on our biggest ad campaigns. Also, AJ wants the position too. Which means I want it more, so I can rub it in her face for at least a year.

Translation: being professional and overly pleasant to Victoria is key for the next few weeks.

Allen's always taken more of a liking to AJ, but that's only because he takes more of a liking to *every* woman in the office.

What a creep.

I might be a suave flirt, but I know how to read the room. I'm not some desperate, screwy guy. Plus, let's be honest, women flock to me. It's not exactly a concern I struggle with.

"Good morning, you two," Victoria says with a smile.

AJ and I shoot each other a look. Victoria's not mean, but she's definitely intimidating and not exactly the small-talk type. AJ even invited her to her wedding and Victoria declined. Though, from what I heard, she still sent AJ an expensive gift.

Now I'm wondering… did AJ get to keep all her wedding gifts, or send them back? Hmm. Might have to ask her one day, preferably when she's really pissing me off. That'd shut her up for a few hours.

"Might I say, Victoria," I begin, flashing a polished smile, "you look incredible in that Chanel jacket." I know my designers. "And you seem to be in an excellent mood," I add, shooting AJ a look that says *yes, I know I'm laying it on thick.*

"Thank you, Jonathan," Victoria replies, pulling a tube of lipstick from her matching Chanel purse. She applies it with one hand, flawless as always. "But I haven't made any decisions yet about Allen's replacement."

"Of course. Just being friendly," I say smoothly.

AJ huffs beside me.

Victoria turns to her. "How are you this morning, Abigail?"

AJ blinks, clearly stunned that Victoria's addressing her with actual warmth.

"I'm good, thank you," she says, smiling politely.

That smile? Ugh. *Too* perfect. Straight teeth, the ideal shade of white. The kind of smile that says, *yes, I probably floss twice a day and my dentist sends me Christmas cards.*

The elevator doors open and the three of us step on. Inside

the elevator is so awkward I half-expect it to start narrating our thoughts. Some low-budget jazz music trickles out of the speakers like it knows it's making things worse. AJ stands just far enough away to make it clear I'm lucky she's not using her purse as a weapon. I hit the button several times for floor seven, our floor. Our office takes up the entire level. The building itself isn't massive, it's got some age to it; old bones with a modern face-lift. It was fully remodeled about ten years ago to give it that exposed-brick-meets-sleek-glass vibe.

Charles, our soon-to-be-retired owner, also owns the building. Which reminds me, I really should look into investing in real estate. Especially in New York. My money's just sitting in a trust. Sure, it's gaining interest, but I could be doing something smarter with it. I never seem to have the time. Or maybe just not the urge. I will admit, lately I've been wanting more out of life. What "more," exactly? I'm not totally sure. Just… *something*. Maybe that's why I didn't sleep last night. Maybe that's why I feel like I'm running on fumes this morning.

The elevator dings and we all step off.

Victoria wastes no time beelining to her office, hers is the best one on the floor. Floor-to-ceiling windows, panoramic city view, total boss energy. She probably wants to prep for the ten o'clock meeting with our new partner, which explains the extra pep in her stilettos.

As I move to step off the elevator, AJ tries to do the same and we bump into each other.

She smells good. Like… *really* good. Floral, with a hint of citrus underneath. How have I never noticed how good she smells?

"Excuse me," she snaps, brushing past me like I'm in the way, which I guess I am.

She isn't always this jumpy. I assume she's more embarrassed than anything. I mean, we did suck face last night. *Twice.* Hard to come back from that in the fluorescent light of day.

I stroll through the floor and into my office. The best part? The giant window overlooking the city, just enough skyline to trick me into thinking I matter. My desk, on the other hand, looks like a crime scene: half-stapled reports, coffee rings and a plant I've never water that somehow refuses to die.

I guess I should be thankful I have plenty of space for my desk, bookshelf and two guest chairs. Once I get that promotion though, it's game over. My new office will have a whole second side; enough room for a couch, maybe a sleek table, possibly even a flat screen so I can flip on the news or watch our latest ad campaigns in peace. *Manifesting*, as the TikTokers say.

Manny, one of my closest friends and one of the only people here who tolerates me, approaches my desk with his usual too-much-energy entrance.

"Man, you left too early last night," he says, half-shouting.

"Why?" I ask. "Did I miss Beau dancing on the tables again?"

"Nah," Manny laughs. "Beau was tame. But someone did say they spotted a Victoria's Secret model."

"Yeah. I saw her," I say casually, opening my laptop. "Actually met her."

Manny freezes. His eyebrows shoot up.

"What? Bro. You didn't even tell me."

I shrug. "She was with AJ's ex."

He blinks, stunned into silence.

"…Wait, why were you with AJ and her ex?" The excitement

fades from his voice. Everyone knows me and AJ don't exactly braid friendship bracelets in our free time. Six years of animosity isn't exactly subtle.

"I wasn't *with* them," I say, waving a dismissive hand. "I saw her talking to them at the bar and walked over. That's when I found out it was her ex-fiancé."

Manny's quiet, clearly trying to figure out what to say next.

"How was he?" he finally asks.

Right. Manny *knows* Marcus. He *was* invited to the wedding. He went. He's also the one who gave me the play-by-play after the fact. After I made the brilliant decision to mock AJ three days later, without knowing she'd been left at the altar. Yeah, not my proudest moment.

"He seemed normal," I say with a shrug. "Shorter than I expected."

"Damn," Manny says, his voice softer now. "That must've been rough for Abby."

I nod, as my mind drifts. Not to Marcus. To her. To last night.

Her full, warm lips. That slow exhale she let out mid-kiss, like maybe, *just maybe*, she was into it. *Did I turn on AJ with my kiss?* Jesus. Now that curiosity is stuck in my brain like a splinter.

"Hello? Earth to Jonathan." Manny waves a hand in front of my face.

I blink the thought away. "Sorry. What was the question?"

"Was Abby okay?" he asks.

"Oh. Yeah." I nod, lying through my teeth. "She seemed fine."

She wasn't fine. She was spiraling. Fiery in that way I weirdly kind of like. But I'm not about to sit here gossiping with Manny like we're swapping stories at a brunch table. I'm too classy for that and too busy to care.

"Go to your office," I say, waving him off. "I gotta look over my presentation."

"Right. Okay. See you in there," he replies, shooting me his half-goofy, half-sincere smile before walking off.

* * *

Once I had the rest of my papers organized, I wander into the break room for a coffee run. The scent of someone's day-old Pad Thai fills the room. I spot Tanya talking to Elaine, the office gossip hens. God love 'em. There's always one. Or in our case, two. They stop whispering the second I walk in.

"Oh. Hey, Jonathan," Tanya says, waving awkwardly like she was just caught hiding a body.

"Hi, ladies." I flash them my best confident-peacock smile. "Whatcha girls gossiping about?"

I grab my usual cup, refill it with coffee, add a splash of creamer and stir like it's the most normal morning ever; despite the fact that Tanya is blinking at me like I'd grown a second head.

"Well…" Tanya starts.

Elaine smacks her arm. "Nothing," she adds quickly. "Just excited to meet the new partner."

I pause mid-stir and glance over at them.

They're lying, obviously. Elaine is the alpha, but Tanya oozes as the weaker link. The one who cracks first under pressure. I turn, zeroing in.

"Tanya," I say leisurely. "What's going on?"

Tanya's eyes dart to Elaine like she's holding in a secret and her bladder at the same time. Elaine rolls her eyes and gives a subtle *fine, go ahead* shrug.

Tanya squeals, then blurts it out. "I saw you and Abby making out last night."

I nearly drop my coffee. The smell of rich, roasted caffeine is suddenly replaced with the stale whiff of the air conditioning. Like the very aroma of *you're so screwed*, drifts around me.

The Yank isn't exactly a massive bar, but it's not tiny either and later in the evening, the lights get low, the vibes get flirty and I *really* thought we were in the clear. The group of coworkers had been sitting way in the back. I figured no one saw the first kiss. Or the second. *Especially* not the second.

I loosen my brand-new Brooks Brothers aqua-blue tie and clear my throat.

Tanya keeps going. "I got to the bar late and when I walked in, I saw you and her... you know. Making out. By the Yankee memorabilia wall."

Ah yes. *That* kiss. The second one. The one that lasted way longer than it should've, mostly because I didn't want to stop. I liked kissing AJ. As much as I despise her, I have to admit she's a hot kisser.

"I see," I say, calm as ever. I'm not a panicker. I'm an improviser. I'm a salesman. That's why I'm great at my job.

"You see, ladies," I begin again, slipping into full-on pitch mode, "AJ and I happen to share a very passionate love for baseball."

They blink, therefore I press on.

"We got into one of our usual arguments and to get her to shut up... I kissed her."

Tanya and Elaine trade a look that practically blares with curiosity, as well as possibly buying my bullshit.

"You know how AJ can be," I add with a casual shrug. "Sometimes she just won't stop talking. Figured I'd try a new tactic."

Elaine narrows her eyes. "Did it work?"

I smirk. "Let's just say she stopped talking… and now hates me even more. So yeah, I'd say it worked." I wink.

They giggle, of course, then grab their matching neon-pink Stanley cups and head for the door.

Just as they're leaving, Tanya tosses a glance over her shoulder. "Maybe I should keep talking to you, Jonathan."

Elaine gasps. "Tanya! You're so bad." She slaps her arm as they disappear down the hall, laughing.

"Have a nice day, ladies," I call out, plastering on my most charming smile.

Damn, that was close. So, now the two biggest talkers in the office know I kissed AJ. I should probably tell her before she finds out the hard way. I top off my coffee, ditch the pretense of a leisurely pace and head straight for her office.

When I walk in, she's finishing up an email. She glances at me over the rim of her blue-light glasses, non-prescription, I know she has perfect vision. She likes to remind me of it every time she catches a typo in one of my presentations.

"What do you want?" she snarls.

"We may have a problem," I say.

Concern flickers across her face, right before her sapphire-blue eyes shift toward the large glass wall at the front of her office. They widen and her entire body goes rigid.

I turn around to see what's got her looking like she's just seen a ghost.

"Everyone! Everyone come out quickly to meet the new partner, Marcus!" Victoria calls out, her voice entirely too cheerful for what's happening. She's arm-in-arm with the one man who absolutely should not be here. The same man I mocked last night for leaving his bride at the altar. The same man AJ was supposed to marry.

I spin back toward AJ, panic starting to rise in my throat. She looks at me like I've just detonated a bomb in her office. My jaw tightens as I white-knuckle my mug.

"Okay," I say. "We may have *two* problems."

5

Abby

I never really understood the phrase "someone walked over your grave." It always sounded like one of those old-timey dialogues people used to sound poetic, even if it didn't actually mean much, just words without weight.

But now? Now I *get* it. Because the second I see Victoria, my boss, arm in arm with *Marcus*, my ex-fiancé; the man who left me on what was supposed to be the happiest day of my life, it doesn't feel like someone walked over my grave. It feels like a semi-truck barreled through it, reversed and parked there for good measure. Around me, keyboards are clacking, someone's Spotify is leaking from too-loud earbuds and the scent of burnt toast is lingering from the break room. Meanwhile, I'm internally combusting. My entire body erupts in goosebumps. A hot, queasy wave rolls through me like my insides are threatening to revolt in spectacular fashion.

I certifiably ponder whether I'd have enough time to pro-jectile vomit directly onto my keyboard, or if I should aim for the trash can. The office, normally spacious and flooded with natural light, starts to shrink around me like a collapsing circus tent and the AC, which is usually set to *arctic tundra*, suddenly feels like someone cranked it to *hellfire on steroids*. My throat tightens. It's that awful combination of hard to swallow and somehow like I've been chewing on gravel.

I glance at Jonathan. Even *he* looks rattled and this is a man who thrives on havoc and has probably stared down both an IRS audit and a live scorpion without flinching.

Most of this office was invited to my wedding. They know who Marcus is. Which means, any second now, the whispers will start. Along with the sympathetic stares and the "Are you okay?" head tilts that make me want to crawl under my desk and live there forever. I hate being the center of attention. Especially when it's because my personal life has turned into the office's favorite soap opera.

Then the memory of last night hits me. Me grabbing Jonathan like we were a couple. Me *saying* we were a couple. Jonathan taking a jab at Marcus for leaving me at the altar. The kiss and then… another kiss. My brain is already a tangled mess and now someone's throwing fireworks into it.

Jonathan steps out of my office to head toward Victoria and for a split second I think about following him. But instead, I pivot like I'm dodging a life-or-death situation and rush straight to the bathroom. My heels click like gunshots against the tile floor, echoing louder than they should. The hallway feels endless, lined with those abstract corporate paintings that look like someone gave a toddler finger paint and a deadline.

Victoria's voice drifts down the way, cheerful and businesslike. She's too busy introducing Marcus to notice my abrupt exit, thank the heavens. She tells everyone to grab their things and meet in the conference room.

The conference room used to be one of my favorite places in the office. It was where I pitched big clients, made even bigger wins and got those glowy, *this-is-why-we-hired-you* looks from execs when I nailed their campaign vision. It's massive too, decked out with plush leather chairs that lean all the way back like you're about to take a first-class nap, a coffee bar with snacks and that magical infuser that always makes the room smell faintly of lavender and lemon. Best of all? The entire back wall is floor-to-ceiling windows, giving you a view of the city so beautiful it almost makes work emails feel poetic.

Those fluffy memories will now be tainted. Now that Marcus will be in there and with him, all the eyes, all the whispers, all the pity.

I push into the bathroom and make a dash for the sinks, gripping the porcelain like it might anchor me to Earth. The bathroom smells of hydrangeas, while the overhead light flickers just once and the white tile floor is cold even through my shoes. I swear the soap dispenser is judging me. I lean forward, trying to breathe through it, trying to brace for the emotional sucker punch that's clearly coming. I lift my eyes to the mirror. My strained, pale reflection stares back and I watch as the sadness creeps in, watch it gather behind my eyes like a swell that hasn't quite broken yet.

No. No crying. I am a professional. I have worked too hard to fall apart in a freaking office bathroom. It's been almost four years since Marcus stranded me at the bridal suite like a rejected Amazon return. That is more than enough time to move on. *Pull. It. Together.* I say it out loud, hoping the mantra sticks to my brain like bubblegum. A paper towel from the dispenser flutters to the floor, like even it's given up on me. I stare down at it for a second, weirdly tempted to follow its lead.

Just as I'm bracing for the floodgates to open and wash away what's left of my dignity, the bathroom door slams open like it's been kicked by a dramatic soap opera star.

Jonathan bursts in, into the *women's bathroom.*

"What the hell?!" I shout, flinging my hands in the air. "This is a whole new level of insane, even for you."

"Okay, okay, hear me out," he pants, completely unbothered by my yelling as he paces across the tile floor like he's plotting an escape route. "I've got a plan." He pauses mid-step and glances around. "Oh. Huh. I've never been in the women's bathroom before." Then, like we're in the middle of a *Better Homes & Bathrooms* tour, he adds. "You guys get fresh-cut flowers in here? That's awesome."

I slap my hands together. "Jonathan. *Focus.*"

He snaps out of his bathroom admiration. "Right. Okay. Marcus thinks we're a couple, yeah?"

I wince. "Unfortunately, yes."

"Then we're still a couple," he says simply.

"What? No. Why?" I incoherently spit out.

"To save you from public humiliation *and* to stick it to him," he replies, like it's the most obvious thing in the world. "This way, you still look like you've moved on."

"I can't ask you to do that," I say, waving my hands. "Besides, what will the office think?"

"No one has to know." He shrugs. "Marcus isn't going to say anything. He'll drop in, make his rounds, pretend to care and leave in three days. That's what these bigwig silent-partner types do."

I stare at him, chewing it over. Then turn to the mirror. I smooth my hair. Wipe the eyeliner smudge from under my eye, trying to make sense of the absolute circus that is my life, complete with fire juggling, emotional acrobatics and zero safety nets.

"Wait," I say, squinting at him through the mirror. "Why are you actually helping me?" My tone is suspicious enough that I might as well be holding a flashlight under his chin and asking where he buried the body.

He smirks. "Because I want your parking spot for six months. *And* first brew choice in the break room for a year."

I whip around. "You devil."

He knows exactly how much I love being the first one to choose the coffee in the break room and that parking spot is legendary. Anita left it to me before she retired. She'd worked here since the dawn of time or at least since the *Founding Fathers of Marketing* started this company. She told me once she saw a lot of herself in me. Never married, no kids and last I heard, owned three cats. So... not *totally* a compliment. But still, she meant well.

"You've been trying to steal my parking space for years," I snap.

"Exactly," he says, practically glowing with enthusiasm. "But also..." He pauses, like he's debating whether or not to say the rest, then finally adds, "What that guy did to you was messed up. And I don't like his haircut, so... he deserves this."

Wow. Never thought I'd see the day Jonathan Slack and I became... what? Accomplices? Friends? Either way, I'm weirdly grateful. For once, he's not throwing me under the bus. He's jumping on it with me and just maybe, helping me make my ex regret ever running out on me. Marcus may never regret leaving me... But that doesn't mean I can't give it the ol' college try.

"So…" Jonathan says.

I hold out my hand. "Deal."

He smirks, pushes it away. "Come on. Lovers hug."

Before I can object, he pulls me into his arms. He smells… infuriatingly good. Like sandalwood and spice and man.

I push off him with an eye roll.

"They kiss, too," he adds with a wink.

"Don't hold your breath," I quip, hitting his arm.

We walk toward the door. I pause and take one deep, grounding breath.

Jonathan glances at me, grinning. "Come on. Let's make this walking midlife crisis hate his life."

He opens the door for me, our footsteps hit against the tile, like we're stepping onto a stage instead of back into corporate reality, ready to sell the performance of a lifetime as my brain circles the drain, screaming: *What the hell did I just get myself into?* The hallway's too bright, too loud, too everything and I already regret whatever pact I just made with Satan in slacks.

6

Jonathan

D amn. AJ went ghost-white the second she saw her ex in our office. I didn't think that was possible until I saw her go pale enough to blend into printer paper. After we struck our deal in the women's bathroom, which, by the way, smelled like sweet vanilla cream and was not-so-shockingly cleaner than the men's, I watched the color start to return to her face. She still looked sickly, but at least she had a little pink in her cheeks again. Like her body was slowly rebooting.

For some reason, I felt bad for her. *AJ*. My work nemesis. A total brat more days than not. Seeing her like this, though? It didn't feel satisfying. Maybe because I wasn't the one who got to torture her today. Or maybe because, as much as it pains me to admit it… AJ's actually a good person. She volunteers at the homeless shelter. She bakes cookies for the office. She throws parties whenever something big happens, like someone signs a huge client, gets engaged, has a baby. She stays late every night working. I should know, I'm usually here too. Sometimes I even trail behind her in the parking garage to make sure she

45

gets to her car okay. She annoys the ever-living hell out of me, but I still don't want her getting mugged. Or hurt.

We both shuffle into the conference room with everyone else. Victoria's already posted up at the head of the table like the queen she is, and Marcus, smug as hell, is seated beside her. He looks at AJ. Then at me. Then back at her. Almost like he expected her to be here… and had no idea I would be.

According to AJ, he knew where she worked. He just never showed up or met anyone. Maybe he didn't realize he was buying into her company. How do you not know where your fiancé works? What a dick. That just makes me hate him more.

Also… what did AJ even see in him? He dresses like a professor and has that "I teach finance at an Ivy school" energy. Okay, sure he looks like James Marsden, so the guy's got the whole clean-cut, charming thing going for him, still doesn't mean he's half as cool as that actor seems.

AJ and I end up sitting next to each other. Not on purpose, it's just the closest pair of open seats when we walk in. If I know her, she'd rather be dangling off the edge of this building than in this room right now.

She inches her chair closer to mine, like she's using me as some kind of emotional life raft.

Under the table, I lightly tap her thigh. She flinches at first, then glances over, realizing what I'm doing, offering support. Her mouth softens into the tiniest smile.

I like this version of AJ, the one who doesn't look like she's mentally setting me on fire. But I don't like the other part, the scared, shaky one she's also trying to hide. People are watching her. I can see the curious glances. Some of them were invited to her wedding. Did they know who Marcus was?

She used to have photos of them in her office. I didn't pay much attention back then. I do remember one of the pictures, some cheesy shot of the two of them in a hot air balloon. I think that's when he proposed.

Totally lame. If it were me, the proposal would've been way more epic. I clear my throat and shift in my chair, brushing off the thought like it didn't just knock the wind out of me mid-meeting.

"Alright. Welcome, everyone," Victoria begins. Her Chanel jacket is off now, revealing a sleek gray blouse with black pearl-like buttons marching down the front. Stylish as ever and rich, thanks to divorces one, two and most recently, three. If anyone's more jaded about love than me, it's Victoria. Once she finds out who Marcus is in relation to AJ, she won't care. Not in a cruel way, just in a *that's life, suck it up* kind of way.

"This is Marcus Taylor," she continues, gesturing toward him. Marcus stands and offers a little wave, like he's accepting an award for *Most Likely to Have Ruined Someone's Life and Still Look Like a GQ Model.*

"He's our new silent partner and will be shadowing our office for the next few days." Then Victoria turns to me. "Jonathan?" Her voice is casual, but her eyes flick to mine with all the sharpness of a thrown dart.

I flinch like the time my mom caught me cracking open every single egg from our fridge on the driveway just to see what would happen in the sun. The market was already closed and yeah… my mom's face? Not exactly glowing with pride. Even then, though, her version of punishment was more of a light tap than an emotional spanking. My mom was sweet. I got more of my dad's edge. Tough, blunt, low tolerance for feelings. Still, they made it work. Called themselves salt and pepper.

"Yes?" I say, sitting up straighter, pretending I didn't just zone out.

"Don't you have a presentation prepared for Marcus?" she asks, like I've personally offended her by not already launching into it.

Right. Presentation. I shoot up so fast I nearly knock my chair over. I adjust my belt, check my shirt's still tucked in and try to push down the weird flutter of nerves that feels dangerously close to terror.

"Yes. Yes, I do," I say, clearing my throat. "I've compiled stats from the last three fiscal years to showcase our revenue growth, client testimonials and a rundown of the *big fish* we're currently working on poaching from other firms."

Luckily, I'd already loaded the slides onto the main conference screen earlier this morning. I did forget my printed notes. It's fine though, I can work the room off the cuff. That's kind of my thing.

I grab the clicker and the massive projection screen drops down from the ceiling. The lights dim. My slideshow begins. With each slide, I walk them through our strongest data points: revenue trends, retention stats, the growth rate of influencer marketing and upcoming prospects. I keep it tight, under seven minutes. I'm no amateur; everyone knows attention spans are toast after that mark.

After the presentation, a few people clap and I feel a mild sense of pride. I glance over at AJ and offer a small smile, like *Hey, not bad, right?*

"Thank you, Jonathan," Victoria says, already moving things along.

I slide back into my seat and take a long sip from one of the water bottles Brooke, our *always-on-it* office assistant, had set out for everyone.

"That was great. Thank you," Marcus adds.

I give him a polite nod and go back to sipping, pretending I'm completely unfazed by the fact that this man left the woman next to me standing in a bridal suite years ago.

He leans forward slightly, adopting that approachable-big-boss energy. "I just want to take a moment to thank everyone for having me. I promise to stay out of the way for the most part. I'd just like to observe a few client meetings, get a feel for the team dynamics here." He scans the room like he's about to break into a trust fall. "Let's go around. Say your name, how long you've been with the company, and something about yourself."

Because nothing says *bonding* like a forced fun fact circle.

AJ and I are seated at the far end, so it takes a few minutes to get to us. Stan kicks things off with how he's into fly fishing and then Marge goes on about how she loves knitting and cooking. Elaine jumps in with a funny story about trying, and failing, to run a marathon. It gets a solid laugh from the room.

By the time it's AJ's turn, her voice is quieter. "I've worked here for six years… and I like to bake," she says, folding her hands in her lap.

"She makes the best chocolate chip cookies," Elaine adds, grinning at Marcus.

Marcus smiles like he already knows that. Of course he does.

Then it's my turn. I keep it simple: a little about my love for classic cars and my lifelong obsession with baseball. As I speak, I catch Marcus watching me with a strange face. It's the kind of look someone gets right before they pour gasoline on a fire because they're *dying* to watch it explode.

"How long have you and Abby been an item?" he asks, casually tossing the grenade onto the table.

Well fuck me. The room goes dead silent. Tanya and Elaine both gasp, loudly. Stan starts to say, "That's funny, they hate—" but Tanya kicks him under the table and he shuts up.

Victoria's eyes dart between me, AJ and Marcus. "I'm sorry," she says stiffly. "Abigail and Jonathan collaborate on campaigns, but they're not... involved like that."

"Oh?" Marcus blinks innocently. "Because when I ran into them last night, they said—"

I glance at AJ. She looks like she's teetering on the edge of either screaming or sobbing. Possibly both. And in a split-second decision, because sometimes the best move is made before anyone else can, I interrupt.

"Yes," I blurt. "We're... seeing each other. For a few months now."

Every eyeball in the building might as well be laser-focused on us. I swear I can hear Tanya's acrylics gripping her Stanley Cup like it's the popcorn bucket in a movie theater.

I reach for AJ's hand and tug her to her feet. She resists for a beat, then stands. We're already knee-deep in this lie, might as well commit.

"Yes," she echoes, her voice calm but tight. "It's... new-ish. We didn't want to cause drama. So..." She glances at me, like we've reached the edge of the cliff and are deciding whether to jump. "We kept it a secret."

"I *knew* it," Tanya squeals, sounding way too satisfied.

"Settle down, Tanya," Victoria mutters, rolling her eyes. Then she crosses her arms. "You two know office policy. All interdepartmental relationships must be disclosed."

"I know. I'm sorry," I say quickly. "We just wanted to make sure it was… the real deal."

Victoria narrows her eyes like she's sniffing out bullshit.

"And is it?" Tanya asks, leaning in like we're on an episode of *The Bachelor*. Seriously, Tanya? Read the room.

Victoria shoots her a glare but then turns to me, clearly wanting an answer too.

"Yes," I say, standing tall. "It is."

AJ takes a breath in, then out. "Yes," she says shaky yet solid.

"I'm sorry, Victoria," Marcus adds. "I didn't realize I was saying anything wrong."

Yes, you did, asshole, I say with my eyes as I shoot him a death glare.

"We met last night and they seemed open with their relationship," he adds, all innocence and fake humility.

"How about you just focus on being a *silent* partner instead of meddling in people's personal lives?" I snap.

"Jonathan!" Victoria scolds, her voice serrated.

But Marcus holds up a hand, pretending to be the bigger person. "No, no, Victoria. He's right," he says with a sigh, all noble regret. "You're right, Jonathan. I'm sorry."

Victoria and half the women in the room buy the performance like it's on sale at Saks. He's one good, calculated bastard, I'll give him that.

"This was great. Thank you, everyone," Marcus says, pushing back from the table. "I need to step out and make a few calls, but I'll be back shortly."

"You can use my office," Victoria offers, already back to boss mode. "Down the hall, on the left."

"Thank you," he says, like he's the fucking president. "See you later, everyone."

He actually waves. *What a prick!*

As soon as he's gone, Victoria turns back to us, her finger pointing like a dagger. "You two. Abigail's office. Now." She strides out.

I glance around at my coworkers, my fellow inmates and most of them are either giggling, grinning, or straight-up whispering already. I catch Manny's eye and he looks stunned. I wink at him. Then I push back my chair and rise, all fake swagger.

I let my lovely "girlfriend" go first, of course.

As we make our way toward her office, she shoots me a look over her shoulder.

"We are so dead," she admits, swallowing hard.

I run a hand through my hair and sigh. "Yep."

$$7$$

Abby

Victoria opens the door to my office and makes herself right at home by sitting in *my* desk chair. My chic-yet-cozy, white sherpa-covered chair. The one I picked specifically for my comfort and taste. She gestures to the two chairs opposite my desk, the ones usually reserved for client meetings and the occasional coworker vent session. They're still stylish, cream leather with gold stems and high backs. But way stiffer. I decorated my office to feel like me. Since I basically live here, it might as well feel like home. A very put-together, productivity-inspiring, Pinterest-worthy home.

Jonathan lets me sit first. Oh, so he's a gentleman now that we're both potentially getting fired.

Victoria leans forward, bracing her elbows on my desk like she's about to interrogate us under a flickering light bulb. She squints at me. Then at Jonathan. I suddenly feel like we're suspects in a crime drama and she's the lead detective who already knows we're guilty.

She lets out a breath. Not just any breath, a full huff. Like we've already wasted her time.

"So," she says slowly, "you expect me to believe that now you're a couple?" She doesn't ask it so much as challenge the very concept.

Jonathan clears his throat. My heart stops. He better not crack.

"I admit," he says, "it does seem… surprising, given our history of office rivalry. But opposites attract. And yes, we're a couple. A *happy* couple, actually."

My heart starts beating again. Good save. For a second there, I thought we were toast.

"Yes, Victoria," I add, channeling every ounce of fake confidence I have. "We've learned to love what makes us different. It's what we admire most in each other." A bead of sweat slides down my temple. It's freezing in here, but I'm sweating anyway because pretending to be in a steamy office romance with the guy I once tried to report to HR is apparently a full-body workout. "I'm sorry we didn't tell you sooner," I express.

Then Jonathan does the unthinkable.

"I take full responsibility," he says, cutting in. "For not informing you sooner. I'm prepared for any consequences."

My mouth almost hits the floor. Jonathan Slack, taking the bullet for us? For me? Who knew he had it in him. Uncannily selfless for a guy who once ordered a mug that said *World's Okayest Coworker* and gave it to me for Secret Santa.

"I'm not going to fire you guys," Victoria protests, leaning back in *my* chair like she owns the place. "You two are my best employees."

I glance at Jonathan, who gives me a small but noticeable smirk, like he knows he's the teacher's pet.

"But," she continues, "you realize you're both up for that

promotion once Allen officially leaves?"

Oh my God, the promotion. I've been so caught up in the last twenty-four hours of my unhinged life choices; kissing my nemesis, fake-dating said nemesis and then lying to my boss about all of it; I completely forgot we're both up for *Vice President of Marketing*.

My mouth opens, the truth ready to tumble out, but Jonathan sees it happening and stops me. He grabs my hand and gives it a firm squeeze. Then he raises our joined hands like we're the poster couple for corporate harmony. "We understand the stakes," he says smoothly, "and we hope our relationship doesn't sway your decision away from either of us."

Victoria glances at our hands, whatever she's thinking is hidden behind a blank stare. She unhurriedly turns my chair toward the window, my favorite part of my office. The view isn't quite as stunning as hers or Allen's, but it's still a dreamy sliver of skyline that makes the long hours almost worth it.

"You two are my best," she says again, still facing the window. Then she spins the chair back toward us and fixes us both with a steely glare. "I'm not considering anyone else. If I choose one of you over the other, you'll need to be adults about it and not let it affect the company." She pauses, then adds with pointed clarity, "And you will certainly not let it spiral into some romantic meltdown that ends up in my office. That's when we'll *definitely* have a problem."

Even though Victoria can be intense, I actually respect her more than anyone else at this company. She's wise. No-nonsense. Everything I aim to be on my most confident days. Also, she's not wrong to have concerns.

I look at Jonathan and slip my hand out of his. Not in a

dramatic way. Just… firmly. He notices.

"I understand completely, Victoria," I say, as composed as I can manage.

"Makes sense," Jonathan chimes in, doing that overly agreeable thing that makes me want to strangle him with a phone charger.

I want to tell Victoria. I want to blurt out who Marcus really is; to me, to my past, to every ounce of mascara I cried off that day. Saying it out loud, though, would unravel everything. Our little "relationship." The lie. The fake boyfriend act. All of it.

Before I can say another word, Victoria slaps her impeccably manicured hands, undoubtedly treated to weekly appointments and some sort of collagen glove treatment, on my desk.

"Okay then," she demands. "Let's get back to work." She spins around in her Louboutin heels and Chanel skirt and struts out of my office like a luxury war general.

The moment Victoria clears the threshold, I let out the breath I'm pretty sure I've been holding since she sat down at my desk. Jonathan steps forward to make sure the door swings fully shut behind her, like he's guarding the scene of a crime.

"Whew," he says, rubbing the back of his neck. "That was close."

His eyes find mine and the deer-in-headlights energy I'm radiating must be blinding.

"This isn't good," I say flatly.

"It's fine," he replies, way too coolly. "We'll ride this out while Marcus is here. Then in a few weeks, we have a very civilized, mutual, totally no-drama breakup. Happens all the time. Not a big deal."

I start pacing, my office suddenly feeling ten square feet smaller.

"What's on your mind, AJ?" he asks, hands sliding into his pockets like he didn't just bulldoze through my emotional peace and expect me to thank him for the renovation.

I stop pacing long enough to breathe.

"The first relationship I've had in almost four years… and it's fake. And it's with the one person I hate more than anyone," I shout, not loud enough for others to hear obviously.

He flinches and throws his hands up like I physically slapped him with the truth. "Well, that's rude."

"Oh, stop it," I snap. "We both hate each other."

"I've never said I hated you," he admits, in a tone I don't recognize coming from him.

My feet stall and I turn to face him. Is he catfishing me? What's his play here? I can't read him and I pride myself on being a human lie detector.

"Sure, I find you annoying and yeah, I can be selfish. But I never said I hated you, AJ." He takes a step closer, his voice lighter now.

For the first time, I think I'm seeing something resembling a nicer side of Jonathan Slack. And it's… disorienting.

"Why did you say you'd take the fall for not reporting our relationship?" I ask, folding my arms. "You could've been fired."

He takes my hands in his, skin warm and comforting. "It's just a job," he says with a shrug. "I love it, but I don't need it."

"Oh and I do? Because I'm poor and you're rich?" I snap, yanking my hands away like they burned me. "Wow, thanks, Daddy Warbucks."

He lets out an exasperated breath. "See! This is why you're

annoying."

"And this is why no one trusts you!" I shoot back. "You act like being nice is some foreign language. I can't tell when it's real."

"I'm *trying* to be real," he bites out, his voice rising just a little. "But with you, it's like no matter what I say, it's wrong."

"Oh, please." I cross my arms again. "You've been a dick to me more times than I can count. So forgive me if I don't throw a parade the one time you *don't* act like Satan's hot cousin."

He goes quiet, forehead creases and for a moment, I think he's ironically considering my words. Like... really thinking.

Finally, he sighs. "I don't know. Maybe you're right." There's a beat of silence before he adds, "Let's just get through the next few days." Then, without another word, he opens the door, walks out and leaves it hanging open behind him.

If I didn't know any better, I'd say I hurt his feelings. But that's impossible. You can't hurt the feelings of someone who doesn't have any. Right?

I go behind my desk and sit down, pressing my head into my hands and trying to control my breathing with a meditation exercise. Whatever, it's not working. I surrender, picking my head up and I can feel the pressure starting to dissipate behind my eyes. Just when I think I've finally wrangled my nervous system into submission, in walks the ghost of fiancé's past.

"Hi," Marcus says, knocking on the door with one knuckle.

I twist my head and I swear all the blood drains from my skull to my feet. A wave of dizziness rolls over me like I've just stood up too fast on an empty stomach.

"May I come in?" he asks.

I forgot how good he looks. *Stupid good.* With his dark, tousled hair, a side-smirk that used to melt me and those bright blue eyes that somehow still hit their target. I used to swoon over this man and now, annoyingly, the swoon still shows up. Traitorous hormones.

"Yeah. Sure," I manage to stutter out.

He walks in and shuts the door. What is it with the men in my life and shutting my office door like we're about to discuss national secrets?

"I'm sorry for just showing up like this," he remarks.

"Yeah, about that." I lift my head and level a look at him. "Why are you here? You knew I worked here."

He sits down in the chair across from me and lets out a sigh, the kind that says *I know I screwed up* but not quite enough to say it out loud.

"When I was approached with this deal, I wasn't sure if you still worked here," he says. "You always talked about starting your own agency."

He's right, I did used to talk about that often. I used to have plans. Big ones actually. But plans require heart and after mine got shattered into microscopic dust, that ambition dimmed. Starting over felt impossible.

"Well, clearly I didn't," I snap.

"I realize that now," he admits. "I was going to bring it up last night when I saw you, but I was caught off guard. I mean… I didn't think either of us expected to run into each other."

He shifts in the chair and it lets out the tiniest creak. Somehow, it sounds exactly like the crack of my heart the day he disappeared.

"Definitely wasn't expecting that," I admit, managing a half-smile that *feels* forced except it isn't. Not when I'm around him.

Marcus's face lights up. "I love seeing you smile."

The words land like a brick to the sternum. Then he blinks, like realizing what just slipped out and shakes his head fast, like he's trying to physically dislodge the thought.

He adjusts his blazer and clears his throat. "I promise I won't get in your way today. Or during the retreat."

"Retreat?" I repeat, my pulse ticking up.

"We're taking the office to Cedar Lakes for a corporate retreat," he says, with the same chill energy someone uses to say *pass the salt* as if this isn't an emotional *Hunger Games* waiting to happen.

"When is this happening?" I ask, already bracing.

"Victoria's announcing it today. We leave Friday," he exclaims, undeniably enthused about it.

Friday. As in, two days from now.

I nod lazily, the muscles in my face trying to arrange into something that resembles a normal human expression. "That's… great."

"You say *great* a lot, don't you?" he teases, flashing a smile before turning and walking out.

I sit there frozen, replaying everything: his vapidly charming face, his carelessly dropped retreat bomb, his exit line cuts like he's walking out of a stage play and I'm the one left behind in real life.

So, in two days, I'll be trapped in the woods with my ex-fiancé… and my fake boyfriend.

What could possibly go wrong?

8

Jonathan

When AJ called me a dick, something twisted in my chest. Why did I care if she thinks I'm a dick? I mean… I *can* be. But most people like me. So why doesn't she?

If I'm being honest, I can't even remember exactly how our feud started. I'm sure there was some moment that lit the match, the spark that set it off. The fire's just been burning for so long now, it all blends together. An argument could be made that it reached full inferno after I mocked her following what I thought was her wedding weekend. I obviously didn't know she'd been left at the altar and when I found out I tried to apologize. She didn't buy it. Didn't believe it was genuine. But it was.

How do you get someone to believe you when they've already decided they can't trust you? It's impossible. She's impossible. *And* annoying. *And* cute. *Too cute.* Which is wildly inappropriate for me to be thinking about right now.

When I told Victoria I'd take the consequences for hiding our "relationship," I wasn't just posturing. I meant it. Mostly because I have a job offer on the table. A good one. A *great* one, truthfully. It's in Boston. Which means I'd have to move. There's no way I'm commuting to Boston from Manhattan unless I develop the ability to teleport or become deeply unhinged. While I love this city, grew up here and have all my friends here, I can't ignore the pull for something different.

Two weekends ago, I went to Boston to meet with the head of *Elite Visions Marketing*. Big-time firm. Impressive clients. They want me to lead their largest division of sales and marketing. The salary's incredible. Still, that's not what's pulling me. It's the change. The newness. The chance to shake things up.

I'd miss Manhattan, of course. The noise, the pace, the fact that I can get dumplings and dry cleaning at 1:00 a.m. Maybe a job change would be good for me.

So yeah, when it seemed like Victoria might fire us, I stepped in. Not just because I had a backup plan, though I did. More because getting fired might be the push I need to actually make a move.

Also, I didn't want AJ to get fired either. She's insanely good at what she does and I know how much she loves this job. So yeah… I'd be, for lack of a better word, upset for her if she lost it because of this mess. She'd never believe me, even if I crossed my heart, hoped to die and swore those were my true intentions.

When Victoria said she wasn't firing us, a small rush of relief hit me. Perhaps I'm not as ready to leave this place as I thought.

I needed time to think, so I spent the rest of the morning trying to steer clear of AJ, dodge Victoria and most importantly, avoid Marcus.

While at my desk, my stomach growls so loud I'm half-convinced the two interns whispering outside my office heard it. I glance down at my TAG Heuer; sleek, silver, a gift to myself for surviving last quarter's hellscape. It's officially lunchtime. I head down to the cafeteria. Say what you want about corporate food, but ours delivers. The paninis are solid, the fries are crispy and the cookies? Legendary. I've already got a roast beef sandwich in hand and I'm just deciding between turkey pesto and chipotle chicken for round two when I catch sight of Marcus across the room. *Crap.* He's already walking my way, sandwich in one hand, cookie bag in the other, like we're about to bond over baked goods.

"Hey," he says nonchalantly.

"Hey," I reply, side-eyeing the cookies like they started this mess. "Best cookies in the building," I remark, mostly just to fill the awkward silence.

"Stan told me," he replies, holding up the bag like he's won something. "Guy behind the counter said I got the last one."

What the hell! Now this guy just officially made my *do-not-trust* list.

"Cool," I say, trying to act unimpressed even though I'm mentally adding have a stern word with Stan to my to-do list.

I make a move to walk away, but he stops me. "Mind if we talk for a minute?"

I give a small nod, even though every fiber of my body wants to say *no* and walk straight into a brick wall.

He gestures to the closest empty table. We both sit, dropping our sandwiches onto the table like it's a summit meeting.

I stare at my food. I wonder if I can eat while he talks. I've got nothing to say, I'm starving and I'm now pissed I won't be tasting one of those damn cookies.

Marcus sits down across from me and starts peeling back

the paper on his sandwich.

Thank God. If we're eating, maybe I can get through this without stabbing myself with a plastic fork.

I start to unwrap mine too, ready to zone out into deli meat and provolone bliss, when he says, "I'm happy AJ found someone."

Is he, though? I pause mid-unwrapping, watching his face. He's trying to look sincere, but something's off. Like he's holding back.

"Yep," I say. "I make her *very* happy."

Then I take a huge bite of my sandwich, mainly to shut myself up before anything dick-ish slips out of my trap.

He stops unwrapping and looks at me again. "There isn't a day that goes by I don't regret what I did to her."

My eyebrows lift. *Bold move, buddy.*

"I mean" —he rushes to clarify—, "you know. Leaving her like I did. On our wedding day." He laughs awkwardly, like that softens the blow. "Not, like, regret ending things… just… how I did it."

Right. Sure. I raise my eyebrows conspicuously. "Well," I say, swallowing my bite, "like I told you last night, if you hadn't walked out, I never would've gotten my shot." I flash a cool smile and take another exaggerated bite of my panini.

He nods and starts eating. We sit there in a silence so thick it could be cut with a butter knife. Probably only lasts three minutes, though it feels like an hour.

"She seems good," he infallibly says. "Not thrilled to see me, obviously. But… good. Victoria says she's one of her best."

"She is," I admit. "One of the hardest working people I know."

"She always was," he protests.

I roll my eyes. I've had enough of the small talk and this weird insight into who AJ was, or maybe still is. I set my sandwich down and lean forward.

"Listen," I start. "we don't have to do this."

Marcus lifts a brow, mildly confused.

"You'll be here for a few days, things will be fine. Drama-free. Then you can go back to your corner of the world and we'll continue being the profitable company you bought into." I tack on a smirk for flair. I feel victorious like I just delivered a passive-aggressive TED Talk.

He sighs and lowers his sandwich.

"I guess you don't know about the retreat either," he says in a tone that feels suspiciously close to pity.

And just like that, my awareness sharpens. The chatter around us. The clatter of plastic trays. The sizzle of the panini press. The smell of warm bread drifting across our table like a warning.

"What retreat?" I ask, already regretting the question.

"We're taking the office to Cedar Lakes for the weekend," he says, casual as hell. "We leave Friday."

Well, this just screams *corporate nightmare*. A company-wide retreat. A secluded escape featuring AJ, Victoria, Marcus… and the entire office. Half of whom know who Marcus is to AJ and all of whom just found out she and I are "together."

"Great. I hear Cedar Lakes is phenomenal this time of year," I say, pretending I don't feel a spike of stress inching up my spine.

Marcus chuckles. "You definitely spend a lot of time with AJ."

I give him a look. "Come again?"

"She says *great* a lot, doesn't she?" he says with a grin that splatters across his dumbass, freshly spray-tanned face.

I blink, then sigh. "Yeah. She does."

He gathers the rest of his food and stands. "Well… see you up there."

Before he turns to leave, because the universe is strange, he holds out the cookie bag.

"Want one?" he asks.

I never say no to sugar. "Yeah. Thanks." I reach in and grab one, watching as he nods and walks away. Is he trying to be nice to me? God help us all. This retreat is going to be a mess.

9

Abby

The fact that I managed to get through emails and even take a client call without flinching or sprinting out of the lobby screaming is, honestly, impressive. But with every tiny win comes a massive slap to the face along with a punch to the stomach.

Victoria finally emerges from her office, where she's been talking to Marcus for what felt like an hour. Lunch has come and gone and I manage to skip eating, chug three cups of coffee and successfully avoid Jonathan… or maybe he's been avoiding me.

"Everyone, come out for a moment!" Victoria's voice cuts through the office like a fire drill announcement.

Our office is laid out like a giant circle, with each private office curving around the central bullpen. In the middle is our glass-walled break room, flanked by the front desk near the elevators, our two assistants' desks and the copier-slash-fax machine combo that sounds like it's dying a painful, dramatic death.

Victoria's made sure the space isn't just functional, it's *chic*.

We've got plush velvet chairs for clients to lounge in while they wait. The desks are all sleek white wood. The walls are painted a modern gray with black accents and pops of color show up in curated art and stylish décor pieces that sit around the circle like little personality sprinkles.

The lobby? It's practically a hotel. Lavish seating, fresh flowers changed weekly by her personal assistant and a flat-screen TV running our ads on an endless loop. Say what you want about Victoria, but the woman knows how to make an impression. Every corner of this office practically screams, *We're successful and slightly better than you.*

So, when she steps out of her office in her Louboutins and calls everyone away from their desks, I already know what's coming. She doesn't do unnecessary drama or spontaneous group bonding. If she's summoning the troops, it means something's up.

Marcus had already let the giant announcement slip earlier: *the retreat.*

"Okay," Victoria says, stepping forward like she's hosting an inspirational movement. "In partnership with Marcus, we're taking everyone on a corporate retreat."

Cue the low cheer. Some people even clap. Everyone's way too eager to pretend this is a vacation, while all I want to do is spend the weekend under my comforter, eating cereal straight from the box and hiding from humanity.

"We leave Friday and will be traveling to Cedar Lakes," she adds.

"I heard that place is amazing," Tanya whispers to Elaine, like she's narrating a travel blog.

Across the room, I spot Jonathan standing off to the side, half-listening, half… somewhere else in his head. He looks up just in time to catch me staring at him like some unblinking, emotionally wrecked raccoon. He nods and shoots me a half-smile. What *is* he thinking?

Victoria continues, "We'll be there all weekend and the property has everything we need, meals, Wi-Fi and activities. That said, make sure to bring your laptops and any paperwork you might need in case a client calls." Her tone sharpens. "This is still a work retreat, so if duty calls, you answer."

And then, like a cherry on top of my mental breakdown sundae, Marcus steps in.

"I just want to say I'm excited to get to know you all more this weekend," he says. "Thank you again for the warm hospitality."

He starts to walk off, waving like a pageant winner. But then he pauses, scanning the room like he's looking for someone. His eyes land on mine and there it is, *that* look. His signature, heartbreakingly handsome smirk. The one that used to make my knees buckle and my heart race like I was sixteen again. Now? It makes my stomach twist so hard I feel like I might hurl all over the very nice office carpeting. Because in that one second, everything comes rushing back; standing in my wedding dress, waiting for a man who never showed. The hollow pit in my stomach. The pity in my bridesmaids' eyes. The sound of my mom crying louder than I was. And here he is again, looking happy, successful, like he didn't steal a piece of me that day.

I don't even know how to explain what I'm feeling. It's a combination of rage, sadness, maybe even a pathetic flash of longing. It's like every emotion in the world is trying to hijack my body at once and none of them are playing nice.

"All right, everyone. Back to work," Victoria says, clapping her hands like she's herding cattle instead of unstable marketers.

I trail behind her as she walks toward her office, practically stepping on her stilettos. She senses me hovering and whips around with the grace of a Bond villain. "Yes, Abigail?" Her tone is formal. She's definitely done with me today.

"I wanted to ask if I could skip the retreat," I blurt out, hands trembling at my sides.

She tilts her head and squints down at me over her towering heels. "You want to skip the corporate retreat?"

I nod like a toddler bracing for time-out.

"Do you have a good reason?" she asks flatly.

I scramble for something. Anything. Grandparents' wedding anniversary? Emergency gallbladder surgery? My dog has explosive diarrhea? I don't even *have* a dog. Nothing lands.

So naturally, my brain jams and my mouth takes over. "I... promised my neighbor I'd watch her cat," I say.

Her eyes narrow. "For the entire weekend?"

"She's very codependent," I add, immediately regretting everything I've ever said in my life.

We stare at each other.

I sigh. "Okay, no. I just... don't think I can go."

"Okay," she says simply.

Relief washes over me for exactly two seconds.

"But if you don't come," she adds, stepping back into full boss babe mode, "I'll assume you're not serious about this company. Which means I can't consider you for the promotion."

In the span of a single breath, I suddenly want to puke in my chic leather flats. This woman could teach a masterclass in psychological warfare while contouring her cheekbones. I know exactly what she's doing. Blackmailing me into going on this ridiculous retreat. But the worst part? She's not wrong.

If I don't go, it'll look like I don't care about the promotion or this company and that's not just wrong, it's insulting. This promotion is everything. I've worked my ass off for it. No way am I letting a little ex-fiancé catastrophe ruin that.

I square my shoulders, standing taller. Victoria eyes me like she's witnessing the miraculous birth of a spine.

"You know what?" I say, my voice more confident now. Her eyebrows try to rise, but the Botox in her forehead doesn't quite allow it. "You're right. I don't know what I was thinking. I'll be happy to attend."

She folds her arms and gives me a slow once-over. "Good to hear." She turns back to her desk. "Don't you have that Zoom call with Johnson & Johnson?"

Crap, I do!

"Yes, heading to the conference room now," I say, spinning on my heel before she can zap me with another mind game.

As I near the glass-walled conference room, I spot Jonathan already inside, spinning slightly in one of the sleek chairs. Because clearly the universe has jokes today.

I open the door and step in. He turns toward me like he's just been caught raiding a cookie jar.

"Peggy got sick," he blurts. "She asked me to sit in."

Right, so sitting next to my fake boyfriend while pretending my life isn't in an absolute tailspin is exactly the vibe I was going for during this meeting.

"Okay," I mutter, sliding into the seat next to him and logging in. I can feel his eyes on me as I type in my password. "What?" I snap without looking up.

He flinches. "Nothing."

I glance sideways at him. "Then why are you staring at me like I'm a bomb about to go off?"

He hesitates, then quietly says, "Are you okay?"

"That's what you're worried about? Me?" I huff out.

He nods *yes*.

"Well," I say, throwing my hands up, "my ex is suddenly back in my life, I've got a bogus boyfriend I can barely stand, a promotion that's slipping through my fingers and oh let's not forget the mandatory retreat where I get to pretend I'm madly in love with you."

I slump back in my chair, exasperated. He runs a hand through his annoyingly flawless hair and the faintest whiff of his cologne hits me. He always smells like a rich country club completed with leather chairs, overpriced bourbon and just a touch of arrogance.

"Yeah. I get it," he says. "That's why I wanted to check in. And… I have a plan."

"A plan?" I repeat, narrowing my eyes.

"Yes!" he exclaims, eyes lighting up like this is a group project he actually wants to lead. "Listen. We've got this. We can spin this whole situation to our advantage."

I raise a brow. "Go on."

"I ran into Marcus during lunch," he starts. "And he seems like he misses you."

I blink. "He does?"

"I'm serious. He looked like he was two seconds away from crying and handing you a handwritten apology," he remarks.

My jaw drops just enough that Jonathan smirks.

"So," he continues, "if we play this right, we'll have him eating out of the palm of your hand. And then when the moment's perfect… BAM!" He claps his hands together so loud I jump. "You crush his soul."

I let out a slow breath. "Well, I'd love to make him feel at least one ounce of the emotional trainwreck he left me in."

Jonathan grins. "Exactly."

"You really think this'll work?" I ask way too desperately.

"Totally," he blurts.

I pause, studying him. "Okay… what's in it for you?"

He shrugs, fortuitously. "It'll look good to Victoria if she sees us getting along. Shows maturity. Growth. The last thing she wants is to promote someone no one can work with."

"And?" I prod.

He sighs dramatically. "The intern. Claudia. Keeps asking me out. If I'm fake taken, she'll back off."

I tilt my head. "Wow."

"What?" he snaps, raising his eyebrows.

"Didn't think I'd live to see the day you turned down a young, eager intern." I chuckle.

He adjusts his jacket and clears his throat. "I may be Vice President soon. Can't afford to piss off the wrong intern or sleep with one who'll make it her life's mission to destroy me."

"Aww. Look at you, responsible and scandal-averse. Who even are you?" I mock, straightening my posture.

"Remember Joaquin?" he asks.

"Oh. True," I admit, instantly remembering poor, sweet Joaquin.

A few years ago, one of the interns developed a crush on him. He was attractive, kind and unfortunately, way too easy to manipulate. She'd stay late to help with his projects, all smiles and fake enthusiasm. Then, when she made a move and he turned her down, politely, might I add, she lost it. She went straight to Victoria and accused him of hitting on her. There was an internal investigation. HR was involved. But what the intern didn't know was that Victoria has security cameras all over the office. She pulled the footage from that night and it showed, clear as day, the intern threw herself at Joaquin. He stepped back, looked horrified and left the room.

Victoria gave the intern a choice: drop it or deal with her lawyers. The intern got a glowing recommendation, a job at an agency in Chicago and had to sign what I'm sure was a terrifying stack of legal paperwork. I don't know all the details, but I do know that despite being in the clear, Joaquin was still asked to leave. Victoria helped him land somewhere else, another agency in the city.

As much as she believed him and we all did, she wasn't about to let a scandal tie itself to her company's name. It was a smart business move. Cold, but smart.

So yeah, I get what Jonathan means. Claudia's… unpredictable. She's the kind of intern who always wants to grab drinks after work and has no concept of personal space. I wouldn't put it past her to stir up rumors just for fun.

I pause for a moment, fingers fidgeting with the corner of my notepad. As much as I hate to admit it, it *is* nice not going through this whole mess completely alone.

I glance over at him. "Thanks," I say quietly.

A smile creeps across his face. "You're welcome, AJ." He throws in a wink because apparently his charm comes with a built-in eye spasm.

Just then, the Zoom call connects and despite the spectacle our lives have become, we actually nail the meeting with Johnson & Johnson.

Maybe we do make a good team. *Platonically*, of course.

10

Jonathan

Did I seriously just strike a deal with *AJ* of all people? That's the thought on repeat as I drive home after work, shaking my head like I can rattle the memory loose and dump it out on the highway. What a day.

My only plan tonight is simple: pour myself the biggest glass of bourbon known to man, microwave a pepperoni Hot Pocket and stretch out on the couch to binge more *Love Island*. Tomorrow's going to be a circus, I can feel it, so tonight, I'll recharge.

I park in the garage and head upstairs, where Frank, my building's overly formal doorman, greets me like he's auditioning for a period drama.

"Good evening, sir," he says with a nod.

"Frank, for the hundredth time, call me Jonathan." I grin as I say it.

Frank's the best. Loyal, punctual, probably takes his job more seriously than the president. He's also a stickler for manners, mostly because half the other residents in this building are rich, entitled jerks who expect to be bowed to.

Not me. Sure, I'm rich and definitely spoiled. I'm just not an asshole. No matter what AJ thinks. *Ugh.* There she is again, sneaking into my brain like she pays rent.

Frank tips his hat. "Yes, sir… I mean, Jonathan." He winces, like the name actually tastes bad.

I laugh and hand him a crisp fifty-dollar bill. To me, it's pocket change. To him, it probably covers groceries for the week. His eyes widen for a second before he gives me a grateful smile. "Thank you, Jonathan. Really."

"You're welcome, Frank," I say, heading for the elevator.

I know this will sound stupid but sometimes I wish I knew what it felt like to be broke. To really struggle. Just to feel something real. Some… edge. Some ache.

Instead, I walk around like a well-dressed zombie, numb, coasting and getting worse by the day. I keep waiting to feel something. Anything. What that anything is, though? I haven't got a fucking clue.

My dad used to say, *If you don't know what to do, don't do anything at all. Let it fall into place.* And damn it, he was always right. He's gone now. Died last year, just before I hit thirty. Hence the full access to my trust fund. Not that I'm complaining. I'd already got dividends of it at twenty-one and twenty-eight, with the final draw scheduled for thirty-five… or sooner, if he passed. Well, he did, so the full amount hit my bank account before his body was even cold.

Cancer. It's always fucking cancer, isn't it?

Prostate cancer to be exact. My doctor told me it can be hereditary, so he tested my PSA early. It's normal, for now. We'll test it every year just to be safe. Weird how a father can pass down both a fortune and a potential ticking time bomb.

I trudge into the elevator and lucky me, run into Mrs.

Whitman. She's holding her demon disguised as a poodle.

"Hello, Mr. Slack," she says primly.

"Hi, Mrs. Whitman." I glance down at the snarling fur ball and tilt my head forward. "Fluffy."

The dog growls like I just insulted her bloodline.

"Fluuuffy," she coos, stroking the back of her head. "You know she hates everyone, even me." She laughs like that's charming.

"Yes. I'm aware," I say, keeping it polite. Sarcastic, but polite. The last thing I need is bad blood with the neighbors. Especially in this building. I surprisingly like living here.

My parents used to live in one of the penthouses, back when my dad was still alive. After he passed, my mom sold it and started traveling the world with her group of equally widowed besties. Occasionally, I get postcards and little trinkets from whatever far-off country they're conquering next.

My mom's sweet. She's soft-spoken, thoughtful but I always had the sense she lived the life *he* wanted, not hers. Now she gets to do whatever the hell she wants. Good for her I guess.

The elevator dings on my floor and I step out. Fluffy lets out another gremlin growl, ensuring I'm aware she's offended by my existence.

I nod at Mrs. Whitman and head down the hallway to my unit. It's not exactly modest, three million when I bought it and worth way more now. In this city, that's just called real estate.

I unlock the door and step into my foyer, shrugging off my slim-cut blazer and hanging it in the coat closet. My place is... open. Some might call it cold. I call it *airy*.

The grand living room spills right into the kitchen, complete with a massive white granite waterfall island and a chef's setup decked out in marble accents. There's pricey art on the walls, nothing over twenty grand though. I like art. I appreciate it. I'm also not insane. I'm not blowing millions on a painting.

Furniture, though? That's a different story. Or at least that's what the interior designer I hired told me. She picked out everything, finished the job and then, well, I slept with her. Didn't call her back. She shockingly didn't take it well. Good thing I changed the locks. Just in case. Never underestimate an angry woman with a master's in fine arts and a grudge.

But come on, was I really going to fall in love with an art major? Or *anyone*? I don't think I've ever been in love. I probably wouldn't recognize it if it smacked me across the face.

After a much-needed steam shower, I head into my pristine, restaurant-grade kitchen, one that would make professional chefs weep. I pull a box of Hot Pockets from the freezer. Yes. Hot Pockets. One of my many guilty pleasures. I don't cook. I eat out often, expensively. But tonight? I need comfort food and silence. The day couldn't end fast enough.

Just as I pop the delicious pepperoni-filled pastry into the microwave, there's a knock at my door.

Who the hell is that? I hesitate, walking over like I'm in a horror movie and peer through the peephole. It's Manny.

"Yo! Let me in!" he calls out, grinning and waving a six-pack of Modelos.

I crack a smile. I love Manny, probably my best friend but the man drinks the worst beer on the market. Seriously, *Modelos*? It's tragic.

I open the door. "What are you doing here?" I ask, keeping the smile on my face even though all I really want is to be alone.

"What? Am I interrupting your pepperoni dinner?" He smirks, stepping inside.

Prick. He knows me too well.

"Yeah, yeah. Come in," I say, waving him through. He strolls in, reeking of booze and woodsy cologne. He's already halfway to drunk. I can see it. Smell it. Feel it radiating off him.

"So what's up, man?" I ask as I walk back into the kitchen to retrieve my Hot Pocket. It's a little too crisp around the edges. Still, it'll do.

Manny plops down on one of the stools at the island and gives it a curious look. "Whoa. New bar-stools?"

I chuckle. "Yeah. Pottery Barn got me again with their summer catalog."

He arches a brow. "Dude… if I didn't know you so well, I'd think you were gay."

I roll my eyes. "Thanks for the support."

"Not that there's anything wrong with that. Love is love," he says, holding up his beer in salute.

I take a bite of my hardened, now mildly disappointing dinner and wince. "This is… a crime."

"Let's order some Chinese," Manny says, throwing his hands up like a deranged cheerleader who just won state.

I glance down at my sad excuse for dinner, then up at Manny, then over to my phone. I sigh like I just lost a war and dial up Mr. Wong's, hands down the best Chinese food within ten blocks.

"What do you want?" I grumble.

"Sweet!" Manny pumps a fist. "I'll take the number three and number five. Oh and two egg rolls. Extra hot mustard."

"Yeah, you got that, Lin?" I ask the woman on the other end of the phone. "And I'll take the number six with one egg roll.

Thanks, sweetie," I add.

She giggles. All women giggle at me. Except AJ. *Never* AJ.

I hang up. "Twenty minutes," I say, flopping down onto the bar stool beside him.

"Cool. Thanks, bro. Plenty of time to talk about whatever the hell is going on with you and Abby." He gives me the kind of look normally reserved for people who suddenly develop a second head.

I sigh and grab the bottle of bourbon off the counter. No glass. Just the bottle. Screw it.

Manny cracks open a beer and we clink like we're celebrating something other than the dumpster fire that is my life.

"I don't even know where to start," I mutter.

"Start with the part where you fell in love with the one person you loathe," he teases.

"Dude. We're not in love," I shoot back. "And we're not really dating."

Manny blinks. "Wait... what?"

I rub a hand down my face and groan. "We're fake dating to make her ex jealous."

Manny pauses mid-sip, beer hovering midair. "Why?"

"Because last night, when we ran into her ex, she kissed me. Total spur-of-the-moment, make-him-jealous move." I shake my head, still annoyed. "Neither of us had any clue he'd turn out to be the new partner. Then he had to go and announce it to the whole room like he's hosting a game show." I take a swig straight from the bottle, then grin. "Now we just have to sell this thing. Make Marcus sweat a little and keep Victoria in the dark." I drop my head back with a groan. "Simple."

"Wowww," Manny says, scanning my kitchen like he's searching for a grip on reality. "So you're not actually dating?"

I shake my head. "Nope. Just for show. Then we'll 'break up,'" I add, tossing in some half-hearted air quotes. "Amicably, of course. Then we can all move on from this flaming disaster."

A slow grin spreads across Manny's face. That look never means anything good.

"You think Abby's looking to date anyone?" he asks like a child wanting to sneak candy before dinner.

"What?" I snap, sharper than intended.

He shrugs, all casual. "I don't know, man. She's a cutie. And now that you've got the inside track, maybe you can put in a good word for me."

I blink at him, my fingers curling tighter around the bourbon bottle until my knuckles go white. Heat flares across my chest. Why the hell do I suddenly feel like my skin's too taut?

"You like Abby?" I ask, trying to keep my voice neutral. It fails, miserably.

Manny doesn't notice or pretends not to. "I've had a thing for her for a while. Just never said anything 'cause I figured you two were mortal enemies."

"I don't hate her," I bark.

He nearly spits out his beer. "Okay, man." He chuckles. "You don't hate her."

"I don't!" I shoot back way too defensively. "I mean. I offered to fake date her, didn't I? Who does that for someone they *hate?*"

He gives me a look. "Exactly."

I lean back, trying to play it cool even though my brain is doing laps. "What would you have done if we were actually dating?"

Manny pauses, thoughtful for once. "I was gonna say

congrats," he says simply. "I just want you to be happy, bro. Even if it's with the chick I'm crushing on."

That's the thing about Manny. He's a good guy. Like, *good good*. The kind of guy AJ probably would go for, if she was into dating anyone. From what I've seen, she's not. In all the years we've worked together, I've never heard her gossip about a crush, never caught her flirting, never seen her even look at someone that way. I always figured the devil didn't need a spouse. Now, though? Maybe AJ does want someone. Maybe she's finally ready. Maybe it'll be Manny. The thought makes that weird heat rise again, this time creeping all the way to my face. I glance down at the bottle. Okay, that's enough bourbon for tonight.

Just then, the intercom buzzes.

"Mr. Slack," Frank's voice crackles through. "Your delivery is here."

I walk over and press the button. "You can send them up, Frank. Thanks."

Within minutes, there's a knock at the door. I stand to open it and Manny springs up like he's been starved for days and grabs the bag from the delivery guy, immediately spreading out the containers like we're hosting a buffet. He's clearly starving.

Me? I've completely lost my appetite. Can I really stomach the idea of my closest friend dating my work nemesis? Correction: my *fake* girlfriend? The thought alone makes me want to double down on the bourbon.

"Here you go," Manny says, sliding my food toward me with a plastic fork.

"Thanks," I say, trying to sound normal.

We eat in silence for a beat. Well, Manny eats and I push

my food around while he inhales his like he's being timed. There's grease on his mouth and I just know AJ would cringe at how sloppy he's eating. Still, he's a good-looking guy. Taller than me, tattooed forearms on full display under a fitted tee. At work, he keeps them covered. Tonight? He looks like a magazine ad with a pulse. I wonder if AJ likes tattoos. Manny could probably hook up with half the office if he wanted to. But he doesn't. Manny's not like me. He doesn't sleep around. He's the *nice, hot guy* of the office.

"Hey, what do you want me to say to AJ?" I ask, my voice more clipped than I mean it to be.

He pauses mid-bite, wipes his mouth and shrugs.

"Just tell her I'm a good dude," he says. "Tell her I take care of my grandma, I want marriage, kids… the whole deal." He glances at me, sincere. "Abby seems like the kind of girl who'd want that." Then he grins. "Also, it's true."

He's got a decent strategy going on. AJ *does* seem like the white-picket-fence type. Golden retriever. Carpool line. Two or three kids. PTA board president. And Manny? He's exactly the kind of guy who'd give her that life.

Dammit. That feeling again. It's crawling up my spine, warm and irritating. Wait… I know this feeling. It's jealousy. Jealousy over what, exactly? AJ and Manny? Please. That's laughable. Right?…*Right?*

Suddenly, the mix of too much bourbon and the smell of Chinese food hits me like a freight train. I shoot up from my stool and sprint to the sink just in time to throw up.

"Bro!" Manny shouts, practically leaping away from the counter. "Are you okay?"

He shuffles his food out of splash range like it's a crime scene, eyes wide.

I wash my face, rinse my mouth with water and grip the edge of the sink like it might keep me standing.

"You think it's the food?" Manny asks, inspecting his takeout container like he's about to disarm it.

"I didn't even eat mine yet," I croak, gesturing toward my still-sealed carton.

"Oh. Right." He blinks. "No offense, dude, but I can't be around vomit. I'm a sympathy puker. It's like a chain reaction."

"I'm fine," I say, waving him off.

He cautiously lowers his hand from his mouth and resumes nibbling like nothing just happened.

"Okay, cool. That was crazy," he says breezily, like I didn't just audition for a remake of *The Exorcist*.

"Yeah," I mutter, wiping my face with a paper towel and heading back to my bar-stool.

We finish our food in near silence, except for the occasional grumble about the upcoming Yankees season.

After Manny leaves, I clean up the takeout containers, toss the bag down the trash chute and make a mental note to never mix bourbon and the smell of egg rolls again.

As I walk back into my pristine apartment, I tell myself the vomiting was the booze. Not the jealousy. Definitely not the idea of Manny dating AJ. Couldn't be that. I'm not some overly emotional girly man freaking out because he might be catching feelings for his fictitious girlfriend. Nope. Not me.

"I hate AJ," I say out loud to my empty apartment. I clear my throat and adjust my shirt. "I *don't like* AJ." I correct my wording. And just like that, the lie echoes a little too loud.

11

Abby

I somehow manage to leave the office and make it home without running into a nemesis, sham boyfriend, suspicious boss, or ex-fiancé. So, suffice it to say, my evening is already looking better than the complete fiasco that was my morning through late afternoon.

I'm not usually one to be overly cautious… who am I kidding? Of course I am. Still, is it just me, or is it weird that Jonathan's genuinely willing to fake a relationship with me? This is a man who once got Selena Gomez to let him buy her a drink and dance with him, without saying a single word. Just a look. Just those stupidly hot features doing all the work. That was pre-Benny engagement, obviously. The fact that Jonathan pulled *her*? Wildly impressive. We love our Queen Selena. I only wish I could've been there to meet her and warn her about Jonathan or at least tell her to schedule a rabies shot just in case.

Okay, that was mean. Also kind of true. He has never made my work life easy and now he suddenly wants to help me? It's giving red flags and hidden agendas. I wouldn't even consider going through with it if I wasn't so utterly desperate.

Why do I feel the need to put on this elaborate show for Marcus anyway? Parade around with my new boyfriend, who, yes, is objectively good-looking and independently wealthy even though Jonathan wouldn't buy me a bagel, let alone dote on me. Still, I need Marcus to see that I've moved on. That the pain he caused by leaving me isn't still wedged in my chest like a bent nail in drywall, impossible to pull out without busting the whole thing open.

So what if I'm lying? So what if I still think about Marcus almost daily, wondering what I did so wrong to make the man who once claimed to love me ditch me on the big day? Not a week before. Not even twenty-four hours in advance. Nope. He waited until I'd woken up with my girlfriends, had my hair and makeup done, slipped into my classy-yet-elegant wedding gown and rode all the way to the venue in a flipping limo… just to be met inside by a very sweaty and visibly anxious best man who informed me Marcus "wouldn't be coming." That was it.

And because we hadn't officially moved in together yet, Marcus had the audacity to send a box of my stuff, left at his place, with the best man to my place. The man didn't even face me himself. The next time I saw him? The other night. At The Yank. *Good grief.* To be fair, the one gentlemanly thing he did manage to do was pay for the entire wedding. He took care of everything. Which he could more than afford to, arguably. So… that's still nice, right?

Of course, my problems didn't end there. I'd already given up my lease, because love makes you blind, so I had to beg, literally *beg*, my landlord to take me back. He'd already promised the place to someone else, so I dropped to my knees, cried real tears and pleaded with him like I wish Marcus had done with me. My landlord relented… not before jacking my rent up by two hundred bucks. Still, I got it back. The only tiny sliver of normal I had left. My sanctuary. The one safe space where I could shut the door, tune out the world and hide from it all; smug coworkers and ghosting ex-fiancés included.

When I walk through my front door, I immediately remember why I love living here. It's modest, sure. In New York City, though, landing a semi-rent-controlled unit that isn't infested with rats or surrounded by sirens is practically winning the lottery. My place sits right between the Lower East Side and SoHo; overpriced for the square footage, yet still a two-bedroom, one-bath with just enough charm to make me feel like I've got my life together.

The best part? My unit has access to a little middle terrace. I've filled it with flowers, started a tiny garden and sometimes sit out there with a book, pretending I'm in a Nancy Meyers movie. It's a far cry from the luxury condo I was supposed to move into with Marcus, but honestly? I'm happy here. I feel lucky, especially in a city where most people can't afford to breathe.

For reasons I absolutely refuse to psychoanalyze, I find myself wondering what Jonathan's place looks like. I don't know why I care. I shouldn't care. But I *should* ask. Just in case someone at work brings it up and I blank. I mean, how can you be dating someone and not know what their apartment looks like?

The office gossip mill is going to feast on this one. Me and Jonathan? It's the juiciest news since Vanessa got caught making out with Xavier, the janitor, in the broom closet. So cliché. So steamy. Tongue-on-tongue, right next to the mop bucket. The joke's on the gossipers though, they're married now. Vanessa's pregnant. Evidently, love really can blossom in the workplace.

Too bad I didn't find love, instead I found Jonathan Slack. A walking, talking, cocky-as-hell ulcer who just so happens to be my new, absurd office romance.

I barely get a chance to set my purse down and grab a water from the fridge before my phone buzzes. It's my best friend, Lila, currently in California filming a sitcom pilot. She's about to become famous and then take me to all the star-studded award shows so I can finally meet Chris Evans and make him fall in love with me. At least, that's the shared dream.

"Hey, girl, hey," she says the second I answer. She always has to speak first.

I chuckle. Just hearing her voice makes the day feel less like a disaster.

"Heyyyy," I say back.

"How's the East Coast, lovey?" she asks with a laugh.

"Missing a star, but otherwise it's surviving," I quip.

"Aww, I miss you too," she replies, her tone warm and genuine.

She's never been away this long. Sure, she's always traveling for acting gigs, but this time she landed a sidekick role in a comedy series filming in Hollywood, so she's been staying there the past month to shoot and charm the NBC execs.

"So… how's Hollywood?" I ask, ready to live vicariously through the glamour and glitz.

"Eh. It's okay," she says. Still bubbly, but something's off.

"What's wrong?" I ask, instantly alert. "Are you okay?"

I'm already mentally packing a suitcase. That's just how we are; if one of us is in crisis, the other shows up. Lila is closer to me than most sisters. I should know, I have a sister who hardly manages a yearly email.

"I'm okay," she says. "But I *will* have to send you a plane ticket soon because my show just got picked up for a full season!" She screams.

"Oh my God! That's *so* amazing!" I squeal.

"Thank you!" she laughs.

A sudden pang hits my chest.

"Wait," I say, a little too fast. "Does this mean... you have to move there?"

Lila still lives in one of the unit cottages down the block from mine and I've been watering her plants like a loyal plant godmother. Yes, *plants*. Dozens of them. Each with names.

There's a brief silence on the line. I can hear her breathing shift.

"Yes," she says softly. Just one word. So short. So final.

"Oh." My voice dips. "I mean... that's amazing. And exciting," I rapidly add.

"I know. But..." She trails off, then shifts gears. "But you can visit me all the time."

"Of course I will," I admit. Because that's what good friends do, they celebrate your big moments, even when their own hearts are sinking like a deflated party balloon.

Lila has always been there for me and I'll be there for her, no matter what.

"I have to stay another week or so to wrap things up," she says. "Then I'll come home to pack up my place. Maybe you can come back with me for a week? See my new apartment, visit set, hang with the cast..."

"That sounds perfect," I say and mean it. I'll need a vacation after this disaster of a week. "Especially after the retreat I have to attend this weekend."

"What retreat?" she asks.

"Victoria's dragging us to Cedar Lakes for some kind of corporate bonding situation," I say, using air quotes for emphasis, though no one in my living room is here to appreciate the gesture.

"Cedar Lakes? That actually sounds… kind of nice," she says.

"Oh, it's *very* nice." I pause.

Or at least, it *could* have been, if my ex, my work nemesis and I weren't about to be trapped together in my own flaming circus of feelings.

I want to tell her everything. About Marcus. About Jonathan. About this whole life spiral I'm currently free-falling through. But I stop myself. This is *her* moment and my emotional disaster will still be here when she gets back.

"All right, girly. They're calling me back to set," Lila says.

"This late?" I ask, surprised.

"Girrrlll. We shoot fourteen, fifteen-hour days sometimes," she groans. "But I freaking *love* it!"

I know she does. It's always been her dream to become a star. And mine? To be her best friend who gets the swag bags and *accidentally* bump into celebrities.

"Okay. Have fun. Text me later," I say.

"Love you! Bye!" she calls, blowing a kiss through the phone.

"Bye," I reply, even though she's already hung up.

I set my phone on the counter and grab a wine-glass from the cabinet. Then I settle onto one of my steal-of-a-deal Pottery Barn bar stools, pour myself a generous glass of Pinot Grigio and lean back against the cushion.

My gaze drifts around my type-A organized, color-splashed home. It's so bright, so cheerful, just like my life used to be.

Lila's out there living her dream, all fast-paced and fabulous while I'm living a lie.

Who could've thunk it?

12

Jonathan

Welp. It's Friday. The day our entire office packs up and pretends a lakeside retreat will strengthen teamwork instead of steadily unraveling everyone's sanity, and I am *stoked.*

That's a lie, of course. I'm not usually someone who gets rattled by the unexpected. I thrive on mayhem, as long as I'm the one orchestrating it. This trip, though? This four-day masterclass in pretending to be romantically involved with the one woman I can only stand in three-minute increments? It's been ruining my sleep and I like my sleep.

Yesterday flew by in a complete blur. I assume I went to work, attended a few meetings, pitched some brilliant marketing ideas, went home, showered, packed. The usual. Can't say for sure though, I might've blacked out somewhere between my second coffee and 4 p.m. No one's called to tell me I missed anything important, my suitcase is packed with my most stylish and strategically casual clothes and this morning I woke up to a text from my client Peter that said:

Great job on the commercial pitch. We want to move forward with it next week. Enjoy your retreat! – P

So apparently, I crushed Thursday. Ever since AJ kissed me, scratch that, ambushed me with her traitorous lips, my brain has been fizzling out. I don't like this version of me. The unsettled one. The overthinking one. The one who actually googled *signs you might have a concussion from emotional whiplash.*

Everyone thinks I'm laid-back, easygoing, the guy who rolls with anything. That's fine. That's the version of me I let them see. Beneath all that, though, I'm a well-oiled, mildly obsessive machine. I like control. I need order. I alphabetize my spices. No one knows that and they don't need to. Because who wants to date the guy who has a color-coded sock drawer? *No one.*

I'm Jonathan Slack. I'm fun. I'm chill. Nonchalant should be my middle name. Even if I'm currently spiraling over a woman who once tried to report me to HR for "breathing too loudly."

When I pull into the building's entrance, I spot one of the largest, glossiest, most obnoxiously impressive coach buses I've ever seen. Blacked-out windows with chrome trim and mood lighting, probably. Yup. That must be our ride to the retreat.

I shake my head, impressed but mostly irked. Marcus clearly isn't holding back on this trip. Flashing his wealth like he's trying to buy everyone's admiration or at the very least, their attention. Whatever, not my problem. AJ doesn't even want him back. She made that clear. Truly? She shouldn't. The guy left her at the altar. That's not just a red flag, that's a fully choreographed warning sign with backup dancers.

Not that I want to marry her or anything. Still… she would make a great wife. I don't mean that in a sexist, "make me a sandwich" kind of way. I mean she's the type who remembers dentist appointments, packs snacks for the road, strategically highlights the family calendar, folds laundry with crisp corners. Might even toss in a little handwritten note with her husband's lunch.

Why am I thinking about this? I blink, shake it off. *Get it together, Slack.*

And just as I finally tell my brain to stop thinking about her, the universe laughs in my face because here she comes, barreling toward my car with the intensity of a woman chasing the last Sephora sale item. I scantily have time to shift into park before she's knocking on my passenger-side window.

I roll it down, trying not to look too amused. "You look like someone about to sell me bootleg DVDs or clean my windshield."

"Shut up," she snorts. "Can I get in?"

I unlock the car and like some chivalry-programmed robot, I reach over to open the door for her. Instinct, maybe. Or muscle memory from some past life where I was polite.

She slides into the passenger seat and I immediately catch the scent of apricot from her shampoo and notice the hint of skin I'm not used to seeing. Normally she's buried under layers of blouses and cardigans, like she's protesting central heating. But today she's in white chinos, long enough to say *I'm classy*, short enough to say *I might ruin your life and look good doing it.* Her mauve cable-knit polo is some kind of preppy Ralph Lauren situation. It's good girl with a hint of bad girl corporate. Either way, I'm digging it.

A horn blares behind me.

"Go," she says, jerking her thumb toward the impatient car behind us.

"Shit." I peel out of the front loop and head toward the employee parking garage. Level one, my go-to spot: far enough to avoid dings, close enough to avoid crime.

"So, AJ," I say, throwing her a glance as I pull into a spot. "What's up?"

She shoots me a look. "Go ahead and get it out of your system now before we see everyone."

"Get what out?" I ask, though I already know.

"My clothes," she says flatly. "Make fun of them now. Get it over with."

I shift into park and turn toward her. "I like your clothes," I admit honestly. "And the way you smell." A smirk lifts one corner of my mouth.

She rolls her eyes, but there's a smile tugging at hers too.

Off to a surprisingly good start.

"Well… thanks," she says, like she's not quite sure how to process a compliment from me. "I wanted to talk to you before we head in," she says.

I leave the engine running and keep the AC on full blast because summer in the city is basically Mother Nature's way of hazing us.

"Talk about what?" I ask, glancing over.

"I was doing some research last night," she says, adjusting in her seat like she's about to drop classified intel. "And it turns out most of the accommodations at Cedar Lakes are shared cottages. So, chances are, we'll be rooming with coworkers."

I nod. "Okay."

"I'm going to request Tanya and Elaine, if possible," she continues, voice lowering like we're being tailed by the FBI. "If I keep the two people most likely to out us close, I can control the narrative."

She leans in conspiratorially. Out of habit, I lean in too. The scent of her floral shampoo hits me again and *dammit,* I need to stay focused.

"Smart plan I guess," I remark.

She jerks back, narrowing her eyes. "'You guess'?"

I shrug. "Yeah. I mean… probably fine."

Her tone sharpens. "Jonathan. Our futures hinge on this lie."

"I mean… possibly," I reply, informally. "But you're making it a thing. No one's going to find out. We're solid."

She stares at me for a second, letting it settle in her brain, then nods. "Okay. Okay. You're right." She exhales and rubs her thigh anxiously. "It'll be fine." She looks up at me and says the one thing I never expected to hear fall out of her mouth in this lifetime or any other. "I think we'll have to kiss again."

I cough, almost choking on my own spit. "Wait. Why? I mean… what do you mean?"

She waves her hand like I'm the idiot here. "I mean people are going to expect us to touch. Flirt. Giggle, even. Maybe even finish each other's sentences. And yes, *kiss.* You know, like real couples do."

Kissing AJ again. I mean it's not like I'm against it. Not even a little.

I smirk. "Whatever you want, babe."

She groans and swats my hand off the middle console. "Ugh. Stop it. I don't *want* to kiss you again. I'm just saying we need to be prepared. Especially if Marcus is lurking around."

"Right. Marcus." I nod, my tone coming off more sarcastic than I planned.

She catches the shift. "What does that mean?"

I glance over. "What's your play here? You want the guy

back?"

She pauses and I can see that she doesn't even know the answer to that question. Not fully at least.

"No. I don't think so," she says slowly. "I just… I want him to feel something seeing me with someone else."

There's a flicker of something raw behind her eyes. She looks down and starts fidgeting with her pink-painted nails.

"It's pathetic. I know," she mumbles.

I take her hand to stop her from wrecking her fresh manicure. "No, AJ. It's not pathetic. It's human."

She looks up at me and for a split second, her gaze drops to my mouth. *Don't read into that, Slack.*

"Thanks," she says, slipping her hand from mine.

I don't know why I ask the next part. I probably shouldn't. "What if he does want you back?"

She shrugs, then smiles faintly. "I doubt it. But… I wouldn't mind seeing him try."

Laughter flows, coming out of each of us. It's unexpected and real, just for a breath, just long enough to feel almost normal again. Then… *BANG.*

Manny slaps the hood of my car like it owes him money. "Wassup, lovebirds!" he shouts into the window.

AJ and I both jolt in our seats.

"Come on." Manny grins. "Time to check in."

I roll my eyes and glance at AJ. She smirks, hands raised in surrender.

"Guess it's showtime," she says.

* * *

Walking onto our office floor, I start to think, maybe this

trip won't be a total disaster. AJ and I just have to act overly friendly, maybe flirt a little, but keep it light. No drama. No emotional dumpster fires. Should be easy.

We head toward the group, where everyone's gathered near Marcus and Victoria. They're standing at one of the reception desks, handing out VIP passes to wear during our stay at Cedar Lakes. Apparently, it helps staff keep track of which guests belong to which corporate group. Makes sense. With a place that big, I'm sure there will be at least one or two other companies sharing the resort.

Marcus reaches for a pass labeled *Abigail* and before he can hand it to her, I step in and grab it myself. I slip it over AJ's head, like the charming boyfriend I now am. She smirks, clearly not hating the attention. I think I nailed it.

I turn back to grab my own pass from Marcus, who's already looking at me like he'd rather be anywhere else.

He hands me the lanyard and says, "Here you go, Jason."

I grin. "It's Jonathan."

His jaw tics. "Ah. Right. Apologies."

I slap a friendly hand on his back, making sure it's just a touch too firm. "No worries. By the end of this trip, you won't forget my name again." And I wink, because allegedly that's my new personality trait now.

As I move back to stand beside AJ, I catch Victoria's expression and let's just say she's less than thrilled with the little pissing contest Marcus and I just had. But she won't call him out. She can't. He's *her* boss now. As for me? She'll play the "cool boss" card during the retreat. So I'm safe... for now.

AJ elbows my side and I turn to see her grinning like she's about to burst out laughing. I didn't realize she caught my exchange with Marcus. Either way, I'm glad she did. I like her better when she's smirking, not snarling.

Marcus steps to the center of the room, all confident allure.

"Thanks, everyone, for coming. This is a corporate retreat, but Victoria and I really want to make it fun and show our appreciation for how astoundingly well the company's been doing," he says, clapping like he just cured world hunger.

The office eats it up. By all means they do. You throw a luxury retreat at a group of overworked employees and magically you're the messiah in tailored khakis. It also doesn't hurt that Marcus looks like a GQ cover wrapped around a Bradley Cooper face. Our office is 80% women. He could offer them a root canal and they'd still applaud.

I lean down and murmur to AJ, "Has anyone even acknowledged the fact that he's your ex?"

She pauses, like the thought didn't occur to her, then shakes her head and looks down.

"What a bunch of pricks we work with, huh?" I add, trying to nudge her mood.

"Yeah," she says with a shake of her shoulders.

Well, that settles it. I'm officially making it my mission to ensure this retreat is bearable for AJ and miserable enough to make Marcus regret ever showing up in that smug little blazer like he owns the place. Funny how I'm supposed to be the office jerk, yet I seem to be the only one giving a damn about how hard this has to be for her.

Victoria claps her hands. "We've assigned two people per cottage."

AJ's head tilts toward the center as Victoria continues. "We've printed out your itineraries, but we've also left plenty of free time for you to enjoy yourselves," she says, like this is also a wellness retreat.

She starts handing out sheets and Marcus grabs a few too, making his way over with the swagger of someone who thinks he invented corporate charisma.

I feel the shift in AJ before she even moves; her whole body stiffens as he approaches. Mine probably does too. I try to loosen my shoulders but it's like the tension's calcified.

"Here you go," Marcus says as he hands each of us a paper. Then he adds, real smooth, "I made sure to put you two together in your own cabin."

I glance down at the paper. *Sleepy Pine Cottage*. Then at AJ whose face is stuck somewhere between shock and horror. Then back at Marcus. "Thanks," I say evenly.

AJ doesn't say a word. Just clutches her paper and pretends to read it like it contains top-tier gossip from the royal family. I've worked with this woman for six years and I know when her brain is unraveling like a Pinterest wedding board after three glasses of wine.

Marcus moves along, handing out more papers like he's Santa Claus with a clipboard instead of a sleigh.

"Yay! Bunk besties!" Tanya squeals, hugging Elaine like they've won the friendship lottery. I roll my eyes so hard I practically see my skull.

Manny strolls over and peeks down at our itinerary sheets. "You're with Abby, huh?" he says, his voice neutral, eyes flickering just enough to register something. "I'm with Cliff," he adds with a half-shrug. Not sure if he's bummed it's not me or pissed I'm with AJ. "Cool. Cool," he says, pushing a strand of hair off his forehead like he's in a slow-mo shampoo commercial. "See you on the bus."

I turn to AJ. "Everything will be fine... right?" I ask, full sarcasm.

She looks up at me, blue eyes locked in and for the first time, I notice there's a hint of violet near the edge of her pupils. Weird detail to pick up on now of all times. She stands a little straighter, grabs my paper and folds it like she's about to brief the troops.

"Yes, it will, Slack," she says, all bite and commander tone.

Oh boy. Here we go.

13

Abby

Considering coach buses get a bad rep for being dirty, cramped and equipped with bathroom stalls the size of a broom closet, the one on this retreat is weirdly luxurious for something on wheels.

"You have to go back out there," I tell myself in the mirror.

I glance down at the sink and suck in a breath like it might oxygenate me with courage. Maybe if I pass out, I can be excused from this whole weekend. That'd be nice. It's clean yet dramatic. Unfortunately, I'm starting to get lightheaded from holding my breath too long and *oh, right,* I'm not literally auditioning for a tragic role in a medical drama.

I exhale, unlock the stall door and step out with my head held high. Too high. Now my neck hurts. Okay, tone it down, Abby.

I once wanted to be an actress, back when I was nine and convinced I'd be the next Hilary Duff. I even pulled off a full-blown sob story about our pet fish Fred "jumping" out of his tank, just so my parents wouldn't find out I tried to set him free in the fountain off 25th Avenue. Turns out, fountains are basically chlorinated death traps and not exactly the peaceful aquatic escape I imagined. RIP Fred. I really did try. Looking back, I think my parents knew the truth and just… pretended they didn't. Which now feels like some gentle parenting 101. Proof that sometimes white lies are totally fine. Harmless, even.

What Jonathan and I are doing is just a white lie. A tiny, barely-a-problem, save-face-at-work kind of fib. It's fine. *Totally fine.*

I slide back into my seat beside him and he reaches into a lunch bag packed with snacks.

"Want a candy bar?" he asks, pulling out a Hershey's like some sugar-coated peace offering.

"Yes," I say, entirely too excited, even though it's slightly past ten in the morning. A sugar spike might be the only thing keeping me upright today. I start to unwrap it, grinning like a kid.

"These are my favorite," I admit.

"I know," he mutters under his breath.

I freeze mid-bite, turning toward him. "Are you stalking me now?" I tease, chocolate already melting in my mouth.

He laughs. "Now *that's* sexy."

I giggle as I chew the massive bite down. Before I can stop him, he grabs my hand, leans in and takes a chunk out of the bar like it's a shared ration in the apocalypse.

"You have your own, you maniac," I protest.

He smirks and unzips his lunch bag again, revealing a stack of candy bars.

"Oh my God," I say, laughing. "You're planning to keep us high on sugar all weekend?"

"And hopefully booze," he adds with a wide smile.

"You've got chocolate on your face." I giggle while pointing to the smear.

"Where?" he asks, immediately wiping blindly at his cheek.

"Here, let me." I lean in and swipe my thumb gently across his cheek to clean it off.

He catches my wrist, brings my thumb to his mouth and sucks off the chocolate, because we're now living in an alternate universe where my appendage landing in his mouth is acceptable. Warmth floods through me. Not the polite kind. The kind that hits places that should absolutely not be lighting up for Jonathan Slack.

He lets go of my thumb, but not my eyes and now I'm just sitting here, blinking like an idiot, frozen in place like Ricky Bobby in *Talladega Nights; I don't know what to do with my hands.* Except mine were just in his mouth, so yeah… new level of awkward.

Jonathan stays silent too, his expression unclear. Regret? Confusion? Did he really enjoy that? Did *I*?

Finally, he breaks the tension with a shrug. "Gotta play the part, right?" Then he turns back to his phone like he didn't just give my thumb the world's most confusing foreplay audition.

"Right," I echo, trying not to choke on the lingering sexual tension in the air.

He lifts one of his AirPods toward me. "Wanna watch *Love Island*?"

I blink, in dismay. "You watch *Love Island*?"

He nods, eased as ever and smiles. "Who doesn't?"

That smile of his is dangerously effective and could probably convince a nun to buy lingerie.

"True," I say with a laugh, taking the AirPod and slipping it into my ear.

He leans back, holding his phone between us, angled just slightly closer to my side. We settle into a rhythm, me trying not to notice the way our shoulders brush, or how he laughs at the same parts I do.

Two episodes and one very steamy British argument later, the bus begins to come to a halt and through the oversized windows, the retreat estate comes into view.

It's stunning. Wooded and serene, like a movie set for rich people pretending to rough it.

Jonathan stands and shimmies in front of me to grab our bags from the overhead compartment. He angles himself so it's his butt near my face, not his crotch, which is gentlemanly... I guess.

Also, his butt looks firm. Like, distractedly so. The man has a face that could make a Greek god jealous and a body that probably came with its own gym membership. Ever since our kisses, I haven't been able to stop replaying them in my head. Not just because I was mortified. Because... they were good.

I'd be lying if I said I'd mind having to kiss Jonathan again for appearances' sake. It's not like it means anything. I'm not about to fall in love with Jonathan Slack of all people. So what can it hurt? ...*Right?*

Except then he had to go and suck chocolate off my finger like some sort of dessert-loving Casanova and now my brain won't stop showing me slow-mo flashbacks of his firm ass in my face. Like, is it illegal to want to squeeze it? Or bite it?

Dear God, Abigail. Pull it together. You are losing it.

I give my head a small, involuntary shake, hoping to rattle the mental image loose. Unfortunately, Jonathan notices.

"What's wrong?" he asks, turning toward me, brows raised.

"Oh... uh, I think a bug flew by me," I lie, far too quickly.

He laughs. "Girls and their bug issues."

"Whatever," I mumble with an eye roll, though… he's not wrong. I hate bugs. *Hate them.* Just thinking about them makes my skin crawl. Like the overthinking, bug-averse nerd I am, I did Google the local wildlife before this trip. The worst-case scenario is a tick, which is objectively gross and potentially life-altering, *Lyme disease, anyone?* But Cedar Lakes' website promised they spray regularly and maintain the tick population. So… whew. One less thing to spiral about.

When I step off the bus, all thoughts of bugs and butts, fly out of my head.

This place is… jaw-dropping. Rolling green hills, perfectly manicured shrubbery and views so idyllic it's like Mother Nature got a glam team. The entire group collectively gasps as we take it all in, like we've just stumbled into a luxury yoga retreat or a catalog for rustic-chic weddings. We get to pretend we're relaxed and thriving here all weekend. Can't wait.

I read that Cedar Lakes used to be a summer camp until someone got the genius idea to turn it into a highly sought-after venue for weddings and corporate retreats. With its tree-lined lakes and the Shawangunk Mountains lounging in the background, I can definitely see the appeal. If you're looking for *wholesome but make it editorial,* this is it.

Which, of course, means a tiny pang shoots through me at the thought. Marcus and I had planned to get married at the Central Park Boathouse. Classic, timeless and elegant, just like I'd wanted. I had designed the whole thing myself: an upscale boho dream, overflowing with florals and greenery. The kind of wedding people would still talk about years later. Well, they *do*, just not for the right reasons. Instead of easy elegance, my guests got me ugly crying on a bench, then making a dramatic escape in a limo with Lila, while my mom had to go out and break the news to the guests.

I blink the memory away as we walk toward the main building to check in. Clusters of people are already sprawled around unlit fire pits while a live band belts out Rod Stewart like they're headlining Madison Square Garden.

Then—over the music—I catch something that sounds suspiciously like Jonathan's voice somewhere off to the left, half-laughing, half-serenading along.

"Wake up Maggie…" he croons in a low, gravelly imitation of Stewart's voice, just enough of a tease to make me squint at him.

"Wow. You've got a surprisingly good voice… for a tall ogre," I say.

He grins and keeps going, his version getting louder, cheesier—absolutely just to embarrass me. The worst part? I kind of like the sound of it.

He's mumbling about being led away from home and something about heartbreak, then—without warning—grabs my hand and spins me into him. People nearby clap along to the beat. Jonathan twirls me again, still holding my hand, still delivering his off-key-but-somehow-charming Rod Stewart performance like the lyrics are his personal confession.

My coworkers are laughing, singing along, and I'm standing there—breathless in the arms of the man I'm supposed to hate—while he hams it up.

What the hell is happening to me?

I glance over and spot Marcus, standing stiffly near the front of the group, designer carry-on in hand like he's about to board a private jet instead of a lakeside retreat. He's watching me and Jonathan while we spin, laugh and dance as if we for-real like each other. He seems confused. Or worse, like he didn't think I deserved to look this happy. Even if it's fake. Except… in this moment, it's not. I'm not pretending. I'm not performing. I'm just… enjoying it.

The realization makes my stomach twist. Maybe it's the way Marcus keeps staring, like he's trying to do emotional calculus in his head and all the variables come out wrong. I feel a peak of rage spark behind my ribs. Then I catch Jonathan's smile. Still easy, still close and I remember, *this is the point*. Make Marcus hurt. Make him jealous. At the very least, make him wonder.

The song ends. The group claps and I slip out of Jonathan's arms and join them. Jonathan, showman that he is, sticks two fingers in his mouth and whistles like we're at a Yankees game. Not shocking, he can whistle and of course he can sing. And dance with two annoyingly coordinated legs. The man is infuriatingly functional.

We start walking toward the main lodge, Jonathan nudging my elbow with his like we're co-conspirators. He gives me a smirk so alarmingly handsome it could knock a weaker woman off her feet. Not me. I'm only weak-*ish*.

Just as that thought shoots across my mind, a woman in a breezy white linen dress steps directly into our path. Well, more *Jonathan's* path. She's wearing large, clay earrings and perfume that screams floral overload, like she wrestled a spray bottle and lost. The kind of scent that makes your eyes water and your soul whisper, *Oh honey, no.*

"That was *some* performance," she says, resting her hand on his arm and wedging herself next to him like I'm just here to carry his fan mail.

She turns her blinding smile toward me. It's the kind of

smile that says *You don't mind if I flirt shamelessly with your man, right?*

I mind. Oh, I *definitely* mind. Except why *do* I mind? He's not my man.

"I'm Sherry," she says. "One of the managers here at Cedar Lakes."

She's the kind of woman who makes you question if you packed enough lip gloss. I have to admit, I do like the shade of pink she's wearing on her lips. Bold choice. Might copy it later.

"Hi, Sherry, thank you for having us," Jonathan says fluidly as he untangles himself from her grip and wraps an arm around my waist instead.

The shift is subtle but firm. Protective even. It's kind of nice. I haven't been held like that in a long time, even if it is just a performance with my insufferably attractive work nemesis.

Victoria, Marcus and the rest of our group approach and Sherry flips into hostess mode.

"Welcome, everyone, to Cedar Lakes," she beams, glancing at me like I'm the garnish on a plate she didn't order. "Please come inside. Mimi will get you all checked into your cottages."

She gestures toward the main building and we follow her across the wraparound porch of what looks like an Ina Garten's guest house during lavender season.

"We also have a karaoke bar that entertains our guests nightly," she says straight to Jonathan, with a wink. "Would love to hear that voice again." She taps his cheek lightly like she's known him since high school.

Jonathan lets out an uncomfortable laugh. "Sounds fun. Thanks," he says, then not-so-subtly guides me inside with a rigid hand on my back.

"Your voice always bring out the cougars?" I tease under my breath.

"She's not a cougar," he mutters. "She's just... desperate."

"What? I thought you *liked* desperate women." I smirk.

"I like to work for my meals," he says with a laugh, like he's joking. But he doesn't blink and I don't think he's joking.

I roll my eyes. "Well, she's not your type anyway."

"Oh yeah? And what's my type?" he asks, releasing my waist as we fall into step beside each other.

"You like them young," I remark confidently.

"And how would you know what I like?" Jonathan asks, his voice dipped in curiosity.

"Because..." I pause. Oh no, I was about to admit I know more about him than I've ever let on. "I think Tanya mentioned it once," I lie instead.

He raises a single brow. "Tanya, huh?"

"Yep." The lie burns on the way out.

"Well, Tanya doesn't know me. And neither do you," he says as we approach the check-in desk.

My eyes roll so hard I'm impressed they stay in my skull.

"Come on. Let's see what our digs look like," he says, pulling out his license for the front desk and walking ahead of me.

Marcus suddenly appears beside me, his voice low and cool.

"That was some show your boy put on," he says, still facing forward like eye contact might kill him.

I give a lazy shrug. "He likes attention."

"From what I remember, you didn't like men who acted that way," he replies, side-eyeing me.

Wow. He really side-eyed me.

"People change their minds," I snap, my voice tight. "You should know that better than anyone."

Before I can start throwing decorative pine cones at his face, I walk straight to Jonathan and wrap my arm through his. He startles a little but catches on fast. He glances over his shoulder at Marcus, then slides his arm around my shoulders and he kisses the top of my head like we're one of those couples who call each other *babe* in public without shame.

A+ recovery. Okay, maybe this weekend won't be a total disaster.

14

Jonathan

This place is fucking epic. AJ and I just checked into the resort and grabbed our keys to the *Sleepy Pine Cottage*. I made the executive decision to rent us a golf cart because the grounds are massive and with this unpredictable summer weather, I want us, okay, mostly AJ, to be comfortable and relaxed.

As if on cue, a line of golf carts pulls up out front with attendants hopping off like valet cowboys. I guess we weren't the only ones with the same genius idea.

"Alright, everyone!" Victoria calls out, hands raised like a cruise director rallying her passengers for morning yoga. "Go get settled, explore the grounds. We'll meet at the amphitheater for sunset happy hour at five, then head to the pavilion for dinner around six. Enjoy!"

I watch her and Marcus disappear into the main house, probably off to finalize tonight's lineup of overpriced wine and forced team bonding.

I turn to AJ, grab her by the arm and pull her toward the golf cart like a kid who just found a ride at Disneyland.

"Hurry," I say, trying not to laugh.

"Whoa. Okay," she says, giggling as she hops in beside me.

I love driving golf carts. It takes me back to the weekends my dad used to sneak me onto his country club course. That was probably the most relaxed and almost-human version of him I ever saw. He'd let me drive while he kicked his foot up on the dash and rattled off his trademark pearls of wisdom; *You teach a man to fish...* and other metaphorical nonsense he never actually lived by.

As I navigate through the winding gravel path, miraculously without hitting any colleagues or squirrels, I glance over at AJ. The wind's blowing strands of her hair across her face and she's trying to tame them with one hand.

"So," I ask, "how are you feeling?"

She turns to me with a little squint against the breeze. "I feel fine." Then, with a sly grin, she adds, "Nice move at the front desk."

Ah, she means the *arm-around-the-neck, kiss-on-the-head maneuver.* Classic.

"I saw it in a movie once," I say with a shrug.

She chuckles and slow claps. "Well, bravo."

Just as I start to pat myself on the back, I catch movement in the rearview mirror, another golf cart barreling toward us like we're in a scene from *The Real Housewives of Corporate America.* It's Tanya and Elaine.

"Jonathan! Abby!" Tanya shouts, waving her arm like she's flagging down a lifeboat.

I ease the cart to a stop and glance at AJ. Her expression? A mix of dread, disbelief and full-body bracing.

What now? her face practically screams.

"Ladies," I greet as their cart practically sideswipes ours.

"Can I help you before we're all involved in a multi-golf-cart pileup?"

"You ask!" Tanya hisses, elbowing Elaine.

Elaine clears her throat and straightens the hem of her miniskirt like she's about to deliver a toast at a sorority brunch.

"We were wondering…" she begins cautiously, "…if you two want to explore the area with us?" She says it like she's bracing for a firm no and mild public humiliation.

"Sure," I say.

AJ's head snaps toward me. I suppose even I'm shocked by the words that just flew out of my mouth. I glance at her and wait. After a long beat, she shrugs. That's as good as a *yes* in AJ language.

"What did you have in mind?" I ask.

"There's this little beachfront area," Tanya says quickly, like she's afraid I'll change my mind. "It's got a zip line, some seating, trails… really cute. Thought maybe we could all check it out together?"

I glance around, half-expecting hidden cameras. Feels suspiciously like a setup. They definitely just want to spy on us being "in love."

"Sounds sensational," I say, slapping on a smile so big it might give me a cramp.

Tanya and Elaine squeal in stereo. "Yay!" Elaine says, clapping. "Let's meet in like, an hour?"

"See you then," I reply, throwing an arm around AJ's shoulder as I drive us off.

Behind us, I can hear the synchronized "Awwww" from the cart of chaos.

"You are laying it on *so* thick," AJ says with a laugh.

"If we've convinced Tanya and Elaine, we've basically won

an Emmy," I shoot back. "They're like the office's in-house lie detectors."

She tilts her head thoughtfully. "Honestly? I think Marcus already believes it. Or at least, he doesn't *not* believe it."

Intrigued, I push a little. "Why would you think that?"

She hesitates, then admits, "He made a comment while we were in line at the front desk. Something about how I used to not like men who needed attention."

I blink, processing that. "Oh," I say. "And let me guess, I'm the attention-hungry man in question?" I throw a hand to my chest like I'm a Broadway diva preparing for her final bow.

She laughs and points at me. "You? No, never."

"Well, if we're handing out awards for attention-seeking tools, I think it goes to the guy who ghosted his own wedding before the vows. But hey, what do I know?" I glance over at her, just to make sure the jab didn't cut too deep. We might be faking this thing, but I'm not trying to be an actual dick anymore.

She just shrugs. "Who knew you'd end up being the lesser of two evils?"

I chuckle. "Ha."

We pull up to our cabin and damn, it's a stunner. Looks like it was plucked right out of a fairy tale, or at least a moody fall-themed Instagram feed. A weathered stone chimney climbs up the side like it's been standing there since the dawn of time, refusing to fall. The roof's blanketed in moss, like nature slowly decided to claim it back. The logs are dark, stacked tight, probably creak like hell in the cold but hold in heat like secrets. Nothing flashy. Just solid. Like it's been here forever.

AJ gasps as she steps out of the cart. "This is amazing."

"Yeah," I say, grabbing our luggage from the back. "Sorry

you have to share it with me."

"True," she replies flatly, already annoyed.

"I'm sure they have two beds, right?" she asks, fully rhetorical and fully expecting me to know the answer.

"Probably." I shrug, because I definitely don't.

She reaches for her luggage, but I beat her to it. "Let me."

"Thanks," she says, giving me a small smile.

We step inside the cabin and, yeah, okay, it's straight out of a Disney movie. White linen, soft throw pillows, floral knick-knacks on every surface and a lingering scent of jasmine that feels way too romantic for two coworkers fake-playing house.

I drop the bags by the door and wander toward the fireplace. It's too hot out to light it, though it's a nice touch. Maybe we'll make s'mores later… if the night doesn't implode first. I glance over at AJ, who's already drifting through the space like she's casing it for a heist.

"Jonathan!" she yells from the back room.

Oh no. That tone doesn't scream *we got lucky.*

I head over and there it is. One bedroom. One giant, king-sized bed. No second room. No twin beds. No lifeboat of any kind.

"Of course," I mutter.

She glares at the mattress like she can will it to divide in two.

I wander toward the bathroom, open the door. "One shower," I call out. "One spa tub." I peer in. "Nice. Big. Roomy. I mean, technically, we could… "

"No way!" she yells before I can finish.

I grin. "I was going to say we could alternate. You shower, I soak. I close my eyes. Or vice versa."

"You're always trying to get women naked," she fires back,

already retreating into the kitchenette like it's a safe zone.

"Not true," I protest, following her like the emotionally unavailable golden retriever I apparently am.

She strolls over to the Keurig, picks up a ceramic mug and raises an eyebrow at me like, *You want one?*

"Yes, please," I say, answering her silent question with a nod.

And then because I apparently enjoy circling back to my own embarrassment, I add, "Also, I don't *always* try to get women naked."

I settle onto one of the bar stools. The kitchen's tiny yet charming, more cozy cottage than luxury lodge. There's a full-sized fridge, three stools at the counter and a teal-colored toaster that looks like it belongs to someone's sweet British grandma.

AJ pops in a K-cup and hits brew. Then she walks back over, leans on the counter across from me and tilts her head with faux innocence. "So… you don't *want* to see me naked?" Her voice drops just enough to land somewhere between playful and criminal.

I feel an immediate shift in my pants. *Dammit.*

I swallow hard. Is this a trap? A hallucination? A very specific fantasy come to life?

"Is that a trick question?" I ask carefully.

She shrugs. One of those maddening shrugs that says *maybe* and *you'll never know* all at once and even in her sexy, snobby-prep school outfit, the way she leans forward makes it very, *very* clear she knows exactly what she's doing.

Her eyes flick to mine, then down to my mouth and she licks her lips.

I cough, shifting on the stool. Subtly adjust the situation in my pants, praying she doesn't notice.

"Do you *want* to be naked in front of me?" I ask, my voice suddenly dipping a full octave below Alvin and the Chipmunks. Not exactly the tone I was going for.

She smirks, twirling a piece of her golden hair around her finger like she's in a shampoo commercial. "What if I said yes?"

Beep. The coffee machine chimes and interrupts the mood.

Son of a bitch.

"Well," she says, grabbing her mug with a dramatic sigh. "Guess you missed your chance."

"Oh, come on. What the hell?" I groan, slapping my hands on the counter.

She laughs, clearly proud of herself. "Now you'll never know. Because I'd rather drink coffee than show you my naked body."

"Tease," I mutter with a smirk.

"Takes one to know one." She winks, tossing the used K-cup and popping in a new one for me. She's still grinning as she backs away toward the bedroom. "Now I'm going to change. In the room. With the door shut."

"How very inconsiderate of you," I say.

She pauses in the doorway and eyes me. "Can I trust you? Or do I need to lock it?"

I give her a look. "After that little performance?"

She chuckles, turns and walks away; coffee in one hand, luggage in the other. I lean back on the stool to enjoy the view like a total creep. She glances over her shoulder and catches me and I whip forward so fast I bang my hand on the counter.

"Shit!" I shout.

She laughs, shuts the door and disappears into the bedroom.

And now I'm left sitting here, nursing my pride and wondering if she actually locked the door.

15

Abby

Flirting with Jonathan is fun. He's such an easy target and honestly, he probably walks around with a boner more often than not. It's gross. Someone should do a medical study. But teasing him? It's the perfect distraction from the impending doom that is this retreat.

Part of me wants to tell him I didn't lock the bedroom door. That he could've walked in at any time and seen me naked. But no, that might literally kill him.

When Tanya said "let's meet at the beach," I had no idea what that meant in upstate New York. Sure, it's summer and pushing eighty degrees, but this is still New York; weather can turn faster than my mood during PMS. I settle on cut-off jean shorts, flip-flops and an eyelet tank with my bikini underneath, just in case. There's also a huge heated pool and hot tub I wouldn't mind checking out later.

Jonathan clearly got the memo as well. He's in swim trunks and a white linen button-down. Except he forgot to actually button it. His annoyingly tight abs and taut chest are on full display, like a cologne ad that personally hates me.

"You want to walk?" he asks as I step outside.

I glance at the cart, then at the gravel road. "Sure. You can protect me from any bears."

"I got you covered," he lifts his arm, showing off his very obvious bicep muscles.

"Covered? Like your chest?" I fire back, as dry as toast.

He looks down, confused. "What's wrong with my chest?"

"You forgot to button like the entire shirt," I say, then immediately swallow because I just accidentally salivated.

"Too much for Tanya?" he jokes.

I laugh, because yeah, Tanya's about to melt faster than an ice cream sandwich on asphalt.

"I think we should both show up with our chests out," Jonathan says, tugging down his Ray-Bans to eye my breasts before shooting me a wink.

"Stop it," I say, smacking his arm.

"Just a suggestion." He shrugs.

For a few seconds, there's this weird stretch of silence. Not awkward, not charged with the usual annoyance either. Just… calm and kind of nice.

"So tell me about your family," I ask, mostly to fill the quiet. But the second it leaves my mouth, I regret it. His expression shifts, like I touched a bruise I didn't know was there. "Sorry," I blurt. "Way too personal."

He takes a second. "My dad was the nicest man I knew," he says finally. "Which is saying a lot, because I don't know many nice men." He lets out a small laugh. "He was tough. Kind when he needed to be. But mostly, tough."

The gravel under our feet suddenly sounds louder, like the whole world wants to avoid the awkwardness that crept into the room.

"You keep saying *was*," I say carefully. "Did he...?"

He bends down to pick something up before I can finish. A shell, it's gorgeous and deep blue, like a tiny piece of the ocean.

"Yeah. Cancer," he says, handing it to me. "This matches your eyes."

I take it, stunned by the softness in his voice and we keep walking.

"You know, you're kind too," I say after a moment.

He laughs. "How?"

"Well, for starters, you're fake-dating me so I can make my ex jealous," I state, factually.

"I don't like the guy. That part's easy," he quips.

"And you brought my favorite candy on the bus," I add.

He leans closer, his voice low. "Hate to break it to you, but... it's my favorite too."

"What?" I ask, turning to look at him.

He nods, a little grin playing at his lips.

"We have something in common," I say.

"We sure do," he says, like there's more he wants to say but won't.

"Okay, I got it," I press on, feigning innocence. "You're going to let me sleep in the bed tonight while you take the couch." I lower my sunglasses and toss him a wink.

He laughs. "Fair enough. You got me there," he says, chucking a few pebbles into the grass beside the path.

Then, out of nowhere, "You know Marcus is an idiot for leaving you."

"Tell me something I don't know," I say with a small smile. "But... thanks."

He glances around, then adds, "You're also kind of an idiot

for not seeing the signs."

And just like classic Jonathan, there it is. The pompous, rude comments, he so easily chutes out.

"Excuse me?" I snap, crossing my arms tight enough to crush a rib. "I should've known he was going to leave me at the altar?"

"Not necessarily" he starts.

I push my sunglasses up onto my head so he can get the full effect of my death glare. "Then what the hell *do* you mean?"

"Whoa." His hands lift like he's about to steady me, but I back away before he can touch me.

"AJ," he says, his voice edged with something close to regret. "The guy's a jerk. Anyone could see that."

"Oh, and you'd know all about that, wouldn't you?" I snap. "You'd recognize a jerk in the mirror every morning."

"Listen," he says, but I interrupt him.

"No. Forget it." I wave him off like I'm swatting a fly. "Just when I was thinking you could actually be a normal, decent person for once." I shake my head. "I take it back. You're not kind. You suck." I pick up my pace, stomping ahead.

He calls after me. "AJ, stop!"

But nope. Not happening. I charge forward and nearly collide with Elaine just as we reach the beach entrance.

The *beachfront* is really just a sandy patch that slopes into the lake. A massive inflatable raft floats nearby, with people already launching themselves into the water. There's a dock, a rope swing, and the kind of serenity that would be great if I weren't daydreaming about using that rope swing to strangle Jonathan with.

"Hey!" Tanya calls out, waving me over to a couple of blankets spread out with snacks, bottles of water and a Coke

I'm definitely stealing. "Over here!"

I head toward her, walking along with Elaine, ignoring the footsteps behind me. At least someone brought snacks. Way more thoughtful than Jonathan right now.

I should've seen the signs. What the hell does that even mean? So what, Marcus left me and it's *my* fault? Like I caused him to ghost me at the altar? As if I could've prevented my own soul-crushing heartbreak? *Fuck. Off. Jonathan.* I scream it in my head so loudly I swear my skull rattles. God, I wish I had the guts to say it out loud.

Jonathan jogs up behind me, slightly out of breath. "AJ," he says, then spots Elaine beside me. His posture straightens like someone yanked a string in his spine. "Oh. Hey, Elaine."

"Heyyy," she says back with a flirty little smile. "You okay, Jonathan?"

He places a hand to his chest like he's checking his pulse. "Yeah. Just getting in a light jog." *Lie.* "AJ and I were racing," he adds, glancing at me. "She's fast."

Elaine gives me a confused once-over. "You're not even out of breath."

"Umm…well, I run marathons," I say, way too casually. Total lie. I *do* enjoy cardio, but if I'd just sprinted like that, I'd be panting like a Golden Retriever in August.

She narrows her eyes slightly, shrugs and heads toward Tanya, who's lounging on a blanket, chomping on an apple like Snow White on vacation. I start walking toward them.

"Wait, AJ…" Jonathan says, reaching for me.

I stop and spin around, getting way too close to his face. Close enough to count his freckles. "Let me remind you of one thing, Slack," I growl, keeping my voice whispered so Tanya and Elaine don't hear. I jab a finger at his chest, then at his forehead. "You don't know me."

He steps back, a little startled.

"You may *think* you do, but you have no clue who I am. What I've done. What I've been through. So get that through your thick, overconfident skull." I give his forehead one final poke for emphasis.

He doesn't say a word at first. Just looks at me. His eyes, bluer than I remembered, almost stormy grey now, flash with something that looks like sorrow. But with Jonathan, who knows? Could be acting. Could be real. I never know.

"AJ, I fucked up," he says quietly. "I say stupid shit sometimes without thinking. But I know you're not an idiot. You're one of the smartest people I've ever met." His voice is sincere now. No jokes. No fake charm. Just him, standing there with his hair wind-mussed and his shirt still open, looking like a damn Calvin Klein model at confession.

I don't want to hear him out but watching him stumble through an apology is... oddly satisfying.

"Maybe Marcus did act differently with you," Jonathan mutters. "Maybe he led you on. You're right. I don't know what happened. But I *do* know you're too smart for a guy like that to have hurt you and I... I..." He trails off, hands half-lifted like his brain crashed mid-sentence.

"What?" I press.

"I just don't want him to suck you back in," he says finally. "I wanted to remind you of your worth." He exhales hard, running both hands through his hair like he's physically in pain. Drama king.

"You are terrible at apologizing," I blurt out, chuckling.

He meets my eyes, like he's searching for some thread of forgiveness. "I am. I really am," he admits, winded like this was the emotional equivalent of running a marathon.

"And I keep forgetting you're incapable of being around a woman for longer than an hour without saying something monumentally stupid," I snap.

"I'm the idiot here. Trust me," he says, palms up in surrender.

"Okay," I say, arms crossed.

"So… are we okay?" he asks, looking like he's about to beg.

I sigh, thinking about what Lila always tells me: *Forgive people when you can. Don't carry that weight.* So fine. He said something dumb. He owned it. Let it go, Abby.

"Yes," I say finally. "We're fine."

"Thank you," he says, his hands landing lightly on my arms.

"What are you two lovebirds whispering about?" Tanya calls out across the beach.

We both turn as Elaine whips out her phone like a tabloid photographer. "Aww! Oh my God, stay right there, that's going to be such a cute pic."

She waves us closer. Jonathan flashes me a grin, slides an arm around my waist and pulls me in. His body is solid. Abs of steel. Damn it.

"Say cheese!" Elaine sings. The camera clicks.

"Okay, now a kissing one!" Tanya demands.

Jonathan immediately stiffens. "No, no, we don't have to do that," he says, already glancing at me… then down at my lips.

"It's okay," I say softly.

His eyes go brighter, full sky-blue now. He leans in, cups my face and kisses me.

I kiss him back. It starts soft, but there's a spark, just enough tongue to blur the line between fake and maybe-not-so-fake. My hands find his torso, and I intuitively pull him closer.

"Yayyy!" Tanya yells.

We don't stop.

"Okay, you two. *Dang,*" Elaine laughs. "I got the pic."

I pull back from Jonathan's kiss, breath caught somewhere between my lungs and my brain. He looks stunned, like he didn't really want to stop. Like he was… savoring it. I also *am* stunned. That kiss felt better than the last, if that's even possible. My fingers touch my lips as if they've been sparked. Maybe my anger acted as some kind of emotional defibrillator, because my whole body feels electrically charged.

Jonathan lets out a laugh and turns to Tanya and Elaine. "Sorry, ladies. I can't keep my hands off her."

He laces his fingers through mine and leads us down to their picnic setup like we're *that* couple, the one who giggles and cuddles and probably have a joint Instagram account.

Jonathan starts unpacking the beach bag he brought and to my surprise, pulls out the book I brought from home.

"Figured you'd want to get some reading in," he says with that smile, half smug, half sweet.

"Thank you," I say, taking it from him. Our fingers brush and his linger just long enough to tug gently at mine before letting go.

I stare at him for a second too long. Am I delusional… or is Jonathan Slack crushing on me? Worse… am *I* crushing on *him?* Ugh, maybe.

16

Jonathan

The afternoon AJ and I spend at the beach feels… natural. Even with the gossip twins, Tanya and Elaine, tagging along. AJ reads some of the book I packed for her, we graze from the charcuterie board Tanya somehow whipped up and we even brave the lake for a swim, until the icy water turns our limbs to popsicles. But I'd freeze all over again if it means getting another look at AJ in that bikini. Siren red. Two-piece. Underwire top that lifts her breasts like two perfectly shaped peaches; perky, round, not too small, not cartoonishly big, just… optimally distracting. The bottoms are high-cut, clinging to her ass in a way that should come with a warning label and maybe a safe word.

She knows exactly what she's doing when she puts that suit on. Sure, maybe she bought it for herself, but the second she saw it on in the mirror, she had to know she looked like a damn bombshell.

"You know that bathing suit is doing things to my head I probably shouldn't admit," I lean over and tell her as we sit on the dock, legs dangling in the water.

She giggles and says, "It's *which* head that worries me."

Okay, then. *Little Miss Flirty Comedian*. I like this sexy side of AJ and because she can't leave it there, she splashes me with cold water. So I do what any mature man would do; I pick her up and launch us both into the lake.

She surfaces, shrieking my name. "Jonathan!"

We laugh. We laugh hard. But then I have to book it from that freezing water. I run up, grab towels for us both and we sit out in the sun longer. Talking. Just talking about everything. My family. Her family. Favorite foods. The usual stuff couples discuss when they're dating. It feels nice to be able to be myself, not having to keep all my guards up, though I still keep some up. I don't tell her about the job offer in Boston, or that Manny likes her. Or even that Manny knows our relationship is fake. It's not that I don't want to help my friend out, get him in good with AJ, it's just that I don't think it's a good fit. I'm saving Manny from heartache… I think.

AJ doesn't want to be with anyone. She wants to make Marcus jealous, and to be real, I think she wants Marcus back but hasn't admitted it to herself yet. So Manny would be hurt if he started to fall for AJ and then she wants her ex back. Manny, yes. *Just* Manny, I tell myself. I'm sure she's kept some things from me, too. It's not like we're really dating and have to confess everything.

We all decide to head back to our cottages around three so we have time to get ready for cocktail hour at five with the whole group. I let AJ shower first, because, well, women take much longer to get ready than men. When she emerges from the bathroom, wrapped in only a white towel, my heart does a backflip. Her wet hair cascades down her shoulders, water dripping onto the floor.

"I left enough hot water for you," she teases, flashing a mischievous smirk.

I laugh, shaking my head. "Thanks."

I shower in under five minutes and change in the bathroom, figuring it's only fair to give her the bedroom for a little privacy.

"Is it safe to come out?" I ask, cracking the door and waving a white face towel like a surrender flag.

"Yes," she calls back from the living room.

I step out and find her sitting cross-legged on the floor in front of a full-length mirror, meticulously applying eyeliner like she's prepping for the Oscars.

"You're not dressed yet?" I ask, genuinely confused.

"I save that for last, in case I get makeup or hairspray on my clothes," she says, still hyper-focused on her eyelid masterpiece.

"Huh. Women." I shake my head and walk into the kitchen. I can practically hear her eyes roll.

"Want a cocktail?" I ask, grabbing the vodka.

"Sure," she replies quickly, then hesitates. "I'm nervous."

"Oh yeah? Why's that?" I ask, trying to sound casual.

"My dress is... kind of revealing," she says.

The second the words leave her mouth, my hand jerks and I knock the vodka soda all over the counter. "Shit," I mumble, scrambling for paper towels.

"You okay?" she calls from the other room.

"Yep," I lie. "Just mentally derailed thinking about your tits and ass in something *kind of revealing*, thanks," I add under my breath.

"What was that?" she asks again.

"Nothing, it's good!" I shout back. "Weather should be nice

out." *Smooth, Slack, real smooth.*

She gets up from the floor and walks into the kitchen, barefoot and relaxed in joggers and a fitted tank top. And yet somehow, even in that laid-back outfit, she looks annoyingly hot. Her hair is still damp from the shower, pulled back in a loose bun that shows off the smooth curve of her neck.

"Wow, you look handsome," she says, eyeing me up and down like she's debating whether to climb me like a tree.

I'm wearing black slacks with a Ferragamo belt, Tom Ford loafers and a slim white dress shirt, also Tom Ford, sleeves rolled up just enough to show off the forearms. It's calculated, but not too obvious. Just the right amount of skin.

"Thank you." I nod slightly, giving her my best *I-didn't-try-that-hard* head tilt.

"You always dress fancy, Jonathan," she teases as she steps closer.

"I have style. What can I say?" I shoot back with a smirk.

She reaches out and runs a hand over my chest, fingers gliding along the fabric like she's testing its thread count or trying to drive me insane. "This shirt is so tight, you can see the shadows of your muscles," she murmurs, almost to herself.

What is she doing to me? I freeze, barely breathing, as her hand keeps moving up and down. It's like the fabric of my shirt has become irrelevant and all I can feel is her.

She laughs and pulls her hand back. "Sorry. I think I have sensory issues. I always need to touch stuff," she says, like that explains anything. She grabs the drink I made her while I try to shake off the image of her hands exploring more than just the cotton shirt attached to me.

I grab my own glass and clink it against hers. "Cheers."

"Cheers to us being the best fake couple ever," she adds, her voice teasing but bright.

We sip our drinks, eyes locked just over the rims of our glasses. All I can think about is how much I want to kiss off the rosy-pink lipstick she's wearing and taste the cocktail on her tongue.

"This is actually delicious," she says, licking her lips like she's doing it on purpose. "What did you put in it?"

"I ordered one of those cocktail baskets with lemon vodka and soda setup," I manage to respond, though I'm far more focused on the shape of her lips, the way they part and move and thinking about how they'd feel tracing over the parts of me that ache for her.

"It's good," she says, taking another sip, this one longer. Then she sets her glass down with a soft clink and I seriously consider launching *Operation: Kiss Her Anyway.*

"Okay, I gotta go get changed," she says, then dashes out of the kitchen, hips swaying in those damn joggers like she doesn't know the damage she's doing.

While I wait, I down the rest of my drink. Then I down hers. Blame it on nerves. Blame it on the mental reruns of her in that red bikini. Or the phantom heat of her lips on mine. Whatever the cause, I need to be at least slightly buzzed if I'm going to survive tonight.

About twenty minutes later, the bedroom door opens and for a second, I swear the earth tilts on its axis. She steps out gingerly, almost uncertain, like she doesn't realize the kind of damage she's about to do. The dress is fuchsia, tight in all the right places, dipping at the waist and skimming along her thighs before giving way to a slit that slices high up her leg. My eyes can't decide where to land, on the curve of her hips, the long stretch of her legs, or the way her breasts are cradled in the sculpted top, like the dress was made for no one else. Her hair is dry now, wavy yet styled and when she tucks a strand behind her ear, something in my chest pulls tight. Her heels are strappy and nude, adding just enough height to make her look like an elegant goddamn vision.

She smooths her hands down her sides, glances up and tilts her head like she's waiting for a reaction. I'm reacting. Just not in any way I can say out loud. All I can do is stare and try not to fall to my knees.

She spins with her arms out. "Too much?" she asks innocently, as if she doesn't know she just detonated every sane thought in my brain.

I can't speak. I might be drooling. Possibly having a stroke.

"Jonathan?" she prompts again.

I shake my head, snapping myself out of the very detailed visual I was having about getting her out of that dress using only my teeth.

"Yes. Sorry. No, not too much," I stammer. I blink, then manage, "I mean… damn, AJ." I clap once. "You look hot."

She curtseys like she's still the same goofball in joggers and somehow that makes her even more devastating. "Thank you."

"Marcus is going to be eating out of your hands tonight," I mutter.

She smirks and struts toward me while her breasts shift in the dress like they're fully aware of their power. And in that moment, I realize something dangerous: I want to bite them.

Jesus Christ, Jonathan. Get a grip.

She reaches for her drink, only to find it empty. She holds up the glass and gives me a look. "Thirsty?"

I rub the back of my neck, clearly busted. "Yeah."

"It's okay," she says, all sunshine and mischief. "You can buy me another one when we get down there." She winks. Then, because she's apparently trying to kill me, she turns, bends over and adjusts her heel, ass lifted like a goddamn invitation.

In this moment, it hits me, this isn't just about wanting to sleep with AJ. It's not just attraction or timing or chemistry. I want to be *the* guy. The only one she wants, now and always. Not her ex. Not some nice rebound. No one else. I want to be the one who gets her laugh at 7 a.m., her stubborn debates at midnight, her brilliantly infuriating opinions and that mouth I haven't stopped thinking about since the day I met her. I don't want to be a chapter. I want to be the whole damn story.

17

Abby

I own a closet full of work-wear staples. Think: Ann Taylor cardigans, Express slacks and enough sensible flats to outfit a kindergarten teacher convention. When it comes to sexy clothes, though, well, my wardrobe is severely underfunded. So, when Victoria told the office we were heading to Cedar Lakes for a weekend retreat with a fancy cocktail hour on night one and then casually mentioned my ex-fiancé would be there the entire time? Yeah. A shopping trip became mandatory. Emergency-level mandatory.

I love shopping as much as the next New York girl, but between work, errands and stress-crying on my couch to *Love Island*, I rarely have time for a proper haul. When I do, I usually default to practical. A new pair of Tory Burch flats or a silk button-down with a collar cute enough to say *I'm responsible* and flirty enough to whisper *I could day-drink rosé*. But a weekend away with my fake boyfriend and my handsome, emotionally unavailable ex, however? That calls for backup.

Thankfully, Macy's at Herald Square understood the assignment. I did some glorious, well-justified damage to my credit card, buying a tight pair of Good American jeans, a black halter top, matching kitten heels… and the fuchsia pink dress I'm wearing right now. The moment I tried it on, I knew Marcus would combust. He always loved when my breasts were front and center; something about "just the right amount of cleavage," like I was a cocktail menu. Misogynist? Maybe, but not incorrect.

What I don't expect is Jonathan's reaction. The second I step out of the bedroom, his jaw practically hits the floor. Even on the golf cart ride to the venue, he keeps stealing glances from behind his sunglasses like I won't notice. Clearing his throat. Fidgeting with his sleeves. Shifting in his seat like he's got ants or unresolved feelings in his pants. He looks like a man trying very hard not to combust.

I also don't expect this dress to cause a full-on commotion with my coworkers the second I walk into the cocktail party.

"Abby!" Tanya shrieks, sprinting toward me like I've just returned from war or Sephora with a limited-edition palette. She grabs my hands and spins me around like one of those tiny ballerina figurines in a jewelry box. "You look soooo stunning," she gushes, drawing out the *so* like it needs its own set of vowels.

Even Victoria, queen of ice-cold professionalism, steps up to give me a once-over.

"Oh, I love this color on you, Abigail," she says, gently tugging the fabric near my waist. "Who made it?"

Of course she assumes it's Dior or Chanel, her default setting is locked on couture at all times.

"Thank you! It's Misha… I think?" I say, fully aware she has no clue who that is. Sure enough, her eyebrow ticks upward in a polite *never-heard-of-her* arch.

"Well," she says with a clipped nod, "it suits you." She takes a sip of her martini and gestures vaguely. "Go grab a drink."

I give her a smile and melt back into the crowd. Somewhere in the tornado of compliments and praise, I lose track of Jonathan. Then I spot him across the room, at the bar, bourbon in one hand, white wine in the other. My drink of choice.

As I make my way toward him, weaving through a sea of sequins and sports coats, I toss out compliments of my own. *Great tie. Love your earrings. Where did you get that dress?* Everyone looks stylish and polished and far more interesting than they do in the office's bad lighting.

And then, like the scene is being directed by fate herself, I see Marcus. He's leaning against the bar, sipping his usual scotch, exuding effortless charm in a navy suit and that stupid smirk that used to undo me. Our eyes lock. He freezes mid-sip, lowers his glass in slow motion and straightens his spine like something ancient just wakes up inside him. I can practically see the recognition hit: *Oh shit, she's still hot.* He pushes off the bar, gaze fixed on me like I'm his next big risk.

I should be nervous. I'm not though. Not tonight. Not in this dress. The sudden wave of confidence from all those compliments still buzzes in my chest like champagne. The kind that makes you walk taller, smile wider and feel just the right amount of recklessness.

"Abby..." Marcus starts, his voice is thick. He clears his throat. "You look amazing." His eyes drag over me with that old hunger I know too well; wanting me, needing me, already calculating how to get me alone.

I smooth my hands down the front of the dress and give him a practiced smile.

"Thank you," I say, like I don't already know.

Just as I'm about to say something else, maybe a full-blown *Why now, Marcus?* Jonathan strolls up beside me.

"There's my sexy woman," he says, winking as he hands me a glass of white wine. "Your favorite."

"Thanks," I say, taking it from him with a smile that feels just a little tight. I lift it to my lips and sip. "Hmm. It's good."

"I made sure they had Andremily," Marcus cuts in nonchalantly. "That's the one you loved in Napa. Remember?"

I freeze, glass halfway to my mouth for a second sip. Jonathan rolls his eyes so hard I practically hear it.

"Oh," I say, glancing at the wine, then back at Marcus. "That's why it tasted familiar." I stare at him a beat longer than I should. "Thank you, Marcus."

For some reason, we just… stay there. Holding each other's gaze like neither of us remembers how to blink. A full twenty seconds of weird, charged silence settles in, thick enough to buzz.

"Well." Jonathan claps his hands together. "Now that we've solved the great wine mystery of 2025, let's mingle."

Before I can respond, Marcus cuts in. "Actually, could I talk to you for a moment, Abby?" He places a hand gently on the back of my arm. "Privately."

I pause, shooting my eyes toward Jonathan like I need his permission. His jaw clenches, not at me… at Marcus.

"Sure," I say, giving a small nod as I turn toward Marcus.

Jonathan catches my hand before I walk away. His gaze flicks to Marcus, then back to me. Then he leans in and kisses me. It's short and gentle. But not casual. There's something in the way his lips linger, the way his hand doesn't let go of mine immediately. Something deeper, more possessive. He pulls away and his eyes are a darker blue now, more ocean storm than sky. He doesn't look away and for a moment, it feels like the room fades and it's just us, caught in whatever this is.

There's a tingle still buzzing on my lips and a part of me wants to lean back in. To see what would happen if we didn't stop.

Instead, I smile briefly and press my palms against my dress, will my face to stay neutral and turn, walking with Marcus across the room, my heart tapping against my ribs like it's trying to pick a side.

When we reach the far wall, Marcus stops, downs the rest of his scotch in one gulp and exhales like he's just walked out of a courtroom. He looks nervous. Not his usual composed, charming self.

I tilt my head. "What do you want to talk to me about?" I ask, folding my arms lightly.

He swallows hard, eyes shifting toward where Jonathan still stands. Then his gaze returns to me. "Are you happy with him?" he asks, his voice shaky.

The question stuns me. "What?" I blink. "Why are you asking me that?"

Somewhere across the room, laughter erupts and cheers for Manny start; he's just thrown back a shot at the bar. The room buzzes with life, like we're not standing in our own awkward, time-frozen bubble of unfinished business.

"I need to know, Abby," Marcus says, stepping closer.

"Yes," I say quickly, cutting him off. "Of course I'm happy."

But the second the words leave my mouth, something twists in my stomach. I thought watching Marcus squirm would feel like victory, the final, delicious full-circle moment. Me, radiant in a revenge dress. Him, rattled and jealous. I built this whole fake-dating charade to make him feel exactly this way. So why doesn't it feel like a win? I don't want him back. At least, I don't think I do. I don't think I'm still in love with him. I just wanted him to feel something. To hurt like I did. To understand what he threw away. Maybe now he does. Maybe I've finally gotten what I wanted.

He lifts his glass like he's going to take another sip, only to pause when he realizes it's empty. He stares at it, blinking, as if it let him down.

"Okay. Good. That's… good. Good," he says, stumbling over the words.

A thin sheen of sweat collects at his temple. Barely visible but I notice.

"Marcus," I say gently. "Why are you really asking me this?"

He hesitates. His mouth opens, then closes again. Finally, he clears his throat and straightens his spine like he's flipping some internal switch. "You know… dating within the office can get messy. And now that I'm part owner of the company, I need to make sure it's not going to affect your job." His tone shifts, cooler now, as if he's forcing the conversation into a professional box it absolutely does not belong in.

I blink. Really? That's the line we're going with? I can't tell if he actually means it… or if it's a last-ditch cover because he doesn't like my answer.

"Okay," I say, lifting a brow. "Well, we're fine. Everything's fine." I give his arm a polite pat and start to turn away. "I'm going to go have some fun."

Before I can get far, he catches my hand, discreetly, but enough to stop me. I spin back around, shooting him a look that lands somewhere between *don't push it* and *what now?*

He drops my hand immediately, both palms raised in surrender. "Sorry," his face says. Even though his eyes say he's not sorry at all.

I head straight for Jonathan. He's standing with Conner, Tanya and Sarah, all of them watching Manny line up another shot like shot-taking is an extreme sport and he's going pro. Without breaking stride, I snatch the shot glass right out of Manny's hand and toss it back in one smooth gulp.

For a second, the group just stares.

Then Jonathan throws his head back and yells, "That's my girl!"

Laughter explodes around us as fanfare follows.

Manny gapes at me. "Damn, girl. You take shots *and* wear dresses like this?" He waves his hand up and down like he's scanning my outfit. "Who even are you?" He grins. "Bartender! Another round for the group!"

Before I can say a word, Jonathan grabs my hand and spins me toward him. I land against his chest, breathless.

"You good?" he asks, eyes searching mine.

"Yes," I say, smiling as the shot zips through my bloodstream, all warm and electric.

He tilts his head, smirking. "What did the wannabe GQ model want?" he asks, clearly referring to Marcus.

I laugh and tug at Jonathan's shirt. "Model? You should talk."

He chuckles and squeezes my hand. His touch is easy and somehow balances me.

"He just wanted to make sure our relationship wasn't going to cause any… workplace issues," I say lightly, though Marcus's words still leave a weird aftertaste I can't quite shake.

Jonathan glances over his shoulder. Marcus is talking with Victoria and a few others, but his attention keeps drifting back to us. Jonathan leans in, lowering his voice until it brushes my skin like velvet. "Your plan's working." His breath hits my ear and it's game over. A full-body shiver rolls through me, heat blooming everywhere at once. He's close, *too close* and the tension crackles in the air like it's waiting to snap.

I pull back just enough to meet his eyes and they're darker than usual. Hungry even. I don't even try to think. I just know I want to kiss him so badly it hurts.

18

Jonathan

I've got to admit, the evening went pretty damn smoothly. Cocktail hour was actually fun. Manny took way too many shots and AJ even downed one herself, which honestly shocked me. Who knew she had a wild streak buried under all that schedule-obsessed perfectionism?

Shots, sexy dresses that show off her sneaky-hot body and kissing me in front of her ex like it was just part of the outfit? Yeah, that girl has layers.

Dinner was solid, too. Victoria and Marcus clearly spared no expense. Prime rib, chicken Marsala, shrimp cocktail, more salads than anyone asked for and two types of dessert, cheesecake *and* some rich chocolate mousse thing that made people moan at the table. Good food, good vibes and one kiss from AJ? My kind of night.

Okay, so the kiss was small, just a quick one, but her lips were soft as hell. My mouth is still tingling like I touched an electric fence and liked it too much.

The best part of the evening was when Marcus spent the whole night practically drooling over her. He even pulled her aside to check if our relationship was "serious." Yeah, right. That wasn't his concern, that was his busted-ass attempt at recon. A Hail-Mary pass to see if he still had a shot.

AJ laughed when I mentioned it, brushed it off like I was being dramatic, but I know what I saw. I know how men think, especially narcissistic ones. It takes one to know one. It's no surprise I can be a narcissist. At least I *know* I can be. I turn it on when I want and reel it back when I don't. Marcus, though, he *is* it. It oozes out of him like expensive cologne. And I don't love that he's got eyes on AJ. Not because I'm jealous or territorial. Okay, maybe a little. It's mostly because I want her to be happy and I know his type. He'll charm her, chew her up and spit her out the second she stops being shiny. Just like he did to her on their wedding day all those years ago.

It's a weird feeling, caring this much. But spending time with AJ tonight, seeing her relax and laugh and actually have fun without biting my head off, it's been… nice. I want to keep it that way. Especially if I get the promotion over her. I'll technically be her overseeing manager and the last thing I want is to go from fake dating back to full-on work enemies. Even though let's be honest, that's probably inevitable. She's still AJ. Annoying, obsessive and always needs to be right. And somehow still has the most insane cleavage I've ever seen in my life. *Jesus, Jonathan, reel it in.*

When we leave the dinner hall, a few people head toward the small bar on the property for more drinks. AJ looks like she's starting to crash; her posture softening, eyes a little sleepy but I still ask anyway, just in case. "You coming?"

She shakes her head. "No. I'm done. But I'll walk back. You can take the golf cart."

As if I'm about to let her walk alone in that dress, at night, on a dark wooded path. Not happening.

"I'll drive you," I say, already climbing in the golf cart.

She doesn't argue. But just before we pull away, I see Marcus lean in and press a kiss to her cheek. The blush that rises to her face is instant and all-consuming and something irritating and constricting happens in my chest. Jealousy? Could be. I don't know. I'm not super well-versed in the feeling. I will say these feelings have been popping up more often than I'd like to admit.

We ride in silence for a bit, the air cooler now, AJ kicking off her heels and letting out a satisfied sigh.

"What are you gonna do now?" I ask.

She lifts her bare feet and crosses her legs in the seat. "Take a long, hot shower. Put on the biggest hoodie and sweats I brought. Then veg out on the couch and binge *Love Island*." She grins like she just described a perfect Friday night, which, honestly, she kind of did.

I laugh. "Sounds like a solid plan."

"Remember we have to be at the main house at *seven a.m.* for that team-building hike," she says with a giggle.

Right. The hike. The mandatory sunrise bonding activity that sounds like it was dreamed up by someone who's never hiked a day in their life. I glance at the time, it's just after 10 p.m.

We reach our cabin and I pause for a second, then kill the engine on the cart.

"What are you doing?" she asks, watching me pocket the key.

"You made a strong case. I'm joining you," I shoot back.

Her brows lift. "Sucker for *Love Island,* huh?"

"And room service ice cream," I add with a wink.

She squeals. "Ooh, great idea."

AJ jumps in the shower first. It takes every ounce of blood and basic decency in me not to knock on the door and ask if she needs help reaching her back. But I rein it in. I don't cross the line. I don't make it weird. Now, if she had asked me to join her? Lately, with how things have been between us, I wouldn't have hesitated.

While she's in there, I order dessert: two scoops of vanilla with rainbow sprinkles for her and two scoops of chocolate with hot fudge for me. I quickly shower after she gets out and by the time I step out, towel-drying my hair, the ice cream's been delivered.

AJ moves toward the door to tip the guy, but I beat her to it, pulling a twenty from my wallet and handing it over.

"Wow," she says, clearly impressed. "I like *Gentleman Jonathan*."

I smirk. "He comes in other versions too."

"Oh yeah?" she teases, eyebrow arched.

"Yeah. There's the version who devours ice cream and binge-watches drama-fueled British dating shows."

She laughs. "*Love Island* is for men and women, thank you very much."

"Sure it is," I say, straight-faced. "Just don't tell Manny. I'll never hear the end of it."

We settle onto the couch. I hand her the vanilla with sprinkles and she beams as she takes it and grabs the remote. The flat screen clicks on and she scrolls to find the latest episode.

We're tucked into the corner of the couch now. Two bowls of ice cream. One reality show. And a whole lot of tension neither of us seems ready to name… yet.

We end up eating our ice cream and watching *Love Island* like we're filming a two-person podcast. We discuss our own rankings within the show with the occasional gasp when someone gets dumped. AJ has strong opinions about the show, the cast, the villa décor, obviously.

"I think I'd be terrible at it," she says, giggling, "but I'd join the cast in a heartbeat just to be there."

She grins at me like it's the most ridiculous dream she's ever confessed and for some reason, I can totally see it. AJ in a neon bikini, yelling at a guy named Bradley because he forgot their matching bracelets.

Time slips away. At some point, the bowls are empty and the cozy buzz of exhaustion starts to settle in. Her head dips against the couch cushion as she says, "I think I'm done once this episode's over."

She leans forward to collect our empty cups, but then stops, covering her mouth, her whole face turning red as she starts laughing and snorts.

"Oh my God," she wheezes, still snorting, "you've had this on your face forever."

I blink. "What?"

She reaches over and wipes a streak of hot fudge from the corner of my mouth. I go to lick my lip, self-conscious now, then I pause and watch her as she licks the fudge from her own finger.

"Tastes good," she says, shooting me a smirk.

And suddenly, the air shifts. The room goes quiet in that pressure-cooker kind of way. The kind that tells you something is about to happen. Or *should* happen. And if you don't move soon, you'll regret it. So I follow my gut. I smile and take her hand in mine.

She smiles back and starts to lean in. Her lower lip trembles slightly before she bites it, like she's trying to keep it still. My eyes flick to her mouth, then her body. Even swallowed in an oversized hoodie, she still looks unfairly sexy. The kind of sexy that sneaks up on you and wrecks your week. She moves closer and I can smell her shampoo, it's a lavender combination with a hint of clean linen. My fingers reach up to her hair and she doesn't pull away. In fact, she leans into my touch, resting her cheek against my hand like it belongs there.

After what seems to be the longest I've ever gone and touched a woman without making a move, I lose all patience. No more waiting. No more stalling. I lean in, ready to kiss her like I did that night at *The Yank*. Maybe even harder this time.

But the universe, in all its cruel, badly timed glory, has other plans and my phone rings loudly. Like obnoxiously, unnecessarily loud, because I cranked the volume earlier in case a client called during the cocktail party.

We both jolt back like we've been slapped. AJ's hand drops to her lap and my heart pounds like it's trying to stage a jailbreak. So much for perfect timing.

She smiles and says, "I think that's your phone," then looks down.

I grab it from the coffee table. "Yeah. Of course it is," I mutter with a mild, sad half-smile.

She stands, scoops up the empty dishes and walks to the kitchen.

I glance at the screen; it's Manny. He texted too, but I didn't hear it, probably because I was mid-horny spiral, pretending to be effortlessly cool.

I answer, already annoyed. "What, bro?" I snap, irritated he interrupted me and AJ's almost-kiss.

"Oh. Hey… it's Tanya, actually," she says, anxiously.

"Oh," I reply, immediately softening. "Sorry. I thought this was Manny." I glance down again, yep, still his name on the screen.

"I'm calling from his cell. Can you come help us?" Tanya sounds concerned, maybe even panicked. "Manny's drunk and won't stop dancing on the tables. The staff doesn't want to kick us out, but they're closing and he won't listen. He keeps asking for you."

I drag a hand over my face and let out a deep breath. "Yeah, Tanya. I'm on my way." I hang up.

AJ walks back in from the kitchen. "Is everything okay?" she asks, her brow creased with concern.

I stand and reach for my jacket hanging off the couch, mostly to cover the thin white Hanes shirt and the half-chub situation happening below my waistband, thanks to her plump, kiss-me-now lips.

"Yes. I mean… no. Manny's drunk and they can't control him," I admit, sliding the jacket on.

"Do you need me to come?" she asks, grabbing my arm.

I need you to sit on my lap and grind the fuck out of me, is what I want to say.

"No, I'll be fine," I manage instead. "It's probably better if I go alone."

If AJ came with me, Manny would probably drunkenly confess his crush on her. And maybe, *maybe*, she'd want to hear it. I don't want her to know Manny likes her. *God, I'm such a bad friend*, I scream in my head.

She raises her eyebrows. "Huh."

"I just mean… when Manny's drunk, he acts like a total idiot. It's better you don't see that," I add, trying to chuckle it off.

"Oh. Okay." She chuckles back. "I'm gonna lie down then. Be safe. Watch for bears." She laughs.

I think she's only half joking, which now has me concerned about Manny *and* possible wildlife attacks.

"I will. Thanks," I quip.

I move toward her and she straightens her posture like she's bracing herself for something. I lean in and kiss her forehead. She smiles and gives me the smallest nod.

I don't know what would've happened if we actually kissed, just the two of us, no distractions, but I like to think I'll get to find out again, hopefully soon.

I walk out to the golf cart and she watches me go, then waves and shuts the door behind me. I let out a giant sigh and turn the key to the cart. The beeping a reminding sound of how agitated my insides are right now. Manny has no idea how much he owes me, probably never will.

* * *

I walk into the bar the retreat calls *The Canteen* and instantly get hit with a wave of firewood and alcohol. The smell isn't bad but when you were just at your cabin, eating ice cream and about to make out with a cute girl, this is the last place you want to be, consumed by bourbon breath and bonfire vibes. Immediately, Tanya spots me and rushes over.

"I am so sorry I called you," she says, hands raised like she's bracing me for impact. "But he won't listen to anyone."

She's clearly talking about the grown-ass man currently dancing on top of a table to Miley Cyrus' 'Flowers' like it's his last night on Earth.

"Manny!" I yell, marching toward him.

He turns around mid-spin, lowers his sunglasses and smiles widely. "My man!" he shouts. "Come up here and join the party!"

"The party's over, bro. This place wants to close up," I say, reaching for his hand and trying to haul him down.

He stumbles over a chair and somehow sticks the landing with two feet on the floor.

"Spiderman at your ass," he says, lifting a hand and miming a web shoot.

Honestly? Pretty impressive for a drunk six-foot-two man. Regardless, he needs to stop drinking, stop dancing and get his ass to bed. We've got a corporate hike in the morning. Well, technically *today* already.

"Do you need help getting him back?" Tanya asks, eyeing Manny like he's a fallen gladiator.

"Nah, I got it. Thanks. And sorry about Manny," I say, apologizing for my friend being a complete jackass.

"It's okay," she says, waving it off with a small smile. "He was entertaining." She glances at Elaine and Stan, who both wave to me from across the room.

"Bye, Manny!" Elaine calls.

Manny, now draped around my shoulders like a wet towel, waves back half-heartedly. Then he slumps further onto me.

"Take me home, Papi," he says.

"You know I love it when you call me that," I joke.

He lets out a belch. "I know."

Somehow, I manage to lug him into the golf cart and start driving toward his cabin. The wind feels good, it's cool and refreshing even. Manny tilts his head back and lets it wash over him like he's starring in a shampoo commercial.

"Ahhhh," he says, eyes closed.

"You okay, buddy?" I ask, genuinely concerned now that the chaos has dulled.

He sits up a bit straighter. "Yeah. Yeah, bro. I'm good." He nods, then blinks a little too slow. "Sorry I woke you up."

"I was awake. Watching TV," I say.

What I don't add is: *I was also about to kiss AJ for real this time. For real, real.* I keep that tiny detail to myself.

"Was Abby awake?" he asks, slurring only a little now.

I pause, trying to decide if I should lie, deflect, or tell the truth. I go with the worst option: lie-lite.

"No. I don't think so. I took the couch, she has the bedroom."

Boldface lie. Lying to my closest friend, wow, that's a new low for me. Manny doesn't press. He just nods like he gets it. Or thinks he does.

We get to his cabin and I help him inside. He leans against me the whole way, swaying like a drunk palm tree until we reach the couch. I gently lower him onto it and he plops down with a groan.

"Who are you bunking with?" I ask, glancing around the room.

"Stan," he mutters.

Stan, the prick, was still at the bar and didn't even try to help Manny get back here.

Manny kicks his shoes off one foot at a time, grunting as he stretches out. Then, just when I think he's seconds from passing out, he cracks an eye open and drops the question I've been dreading all night.

"Did you ask Abby yet what she thinks of me?"

Shit.

"Not yet," I admit. "There hasn't been a good time to… slip it in."

Which, technically, isn't a lie. But it's also not the whole truth. The real truth? I haven't asked because I don't want to know. If she likes Manny, then fine, she can pursue that on her own time. She's a grown woman. But the thought of it makes my stomach twist into knots. I run a hand down my face and shake my head like I'm trying to physically push the thoughts out.

"You good?" I ask, trying to shift the subject.

He nods, eyes already closing, his breathing slower now.

I grab a pillow from the nearby armchair and tuck it under his neck. Then I head to the kitchenette, grab the tiny trash can and set it next to the couch in case he needs to puke up the fireball and poor decisions.

He doesn't open his eyes, but he mumbles, "You're a good friend, man."

His hand lifts for a fist bump or handshake, I'm not sure which, so I grab it and shake.

Good friend. Ouch, that stings a little considering I'm actively keeping AJ for myself. Doesn't really qualify as friendship gold-star behavior.

I fish his phone out of his pocket, set an alarm for 6 a.m. and place it on the coffee table beside him. "Remember, we have the hike tomorrow," I say.

Manny gives me a sleepy thumbs-up and I can't help but chuckle.

When I walk outside, I spot Stan strolling up with Elaine; they're holding hands. Curiosity flickers, but I'm way too tired to fully care.

"Stan. Elaine," I say, passing them with a nod.

Stan nods back, and Elaine gives a small, shy wave. Good for them, at least someone's getting some fun in tonight.

I drive the golf cart back to my cabin and step inside. The place is quiet, dim, the leftover scent of AJ's lavender shampoo still floating faintly in the air.

I peek into the bedroom and there she is, fast asleep.

I move closer, slowly pulling the blanket up over her shoulder. She shifts, cuddling into it and a small smile touches her lips. That smile could kill a man. I lean down and press a kiss on her cheek, letting it linger a second longer than I probably should. I make my way to my bed, known as the couch, and grab a blanket from one of the armchairs. I toss it over myself as I settle onto the warped leather.

The clock on the wall blinks at me; four hours and forty-seven minutes until the team hike. It doesn't matter much anyways because I can't sleep. Not with the image of her in bed, wrapped in that blanket, stuck in my head. All I want to do is crawl in beside her, pull her close and hold her all night. *My God!* I think I'm falling for Abigail Jean Madison.

19

Abby

Waking up at 6 a.m. came way sooner than I'd hoped, even though I'm actually looking forward to this hike. I'm not exactly a seasoned outdoorswoman, but I love a good scenic trail and I love fishing. It reminds me of being a kid, when my dad used to take me and my sister camping. My mom wasn't into nature and since they didn't have any sons, it was up to us girls to play the part of what typical little boys like growing up. My sister hated it; bugs, dirt, silence, all of it. But me? I didn't mind, except for the bugs. My dad noticed my interest in it and it became our thing. Our time to bond. I still cherish those memories, even if I gagged every time I had to take a fish off the hook. Their slimy little guts always found a way onto my fingers.

When I was thirteen, my parents divorced. My dad remarried, started over, had new kids. And honestly? I can't blame him. My mother isn't the easiest person to deal with. Still, losing that closeness with him was one of the hardest parts of growing up. We try to keep in touch now, but it's mostly sporadic calls and the occasional FaceTime. The last time I saw him was on my wedding day. He was going to walk me down the aisle; until Marcus ruined that, too. I haven't seen him since. I'd planned to visit him last Christmas, then like always, work got hectic and I canceled.

I decide to dress more sensible than cute for the hike this morning, for two reasons: one, the hike starts at 7 a.m. and two, I'd rather be considered practical and smart than stylish and freezing. That said, I throw on my black leggings, the ones that hug my butt just right and my Victoria's Secret blue sports bra that gives just a peek of cleavage while holding the girls in place like a dream. I'm sure Marcus will recognize the bra. He is, after all, dating one of their Angels.

As I step out of the bedroom, the sight of the couch brings up the memory of last night. I almost kissed Jonathan, and not out of obligation. Not to make a show. Not even to stab Marcus in the soul with a well-timed display of passion. No! I nearly kissed Jonathan Slack because I wanted to. Because I was lost in the moment and something about the way he looked at me made me want to dive straight in, no overthinking. But then his phone rang just in the nick of time. *Thank God* it rang. Because whatever this is with Jonathan, this faux relationship, this real attraction, this confusing in-between; it's already complicated enough. That kiss would've made it messier. Sure, it would've been amazing. He would've been amazing. But then what? More kissing? More… everything? That's exactly what I don't need right now in the middle of this professional, emotional, fake-dating nightmare I've created for myself.

Just then, as my brain is about to spiral even more, Jonathan steps out of the bathroom, shirtless, towel slung over his shoulder. "Oh hey," he says casually, hand raised.

"Good morning," I say with a tight-lipped smile that probably doesn't hide the way my eyes just dipped below his neck. "Want coffee?" I ask, walking toward the Keurig before I start saying things like *want abs with that too?*

"Sure, thanks," he says, following me to the kitchen.

I pop a K-cup into the machine, hit brew and grab another mug from the cabinet. I turn around and set it on the counter, pretending my brain isn't still stuck in the mental replay of last night's almost-kiss.

"AJ, about last night…" he starts, his voice a little unsure.

"We don't have to talk about it," I say quickly, waving my hand like I'm shooing away the memory itself.

"Oh. Yeah. Okay," he stumbles.

"It was silly," I add, trying to keep it breezy. "And honestly, it would just make this whole thing messier."

He pauses, eyes locking on mine like he can tell I'm full of it. Like he knows I wanted that kiss last night. And… yeah, he'd be correct.

"You're right," he says, exhaling a breath that sounds way too heavy to match the casual tone we're both pretending to have.

The Keurig beeps, rescuing me. I turn, grab the first cup and slide it across the counter toward him. As I hand him the sugar dispenser, our fingers graze and just like that, the air sends some mystic, electric pulse through my body. The same *what are we doing* vibe. He doesn't look at me. He looks at my hands. Then my fingers. Then finally, my eyes.

"It would've been an amazing kiss, though," he says with a quiet chuckle and that annoyingly charming smile. He pours sugar into his cup and adds, "Not like we don't already know what that feels like."

I laugh despite myself, tucking a strand of hair behind my ear to do something with my hands.

"I guess that's true," I admit. "Our kisses have been…" I trail off.

"What?" he asks, too eagerly.

I shrug and pop a fresh K-cup into the machine.

"What?" he asks again, like he needs the answer more than the caffeine.

"They've been intense," I say.

He smiles and takes a sip of coffee.

"But probably because we hate each other," I add, only half-joking.

He doesn't laugh. Just lifts the cup again, eyes holding mine over the rim.

"I've never hated you, AJ. Trust me. I couldn't even if I tried." His voice is deeper now.

It hits something in my chest I'm not ready to name. I turn as the machine beeps again, grabbing my mug like it's a life raft. I open the fridge, pour in some creamer, then add sugar at the counter. I blow on the surface, trying to cool both the coffee and the mood. When I glance up, Jonathan is staring at me over the edge of his mug.

"I don't hate you either." I say with a smile.

He winks. "Good to know," he adds, standing now and grabbing his mug. "Did you pack a bag for the hike?"

I'm taken aback, going from talking about kissing to suddenly talking about hiking.

"Um. Yes. I am bringing a small drawstring bag I have." I blink myself back into reality.

"Okay, good." He nods. "I'm also bringing a small backpack with extra waters and protein bars I grabbed from the front desk," he admits.

I raise an eyebrow. "Wow. Someone came prepared."

"Always," he says as he shrugs his very toned, *very sexy,* bare shoulders while flashing a grin that, unfortunately, makes me want to kiss him. Or run away. Possibly both. It's a toss-up.

* * *

The retreat sends us on a scenic trail hike, led by two overly enthusiastic guides and a pull cart stocked with snacks, water bottles and picnic blankets for a breakfast setup once we reach the top. As we hike, Victoria and Marcus take turns sharing their vision for the company. At one point, we pause for a break and Victoria has us split into small groups to brainstorm one idea that could contribute to this "new era" of the company.

Naturally, I end up in a group with Jonathan, Tanya, Elaine, Stan and a very hungover Manny, who can barely keep up with the hike, let alone form a coherent thought about company strategy. Still, we pass around some protein bars and manage to come up with a solid idea: highlighting our team's diverse perspectives in future marketing campaigns. We also pitch the concept of collaborating with other firms, doubling up on creative teams to offer clients broader, bolder ideas. Two marketing firms are better than one, right?

Victoria and Marcus seem genuinely impressed with our suggestions. Some of the other groups throw out clever pitches too. One of the groups even suggests installing a vending machine stocked with healthy snacks, which, honestly? I love.

After the break of *team bonding* as they put it, we continue the hike. Marcus somehow manages to sneak up beside me.

"This is beautiful, isn't it?" he asks, trying way too hard to keep his tone breezy.

Startled, I blink and turn slightly toward him. "Yes. It is," I say, leveling my breath as I keep climbing.

Never one to pass up a strategic opportunity, I decide now's the perfect time to take off my jacket, revealing both my fitted sports bra and the very flattering way my leggings hug my hips. I don't work out to show off, but I'm also not blind. I know what I look like in this outfit and I'm proud of it.

Marcus clears his throat as I roll up my jacket and stuff it into my bag.

"It's getting hotter the higher up we climb," I say.

Lie. It's definitely cooler as we gain elevation.

He takes a second to take in my body, then nods, tugging at his shirt. He keeps pace beside me, clearly not ready to let the moment pass.

"Remember that time in Greece?" he asks. "When we got so lost we just gave up and stayed in that random cottage?"

Okay... what is this about? That trip was one of the best vacations I've ever taken and not just because of the scenery. It was also the most thrilling week of sex I've ever had. The kind of wild, breathless, are-we-seriously-this-in-sync kind of sex you never really forget.

I slide my sunglasses up and look him straight in the eyes, even though his are still hidden behind his Ray-Bans. A few seconds pass. Then he lifts them too, revealing that familiar blue-green stare and a half-smile that still knows how to punch me right in the gut.

"Umm. You know I do," I say, matching his smirk.

Marcus lets his gaze linger, not on my eyes, but slowly scanning down to my athletic bra and leggings before meeting my eyes again. Another smirk. Then we both slide our sunglasses back into place like we haven't just had an entire unspoken conversation. He steps a little closer and breathes in like he's about to say something.

"What's going on?" Jonathan suddenly steps up and asks as he wedges himself between me and Marcus, placing a hand firmly on my waist. His eyes dip for half a second. "Wow," he mutters. "You look hot."

Then, without missing a beat, he turns to Marcus. "Does your Angel look this good in a Victoria's Secret bra?" He grins. "I bet not."

Marcus drops his gaze. "We're not dating anymore," he says.

Neither of us responds right away.

"Oh. I'm sorry," I finally offer.

"Tough break," Jonathan adds, clapping Marcus on the shoulder. "But hey," he continues, his voice obnoxiously chipper, "there are more models out there, right?"

Marcus just nods.

"Let's go, babe," Jonathan says, leaning into the word like he's announcing it on a red carpet. He wraps his arm tighter around me. "I've got a view I want you to see."

As we walk away, I glance over my shoulder. Marcus is still watching, his expression somber as Jonathan leads me toward a more secluded hilltop.

Once we're there, Jonathan slides off his sunglasses and lets out a low whistle. "First of all... damn, girl." His gaze trails from head to toe like he's seeing me for the first time.

I laugh and nudge him.

"What did Marcus say to you?" he asks, a little too casually.

"Nothing much," I reply. "Just bringing up old memories."

Jonathan pauses. "Did it work?"

"Did what work?" I ask, confused.

He lifts an eyebrow. "Are you falling for him?"

I laugh and shove at his chest, though he barely budges.

"No. Definitely not." I hesitate. "I mean… it's nice seeing him squirm. Or at least, I think that's what's happening."

"Oh, it's happening," Jonathan says confidently, sinking onto a flat rock and tugging me down beside him. Then his tone becomes softer and he asks, "Are you happy?"

I turn toward the view, the rolling green hills, fluffy clouds, a horizon that feels endless; then back to him.

"Yeah," I say, smiling. "Still can't believe I'm doing this. But… I'm happy."

"What about you? Are you happy?" I ask back while leaning into his arm.

He looks out over the view again, then back at me. His answer is a leisurely nod before he wraps an arm around my shoulders. He's warm and solid in that quiet, comforting way.

"I still can't believe the last few days," he says, pulling his arm back to his side but keeping close. "I'm seeing this side of you I didn't even know existed."

I blush. "I feel the same," I admit. "We're not biting each other's heads off and we both like the same TV shows."

He laughs. "Bare minimum for soulmates, right?"

I stare at his face and see that usual hard-edged jawline of his ease.

"Can I ask you something?" I grin.

"Oh boy. Here it comes," he says, mock-bracing himself.

I tuck my hair behind my ear, a little shy. "Why don't I ever see you dating anyone?"

He pauses, then picks up a small rock and tosses it off the edge of the hill.

"I guess most women don't want to date me," he says with a shrug.

"That is such a cop-out," I respond, nearly laughing.

He lifts a brow, shifting his body toward me. "How?"

"Because I'm sure there are plenty of women who've wanted to date you," I say.

He gives a reluctant chin drop. "Okay, you're probably right." He picks up another rock and tosses it again. "If I'm being honest… I haven't met anyone worth dating."

I tilt my head. "And what qualifies as *worth dating* in Jonathan Slack's eyes?" I ask, throwing air quotes around the words.

He brushes his fingers through the sand, trailing them in lazy circles, then tosses another rock. "I don't really know," he mumbles. "Maybe… someone who'd serenade me with a love song like…" He pauses, like he's actually thinking of one. "Like 'Hopelessly Devoted to You.'"

I blink. "The song from Grease?"

He nods. "Yeah. Olivia Newton-John."

I narrow my eyes, trying to decide if he's joking, but he looks completely serious.

"It sounds corny, but you can hear it in her voice," he adds.

"Hear what?" I reluctantly ask.

"The love she has," he says simply, staring down at the ground like he wishes he could disappear into it. "Someone who could feel like that about me… that's the kind of woman I'd want."

I don't know what kind of response I expected, still it wasn't that.

I mildly nod, reaching down to pick up a rock of my own

and tossing it over the edge.

"But how can someone love you if you won't let them in?" I ask, more to the wind than to him.

He lets out a laugh. "Fair point," he says. "Maybe I won't ever be in love then."

"You've never been in love?" I ask, now turning, facing him completely.

"Nope." The answer is fast and firm. No explanation offered, just fact.

It makes sense to me, suddenly. Why he's guarded. Why his jokes sometimes hide real things. Why he always looks a little surprised when I'm kind to him.

"Wow," I say, not hiding my surprise. "That actually explains… a lot."

"Right?" he says, like he already knows.

He looks at me then, really looks at me and for a moment, I forget how to blink. There's something so open in his face, so unguarded, it tugs at something deep in my chest.

I reach out and take his hand, threading my fingers through his. His smile is easy and immediate and he starts to lean in and surprisingly to my brain, so do I. I can't help it. I'm drawn in by his honesty; it's powerful. His palm is sandy and cool against mine, grounding me as everything else starts to blur.

Manny suddenly appears and plops down, breaking the space… and our fingers.

"My favorite couple," he announces with a wink in my direction.

I shoot Jonathan a look. "He knows," I whisper.

Manny chuckles and throws an arm around Jonathan's shoulder. "Of course I know. We don't keep secrets from each other."

Jonathan stiffens. "I did…" he starts, then falters. "I did tell him," he says, rubbing the back of his neck like he's searching for the right words. "Because Manny…"

Before he can finish, Victoria's voice cuts through the trees. "Okay, everyone! Let's keep moving!"

Manny taps Jonathan's arm and they both hop up. Jonathan turns to me, offering his hand. I take it, letting him pull me to my feet and he mouths, *I'm sorry*.

I shrug and offer a tiny smile. *It's fine*, I mouth back, because it is. Of course he told his best friend the truth. We aren't a real couple. And it's just wild that I keep having to remind myself of that.

20

Jonathan

The hike is impressive. Wide open air, the crisp scent of pine mixed with the faint, earthy tang of the Hudson Valley water. It's scenic, sure but more than that, it's peaceful. This kind of quiet clears your head. Just your breath, your legs and the rhythm of moving forward. No forced small talk. No noise. I work out every other day, so this? Feels easy. Too easy. A few of my coworkers are already winded, trying to pretend they're not. Victoria, for one, looks like she got lost on the way to a Vogue shoot. I don't even know what she's wearing, some custom Chanel workout set with shoes that scream style over support. She still manages to look like she's effortlessly conquering Everest, probably for content.

Marcus, annoyingly enough, is keeping up just fine. Mid-forties, sure, but annoyingly fit. Youthful even. He's like a walking advertisement for men's skincare and strategic cardio. And of course, he's conveniently drifting closer to AJ every chance he gets, pulling out memory-lane stories designed to hit her right in the emotional kneecaps. Like *Greece.* Really, dude? I don't know the full backstory, but judging by the way she looked at him, that one hit a little too well.

So, naturally, I challenge Marcus to a push-up contest. Nothing aggressive, just a friendly, testosterone-fueled ego check. Just two men showing off their strengths. He doesn't back down. Would've been real convenient if he said no and saved himself the embarrassment, but nah. A guy like Marcus? He's not gonna show weakness in front of his ex.

I pull off my shirt, I mean, the sun's out, so abs out. Let's be honest: this is 100% for AJ. She looks over at me and I see her face light up. Mission accomplished.

Marcus pulls his shirt off too and unfortunately, he's jacked. Not midlife-crisis-jacked either. It's more like annoyingly functional muscle mass jacked. I roll my eyes and hit the ground, hands in the dirt.

Victoria is way into the competition and happily pulls out her phone and offers to count, clearly thrilled with the corporate Hunger Games unfolding in front of her. A few coworkers start cheering us on like we're the halftime entertainment at the Super Bowl.

I keep pace, glancing sideways every few reps. Marcus doesn't even seem to be breaking a sweat. *Prick.* Must be genetics. But eventually, age wins and I see his form falter around push-up seventy and he drops.

I squeeze out five more just to flex, literally, then collapse beside him. Sand in between my fingers. Sweat sliding down my back.

The group of coworkers cheers and Marcus gives me a nod of respect. I nod back. Some kind of mutual alpha moment I suppose.

I stand, brush off my hands and walk straight to AJ. I lean down and kiss the top of her head. It's for show but not entirely. She's the prize. Even if our relationship is fake, Marcus doesn't need to know that.

After the hike, we move into more team-building exercises on the retreat grounds. One of them is a human triangle challenge, apparently that's a real thing. We have to group off and stack ourselves into a literal human pyramid. Elaine, being the tiniest of the group, is naturally perched on top. Tanya and AJ take the middle layer and me, Manny, and Stan form the base.

Our group wins for holding the triangle the longest, probably because Stan's built like a boulder and Manny never skips leg day. But personally? I think I'm the MVP. I've got AJ on top of me; well, my back and even though her knee digs into my spine like a dagger, I don't care. There's something kind of satisfying about literally supporting her. I mean, how many guys can say they've physically held up the girl they may or may not be crushing on during a corporate icebreaker?

At one point, she smacks my butt. So does Tanya. I don't know if it's just playful team spirit or AJ making a move. Either way, I'll take it. My ass is basically a stretched rubber band and if AJ is noticing, then I'll take it.

After the triangle chaos, we head to the main house for lunch and a Bloody Mary bar. The set-up is classy, rustic vibes. I have the bartender make mine and AJ's spicy, extra horseradish, pepper rim, the works. She trusts me with it and when she takes a sip, her eyes go wide.

"Oh my God, Jonathan," she says, breathless like she just tasted magic. "This is so good."

I grin and give a smug little shake of my head. "Told you."

She smiles back at me with her glossy lips, perfect teeth and that sparkle in her eyes she doesn't even realize she has.

I'm so screwed.

"This was such a fun day!" Victoria shouts to the group, her arm raised like she's leading a pep rally. "Now go relax for a bit and we'll all meet back here around six for drinks and dinner. Then we're taking the coach to a dance bar down the road!"

"Yay!" Tanya and Elaine cheer in unison like they're auditioning for a musical.

I glance over at AJ and shrug. "Do you like to dance?"

She smirks. "I guess you'll have to wait and see."

I'm going to kiss that smirk off her face. Maybe not now. But soon enough I will.

"Let's go to the hot tub," she says, suddenly lit up with excitement.

Yes, finally, some alone time with her. I've been craving this all day.

"Hot tub?" Manny echoes with the same level of enthusiasm.

"Hell yes!" Elaine chimes in, grabbing Stan's hand like they're heading into battle. "We'll meet you there."

I look at Manny, then at Elaine. I guess it's not going to be as private as I hoped.

We drive back to the cabin to change. AJ heads into the bedroom and comes out a few minutes later in a bright yellow bikini, cleavage on full display and thigh-cut bottoms that should be illegal. She looks unreal. She breezes past me to grab her bag and a wrap, bending slightly as she reaches down. She catches me watching.

"See something you like?" she asks, sly and knowing.

I clear my throat and over-nod. "Yep."

She wraps the cloth around her waist, then walks right up to me, close enough that her chest brushes mine. She looks up at my lips, then makes a tiny moan.

"Mmm… let's go," she says, then she turns and heads for the door.

What a tease.

I shake my head, chuckling. "You don't know what you're doing to me."

Without turning around, she calls back, "I know exactly what I'm doing."

I smack her ass as she lets out a delighted scream.

Yeah. She definitely knows.

Down at the hot tub, it turns out more people got the memo. Not just Manny, Elaine and Stan, but Tanya showed up too, dragging Curtis, Tommy and Billie Jean along with her. Apparently, this is now a full-blown office soak session.

I'll give Victoria credit, she knows how to hire. Our team skews young and attractive, a well-curated mix of mid-twenties to late-thirties. Sure, we've got the outliers like Allen and Dolores, the elder states people of the office, but the majority of the team could pass for the cast of a CW reboot. Victoria herself looks like she's in her late thirties, though I'd bet she's well into her forties. Maybe older. Either way, her plastic surgeon deserves a holiday bonus.

The hot tub feels amazing. The heat seeps into my muscles and softens every part of me that was tense. AJ slides in beside me and I casually drape my arm along the edge behind her shoulders. Our thighs float into each other, skin against skin, her warmth curling around me like a secret. Every so often we glance at each other and smile, knowing looks that buzz with unspoken tension.

Then Manny plops down on AJ's other side and starts chatting her up. His voice is loud, animated and competing with the group's chatter and the constant churn of the jets, but I can still make out a few bits of their conversation. Mostly him trying too hard. Her laughing politely.

I lean back, pretending to relax, even though I'm definitely eavesdropping. Not jealous. Just… observant. Only observant.

"How's things?" Manny says and flashes his suave smile. Why does Manny have to be so tan and attractive too. *Fuck.* I can sense AJ isn't angry with Manny talking to her. She likes it but AJ is nice to everyone. It doesn't mean anything. Then Manny makes his too obvious move.

"When we get back into town would you want to grab a bite to eat together?" he asks her. He actually asks her out right in front of me, in front of the group. Obviously low enough so no one hears but I fucking hear it.

I pipe in. "Bro," I say then gesture toward the group of unsuspecting co-workers who still need to believe me and AJ are a couple.

Manny dips his head down and whispers. "Oh, sorry." He smiles at me and then AJ.

AJ smiles back and covers her lips with her finger, signing quiet.

Manny laughs. "We'll talk later," he manages out while winking at AJ. She nods her head as he slides down the water and starts talking to Curtis. I roll my eyes so hard I think they fall out into the hot water. I turn to AJ.

"Sorry about that," I say with a huff.

"It's okay," she replies casually. "Manny's sweet."

That statement catches me off guard. "Oh, is that so?" I ask, raising a brow. "So… you want to go to dinner with him?"

She laughs and nudges my side under the water. "Are you

jealous?"

"No. I don't care," I say, shooting her a sideways glance.

"Hmm," she purrs, dragging it out like she knows exactly what she's doing. "Okay, good. Because you know you're not actually my boyfriend, right?" she whispers with a smug little smirk.

She slides closer, her thigh crossing over mine beneath the water. Suddenly, it feels like the hot tub jumped up a hundred degrees. I swallow hard.

"I know," I say, meeting her gaze.

"So I could go on a date with Manny… if I wanted to." Her body shifts again, now her round, juicy breasts are pressed lightly against mine.

Jesus Christ. If she keeps this up, I'm going to have a full-blown situation happening under the water. Like, physically unstandable. I clear my throat and subtly adjust my position.

"I know," I repeat.

She leans in, lips just inches from my neck, her breath skimming my skin.

"Mmm," she murmurs. "You smell good."

Then she licks the side of my neck. *Licks it.* How is no one else witnessing this woman turning me on like a clap-on, clap-off light switch?

I swallow again, but it feels like my throat's made of cement. My whole body's on fire and not just from the hot tub.

"AJ," I start.

"Yes, Jonathan?" she replies, all innocent mischief.

"I want to take you to dinner when we get back into town," I blurt out. It comes out like I've been holding my breath for days and finally couldn't anymore.

She leans back, studying me, then she smiles and places her

hand on my thigh.

"I think I'd like that," she says, then winks and bursts into laughter as she shifts to her side.

She was totally fucking with me.

I laugh, shaking my head. "God, I hate you."

"No you don't," she says, splashing water onto my chest and face.

I grab her thighs and start tickling her. She squeals, laughing uncontrollably, trying to climb out of my grip. In the process, she ends up climbing *on* me, practically sitting on my lap. Her face is inches from mine, millimeters, really. She smiles and starts to lean in.

I wipe my lips, so unbelievably ready to kiss her again.

"Oh my God!" Tanya yells. "Can you guys take it inside?"

AJ pulls back, giggling and slides off my lap. We both laugh awkwardly, trying to play it cool.

"You're right," AJ says, just as Elaine scoots up next to her and grabs her hand.

"So, you have to tell me where you got this bathing suit," Elaine says.

AJ turns and gives me a grin over her shoulder. *Dammit.* Another almost-perfect kiss, ruined by my uncanny magnetism for the worst timing ever.

21

Abby

Another almost-amazing kiss… ruined. Again.

After we leave the hot tub, Jonathan barely says two words to me on the drive back to the cabin to get ready for dinner. No flirty banter, no shoulder brushes, not even a cocky grin. Just… silence. I let him take a shower first because I have to hop on a call with an anxious client and put out a few metaphorical fires. The kind of fires where everyone's panicking over something that could've been solved with a simple email.

By the time I'm off the phone, he's out of the bathroom, towel-drying his hair. His phone starts to ring and he glances at the screen. The face he makes tells me everything. Whoever's calling isn't just anyone, it's *someone*. Someone he doesn't want to talk to in front of me. He mutters something vague, like he's taking it outside and steps onto the porch. I guess he needs total privacy. The call's probably from one of his tall, impossibly perfect girls, no doubt. The type with sculpted cheekbones, fashion degrees and "brand collaborations" that involve sipping matcha on yachts. Girls he's always wining and dining around the city like it's his full-time job. It's not like I care. If he's into picture-perfect, airbrushed women with symmetrical faces and fashion-week outfits, that's his choice. Cool. Whatever. He can do what he wants. I don't care…

Once he disappears, I shower, blow-dry my hair and decide to leave it a little curly tonight. Eased waves that highlight the gold in my blonde strands and look just messy enough to feel effortless, just done enough to feel sexy. Because tonight, I want to feel like that girl. One of those modelesque women Jonathan and Marcus, for that matter, always seem to orbit. Girls who walk into a room and own it. Even if I don't care what those men do. Obviously.

By the time I finish my hair, I spritz on my Gucci perfume. One thing I'll never skimp on is fragrance. If I'm going to walk into a room, I want the scent to do half the talking. Jonathan wears Armani, because of course he does. I recognized it the second I met him six years ago. It's a sophisticated, self-assured and expensive scent. Classic Jonathan.

When I step out of the bedroom, he's already dressed and sitting at the counter, sipping from a to-go coffee cup you can get at the front lobby.

"You went to the front desk?" I ask, unable to keep the slight jealousy out of my tone. Caffeine envy is real.

"Yeah," he says, casually gesturing to his ears. "Needed Q-tips."

"Oh." I nod.

"I got you a coffee, too," he adds, sliding a second cup toward me.

My eyes soften instantly. "Thank you," I say, smiling as I take it. That was thoughtful. I definitely needed the brain fuel.

If I ever get a paper cut, there's a solid chance it'll bleed dark roast.

I step a little closer and immediately notice something. He's distracted. His phone's in his hand and he hasn't even looked up at me.

"I just have to put on my makeup and then we can go," I say, trying not to sound weirdly deflated.

"Okay," he says, finally glancing up. His eyes widen a little and he straightens in his seat.

"You look…" He pauses, struggling for words, which is rare for him. "Really… really pretty."

"Thanks," I say, brushing a strand of hair behind my ear to hide the stupid grin threatening to break through.

I'm wearing light blue skinny jeans and black heels, with a black halter top that shows off my newly sun-kissed shoulders and my bare back. No bra required, thankfully, because this top is doing all the work. The girls are cradled high, tall and proud.

Jonathan stands, walks over and takes my hand, twirling me gently. I laugh in surprise as he grabs my other hand and starts swaying with me like we're already on a dance floor.

He looks down at me, smiling that signature smile that turns my stomach inside out. "You better save a dance for me," he playfully demands.

I nod, already blushing. "Of course."

Then I twist out of his arms before I turn fully into mush and head for the mirror to do my makeup.

Fifteen minutes later, we're off in the golf cart heading to the main dinner hall for cocktails. The air is cooler now, wind brushing against my skin as the sun dips lower behind the trees.

As we drive, I get this boiling urge to ask if he's alright. It's been sitting in my chest since before we left the cabin and I can't shake it.

"Are you okay?" I ask, carefully hesitant. I don't know if he'll answer truthfully or shut down and throw a wall up like he sometimes does.

He keeps his eyes forward. "Yeah," he huffs.

I let the silence ride. Give him space with his own thoughts. The tires crunch over the gravel path and just when I think that's all he's going to say, he shocks me.

"My mom called," he admits.

"And you don't get along?" I ask, reading into his tone.

"No, we get along fine," he says quickly, but there's something under it. "It's just… every time I talk to her, it reminds me that my dad's gone. And she's just so…" He trails off, struggling to finish. He swallows hard and lifts a hand, running it through his hair, the wind tugging at the strands as he exhales. "It's like she doesn't care he's gone. Or maybe she's just… past it." He doesn't say it with anger. More like quiet confusion. Hurt, maybe.

"Maybe she does think of him often," I say tenderly, "but she doesn't bring it up to you because she doesn't want to upset you."

He doesn't respond right away, so I glance over at him. He suddenly pulls the golf cart over and shifts it into park.

I blink, confused. "What are you—"

He turns toward me, his whole body angling like he's about to say something important.

"You know," he starts, his voice low, "I've gone to therapy. I've talked to my brother. Even Manny. Hell, probably some random woman I was drunk around." He lets out a heavy breath. "And I've told all of them this same thing. Over and over." He looks at me, really looks at me. "And none of them have ever said what you just did. Not once."

There's something calm in his eyes. A flicker of glossiness that catches the dimming light and my heart catches a little. Jonathan Slack showing me his deepest feelings. I reach over and take his hand, even if I feel a little unstable myself with the rush of emotions from him.

"Jonathan," I say quietly, "people grieve in their own ways. I'm sure your mom thinks about your dad all the time. How could she not?"

He watches me, listening without interrupting.

"But maybe she doesn't bring him up because she's trying to protect you. Maybe she thinks it'll make you sad. And she doesn't want that for you." I give his hand a squeeze. "It makes sense to me, how she acts. It really does."

He looks down at our hands, his inside mine and then places his other one over the top, enclosing me.

"Why do you always seem to help me when I can't even help myself?" he asks, a smile tugging at his mouth.

"Maybe I just know you too well," I say, letting out a chuckle, my cheeks already flushing. I feel the warmth rise up my neck, part comfort, part... something else entirely. I'm half emotionally fulfilled that I helped him open up... and half distracted by the fact that his lips and bone structure are doing unspeakable things to my self-control.

His hand moves to my face and his thumb grazes my cheek, then trails down to my lips. He strokes my bottom lip back and forth before tugging it down slightly, pulling it toward him.

My heart kicks into high gear. The touch is so small, so

subtle, but it sends sparks zipping through every nerve ending I have. I'm going to get whiplash from the emotional ping-pong game this man has me playing.

"I'm going to kiss you now," he says, rough but not in an aggressive way, "and I don't care if a fucking bear comes barreling out of those woods. Nothing is stopping me this time."

I nod, giving him the green light, my throat tightening as I swallow.

Then he makes good on his promise. He leans in and kisses me and it's immediate, deep and hungry. His tongue slides against mine, unhurried but possessive. I taste his mint toothpaste and the warmth of leftover coffee and somehow, it's a ridiculously perfect combination.

I slide closer, wrapping my arms around his neck, meeting him kiss for kiss. He pulls me onto his lap, one arm around my waist as his other hand cups the back of my head. The angle deepens, the kiss growing hotter and more intense. I tighten my hold on him and shift my hips, grinding instinctively. I can feel him hard beneath me and the pulse of arousal it sends through me is near blinding.

He breaks the kiss just long enough to breathe against my mouth and I moan into the sliver of air he leaves behind. His grip on my face tightens and he kisses me again, more sensual this time. It's the kind of kiss that makes you forget where you are, who's around, or what time it even is.

It's been a long time since I've felt this way. Sure, I've had a few casual hook-ups over the last few years, mostly just to remind myself I'm still a breathing woman with hormones, but this? This is something different. This is seductive and safe. Electric and easy. And, holy hell, I think I might combust if we keep going.

After what's probably only a few minutes but feels like an eternity of heat and hunger, he pulls back, one hand resting on the back of my neck.

"You are so amazing, AJ," he says, his voice almost submissive. Then he smiles and it's that boyish, slightly crooked grin that makes my heart lurch.

He doesn't wait for my response, leaning in and kissing me again. His hands glide down my back, then lower, tracing the curve of my hips and squeezing fiercely. His fingers dig in as he groans into my mouth. He pulls away from my lips, tilting my head back so he can trail kisses along the sensitive line of my neck.

I moan again, louder this time and I can feel his breath growing faster, his restraint unraveling. There's a kind of frenzy to it now, like we're both seconds from completely losing control. It's going to take a natural disaster to kill this momentum. Just as he comes back up to my lips, mouth inches away, his phone blares from the back of his jeans. So, apparently, a phone call can kill this momentum.

Out of breath, both of us still buzzing from the make-out rage, we stop kissing, stop grinding, stop moaning. He lifts up, still holding onto my butt and reaches into his pocket for his phone. The screen lights up with *Manny*.

"I think we're late," he says, glancing at me. He doesn't answer the call. Just shoots off a quick text, then shoves the phone back into his jeans.

I smooth my hair, swallowing hard and trying to catch my breath. "Yeah," I breathe. "We probably should go."

"Yeah," he echoes. But before he slides me back over to the passenger seat, he cups my face one last time, kissing me on the lips, then moving to brush his mouth to the tip of my nose. He smiles, his voice dazed. "That was… wow."

"I know," I say, still breathless.

He wraps his arms around my waist and pulls me into a hug, resting his chin against my shoulder as he breathes in my hair. "Mmm," he murmurs. Then, after a few seconds, he pulls back just enough to smirk. "Okay, temptress. Let's go."

I laugh as he lets me go, both of us still a little drunk on the moment.

I slide back over to the passenger seat and start adjusting my top and jeans, trying to tame the aftermath of the whirlwind that just happened. Beside me, Jonathan shifts and readjusts his… well, let's just say his very enthusiastic friend down in his pants. Which, by the way, feels pretty impressive, like I needed more reasons to be into this man.

He glances at me. "You good?"

I nod, still a little short-winded. "Yeah."

He puts the golf cart back in motion and we head toward the clubhouse like two totally normal coworkers who absolutely did not just dry-hump in the middle of the woods.

Did Jonathan and I just have one of the hottest make-out sessions of my life, surrounded by pine trees and potential bear attacks?

Yes. Yes, we freaking did. And it was mind-blowing.

22

Jonathan

I probably look like a full-blown stalker at this point. I can't stop staring at AJ from across the room. She's mid-laugh at one of Allen's terrible dad jokes and somehow even makes that look hot. Her nose crinkles in this adorable ripple, her mouth stretches into a wide, full smile and her laugh is that deep, unfiltered kind: equal parts sexy and playful. The kind that makes everyone around her want to laugh too, just to be part of it.

She tucks a piece of hair behind her ear and glances over at me. I'm standing beside Victoria, nodding along like I care about her latest girls' trip to Aspen with her overpriced coat rack of friends. AJ catches my eye and waves subtly, hand low at her side. I give her a small smile and tilt my head toward Victoria, then roll my eyes for good measure.

AJ giggles and covers her mouth like she's trying to stay composed. It only makes her more irresistible. She's this impossible mix of sexy and sweet and it's driving me crazy.

I can't believe it. AJ. The woman who once made work feel like a competitive sport. The one who's been embedded under my skin for years in all the worst ways. And now? She's making me flushed, restless and horny as hell.

The way her jeans hug her body should be illegal. Every curve of her ass, the perfect lines of her thighs; it's like they were custom-made to ruin my concentration. That halter top sits just right at her hips, revealing a sliver of sun-kissed skin above the waistband. The neckline dips low enough to hint at cleavage without giving it all away. It's… criminal. Sensual in that effortless, sneaky kind of way that makes you look twice and then a third time when you think no one's watching.

Her golden blonde hair is curled in those soft waves that practically beg to be touched. And don't even get me started on how she smells. Like wildflowers and danger. Feminine and bold. The kind of scent that hits you once and lingers in your head for days.

She doesn't need makeup. AJ's the kind of naturally beautiful that makes people stare without realizing it but the swipe of eyeliner and mascara she put on earlier makes her blue eyes even more dangerous.

It's taken me six long years to get here, but the truth is finally slapping me in the face: AJ is sexy as sin and I'm completely gone for her.

The best part? She kissed me back in the golf cart. Sure, I didn't exactly make it easy to resist, regardless though, she leaned in. She wanted it. And the way she's looking at me from across the room right now? She wants a round two.

As usual, dinner here doesn't miss. Tonight's Italian night: chicken Alfredo, shrimp scampi and lasagna so close to my grandma's I almost pull out my phone to call her. Add in the endless wine, background Sinatra and dim, romantic lighting and it's basically a date night fantasy.

Except, of course, Marcus has to sit on the other side of AJ and talk to her the entire damn time. She's polite. She giggles at his dumb jokes. But I can tell she's not totally into it. Her smile doesn't reach her eyes and every so often she glances my way like she's searching for a lifeline. I want to reach across the table and shut him down mid-sentence. But instead, I sip my wine and wait for the bus ride.

Victoria and Marcus have this whole group outing planned, some local bar for dancing. Fine. Whatever. I'm counting down the minutes until I can sit next to AJ, alone, for the twenty-minute ride. I let her get on the bus first, partly to be a gentleman… mostly to enjoy the view. And damn, what a view. Her hips move with just enough sway to make me question every good decision I've ever made.

I follow close. Real close. Close enough she can probably feel the heat off my chest. At one point, she reaches back and brushes her fingers against my jeans. It's just a light touch but it sends a jolt straight through me.

And then Tanya ruins everything. "Abby!" she screeches, waving AJ toward the seat next to her. "Elaine's sitting with Stan. Please sit with me!" she whines and protests.

AJ glances back at me, clearly torn. I give her a nod, trying to play it cool even though internally I'm screaming into a void. She smiles, leans in and kisses my cheek. It's enough to fry every neuron I have. Then she slides into the seat next to Tanya, who immediately launches into a full-blown TED Talk about her outfit.

I drop into a seat a few sections behind them, staring out the window, silently fuming. Of all the things that could've cockblocked me tonight… it had to be the company gossip queen in fuchsia wedges. At least I'm still close enough to hear

AJ laugh and far enough to avoid Tanya's constant babble.

Suddenly, because of course, karma's got jokes, Marcus slides into the seat beside me like we're old friends about to share a beer, not mortal enemies locked in a fake-dating love triangle.

He nods. "What's up?"

I nod back, barely. "Not much."

"I think this place is going to be fun," he says, adjusting his overpriced jacket like we're discussing dinner plans and not silently battling for the same woman's attention.

Before I can fake a polite grunt, Tanya twists in her seat, two rows ahead of our row, leans over AJ and waves back toward us. "Hi, Marcus!"

"Hi, girls," Marcus replies smoothly from beside me but the grin he sends forward is locked on AJ. Even though she's not looking his way.

Just like that, every muscle in my jaw tightens. I can feel the heat rising behind my ears and I'm pretty sure my face is now a shade somewhere between "blood pressure crisis" and "fire engine."

He leans back fully in the seat like nothing happened, pulls out his phone and starts scrolling through his email. Meanwhile, I'm stuck, physically and emotionally, between the girl I'm fake-dating, who I absolutely want to be real-dating and her smarmy ex-fiancé who smells like money and smug entitlement. *Cool.*

The bus rumbles to life and we pull onto the winding road toward the club. I'm already planning how I'll steal her away; maybe a slow dance, maybe a whispered excuse to step outside, maybe I'll kiss her senseless in a dark corner of the bar or hell, even the back alley. I'm not picky. I just need her lips on mine again.

And then, like the human equivalent of a wet sock, Marcus turns to me.

"I want to talk to you," he says, his voice serious.

I arch an eyebrow. "What's going on?"

I assume it's about the company. A merger. A pitch. A budget review. Anything but *her*. Naturally, I'm wrong.

He leans in, like we're bros swapping secrets and lowers his voice. "I want to be honest with you. Man to man."

Oh, here we go. I lean toward him out of reflex, body language habit, but the second he speaks, I regret everything.

"I want Abby back," he blurts out with the confidence of the strongest man in the world.

The words hit me like a slap to the face. No warning. No buildup. Just a straight-up, sucker-punch confession and for a second, I forget how to blink. *Did he seriously just say that? Because if he thinks he's getting her back… he has no idea who he's dealing with.*

I shake my head like I must've misheard him. "Huh?" I say.

He doesn't miss a beat. "I'm going to win Abby back," he says casually, like he's talking about picking up dry cleaning. "Just wanted to give you a heads-up so there's no hard feelings. You know—" and then, the smirk "—because I'm kinda your boss now."

He shrugs like that's a totally normal thing to say, then leans back in his seat and starts checking his emails again, as if he didn't just throw down a gauntlet mid-bus ride.

I'm not the kind of guy who backs down from a fight. Never have been. But for some reason, I sit there in stunned silence. Maybe it's the audacity. Maybe it's the arrogance. Or maybe it's the fact that I don't want to cause a scene with AJ a few feet away. Either way, I don't say a damn word the rest of the ride.

Marcus, on the other hand, sits there proud as hell, oozing that overconfident, I-always-win energy like he just scored the first point in a game I didn't agree to play.

Minutes later we pull up to the club and you can already hear the bass thumping from outside. Neon lights pulse against the building and there's a line wrapped around the block. Clearly *the* place to be on a Saturday night out here.

Because we're rolling deep, the staff comes out and leads our group inside to an elongated booth area right by the dance floor. It's prime real estate with velvet couches, bottle service, the whole deal. As we walk in, I catch more than a few guys eyeing AJ and it lights something hot and territorial in my chest. They all think they've got a shot. Especially Marcus. But they're about to learn the hard way that AJ's going to be on that dance floor with *me.*

We crowd around the booth, settling into the space. Three women in sleek black dresses come over carrying bottles of champagne, Victoria's doing, obviously. Moments later, a guy with too much cologne and too-bright teeth strolls over.

"Hello, everyone!" he announces, arms thrown wide. "I'm Ricky and this is my club. If you need anything, just let me know." He kisses Victoria on the cheek then disappears toward the bar like he owns the whole planet.

"I've known Ricky since college!" Victoria shouts to the group, but the music's so loud all we can do is nod and pretend we heard her correctly.

Marcus, trying a little too hard to play host, stands and starts pouring champagne like he's the man of the hour. When he gets to AJ, he leans in close, says something low in her ear and hands her a glass.

She blushes, then mouths *thank you* as he winks at her.

I swear, it takes every ounce of restraint not to deck the guy right here. Right now. But professionally? I can't. What kind of audacity does it take to tell me to my face that he's going after AJ and then turn around and start laying it on thick like I'm not even standing here? Sure, technically AJ's not *my* girl but Marcus doesn't know that.

I turn to AJ and ask, "What did twat waffle say to you?"

She chuckles, sipping her champagne. "He said he ordered my favorite kind."

Of course he did. I shake my head. "Dude's really trying to win you back, huh?"

She takes another sip and glances over at him. "I don't think so," she says but it's not exactly convincing.

Marcus is already staring and then lifts his glass in a toast. To her, I assume. Though I'm sitting right next to her, so maybe it's for both of us. Either way, I don't raise shit. I just glare. Fuck that guy.

AJ humors him, lifting her glass with a polite smile. Before she drinks, I reach out and grab her hand.

She looks down at our fingers, then up at me with a nervous but excited gleam in her eyes. There's something electric in the air, like we're both waiting for the spark to fully ignite.

She leans into my ear and whispers, "I have to find the bathroom," then laughs. "Bathroom squad!" she yells, turning toward Tanya. "Come with me?"

Tanya bolts over like a golden retriever offered a treat. "Yes! Let's go!" she squeals, shooting me a double eye squint like she was invited to a secret girl ritual. Off they go.

Time passes, too much time, and they still haven't come

back from the bathroom. I start to get actually concerned, so I head down to the dance floor and scan the crowd and there they are. AJ's dancing like she owns the place, all wild blonde waves and carefree energy. Tanya's beside her, flailing with zero rhythm but full commitment. AJ spots me and grins, then runs over, laughing.

"Tanya and I did two shots in a row," she giggles, covering her mouth like she's just confessed to a crime.

I laugh, too. She's so fucking adorable. Especially buzzed, which judging by the flush in her cheeks and the sparkle in her eyes, she very much is.

Tanya waves me over from the dance floor. "Come dance with us!" she shouts, already mid-spin like she's starring in her own music video.

AJ turns to me with that cute, intoxicated smile that could melt steel. "Come on," she says. "Dance with us."

I chuckle. "Okay, let me grab my drink first," I say, giving her hand a quick squeeze before I pull away. Her skin's warm from dancing, her energy electric. I can practically feel it pulsing off the dance floor. The heat, sweat, half-dressed strangers and cologne clouds thick enough to choke a small horse.

I weave through the crowd, heading toward our velvet booth, but Manny stops me mid-stride.

"Hey man!" he yells over the music. "Can I talk to you?"

Now? Seriously?

"I was just about to go dance with AJ," I say, hoping he catches the hint and lets it go.

But he shakes his head. "That's what I wanna talk to you about."

Nothing like a potential romantic ambush to go with my overpriced cocktail. I sit down next to him, already feeling a tightness in my chest. What if he knows? What if he saw something? Maybe it wasn't just the local wildlife catching our X-rated golf cart moment earlier.

He takes his sweet time, then drops it. "I have a feeling she might be into me."

I blink so hard it hurts my eyes. "Um. Okay…"

"I'm thinking about making a move," he adds. "Tonight."

My brain spins. For a split second, I'm not sure if I want to laugh, puke, or throw myself off the back of this booth. What is happening? Do I say it? Do I just blurt it out? Tell him I'm into her, that I kissed her, that I'm already picturing her in my T-shirts making breakfast in my kitchen with me and moving her stuff into my place.

No, I do what I always do. I spin the truth.

I slap a hand on his shoulder and lower my voice. "I don't know, man… Marcus sat next to me on the ride here and told me he's planning to fight for her."

Manny's brows shoot up.

I shrug, letting that little, not really a lie, simmer. "I just think it's about to get… complicated."

Manny looks stunned and pissed. "What the fuck?" he shouts over the music.

I shake my head like, *I know, man. I know.*

"He told you that, *knowing* you're 'with her'?" he asks, complete with air quotes.

"Yep," I say, popping the p. "Fucking prick, right?"

Manny shakes his head in disbelief. "Wow, bro. Does AJ know?"

And here's when I stretch the truth so thin it might snap in half.

"Yeah," I say casually. "I think so. And I think… she wants

it."

Technically not a lie. I mean, maybe? I haven't exactly asked her. Haven't had the time since Marcus hit me with his tyrant, pathetic threat on the bus ride over. For all I know, she could be playing both of us. Or neither.

"Damn," Manny mumbles, deflating right in front of me. He throws up his hands. "Well, figures she'd want him back."

I slap his shoulder again and give it a friendly shake. "It's okay. There are plenty of women out there. Seriously. Look around."

I nod toward a group of girls a few feet away who are very much checking us out. Normally I'd be all in, but tonight? I've got tunnel vision and her name is AJ.

Manny spots the girls and they all start whispering to each other. He smiles and waves. They wave back.

"Come on," I say, nudging him toward them. "Go talk to them. Be the strong, sexy man I know you are."

He laughs, shaking his head as I give him one final push. "Thanks, man," he says, clapping my hand in his. "You're my best friend, dude."

Then he pulls me into a bro hug and now I feel like the biggest traitor on the planet. My chest sinks in and the guilt and bourbon slosh together in my stomach.

"You got it," I say, patting his back like an idiot. Like a lying, kiss-stealing idiot.

He heads toward the girls. They all light up like Christmas morning. He'll be fine. Manny always bounces back. I just don't know if he'll forgive me when he finds out I've been lying this whole damn time.

I shake off the shame. The only thing I'm focused on right now is AJ. No matter the destruction I cause. Or… the destruction *she* might.

I glance toward the dance floor and there she is. Front and center. Spotlight in human form. She's dancing with Tanya and a few other women from the office, but all I see is her. It's like someone pressed slow motion. Her hips rock, just enough to be unpredictable, her ass shifting with every beat. Her arms are in the air, head tipped back, smile wide, lips mouthing the lyrics like she doesn't have a single worry in the world. Like she's free, wild and unbothered.

Damn, she's so luscious it hurts. Her hair brushes forward, over one shoulder and when she dips low to the beat, her halter top shifts just enough to give me a perfect view straight down her cleavage. Her curves are unreal. The kind of curves that make a man stupid enough to ruin friendships, careers, maybe even his entire life, which is clearly what I'm doing.

Her jeans cling to every inch of her lower body, taunting me. Daring me. And I know, in my gut, in my bones, in every throbbing cell of my body… tonight's the night. I'm going to make love to that woman. No more pretending. No more fake dating. Just us. Real and raw and way past the point of no return.

23

Abby

When I've had a few drinks, I *love* to dance. Sober Abby loves it too but she usually needs a pep talk, a dark corner and at least one Dua Lipa song to let loose.

But right now? I'm floating. Two shots with Tanya, two glasses of champagne before that and now I'm smack in the middle of the dance floor, living my best life.

The DJ is spinning Cee-Lo Green's "I'll Be Around," and it's hitting just right, funky and loud, with a deep jazz groove that makes your hips move whether you want them to or not.

Then I hear Tanya scream, "Yay!"

I turn and there he is… Jonathan.

He smirks as he steps into my space, hand sliding to my hip like it belongs there. He pulls me toward him and suddenly we're dancing, bodies aligned, the rest of the room fading out like an overexposed photo.

His eyes meet mine, playful at first, then shifting into a hotter, even hungrier stare. I feel the weight of his gaze drop to my lips and I bite the bottom one, teasing him.

His smile slips into something darker. He leans in, grinding his hips against mine and *whoa.* I can *feel* him through his jeans. And I'm not even sure he's hard yet. That's just… him? At baseline? I gasp. Like actually gasp.

Jonathan spins me around, pulling my back flush against his front and now I get an even clearer sense of *exactly* what I'm working with. His hands slide down my sides, then lower, gripping me with this confident authority as I grind back into him, matching his rhythm. We're dancing, technically. But honestly? We might as well be having sex with our clothes on.

It's hot in here, filled with the steamy, sticky crowd but he still smells *so* good. That scent I used to associate with irritation and unsolicited arrogance? Now I crave it. I want to drown in it. I want it soaked into my sheets. Into *me.* I lean back into him, letting the back of my head rest on his chest. His chin dips down beside my face and I catch the flick of his tongue across his bottom lip.

I know what's coming. I rise onto my tiptoes, bridging the height gap just as he drops in. When our mouths meet it's fireworks. It's not just a kiss. It's a kiss that melts time. One of those kisses where your knees go weak, your brain forgets how to function and your entire body just says *yes.*

His arms tighten around me and I swear I could fall backward into nothing and he'd catch me. I feel safe, which is insane because this is *Jonathan.* But right now? His kiss is movie-scene hot. Lift-your-leg, hold-your-breath, forget-your-ex hot. And I'm not ready for it to end.

His tongue continues to slide more into my mouth and I welcome it, kissing him back with eager pulls. At one point, I even suck on his tongue, just a little and that earns me a reaction. I feel him shift against me, hardening through his jeans. Oh… he definitely likes that move and I definitely want more.

I twist to face him, gripping his jaw and pulling him even closer, like our mouths haven't already fused together. His hands slide down, finding the top of my butt again and this time, he squeezes it with a possessive edge that sends a fire straight through me.

My breathing goes erratic. I can hear myself moaning into his mouth, though the music is so blaring it swallows the sound.

He doesn't stop kissing me. If anything, it becomes messier, needier, more desperate by the second.

Eventually, he pulls back, his eyes wild and dark as they lock onto mine. Then they flick down to our joined hands. He tightens his grip and starts walking, dragging me with him off the dance floor. I follow without hesitation. He's searching for something. I don't know what until I see it; a dimly lit hallway off to the side of the bar, nearly hidden from view. There's no one in it. Just shadows and hazy, golden light.

He glances back at me with a silent question in his eyes.

I nod, gulping, while my brain screams *God, yes.*

He yanks us into the hallway and doesn't waste a second, lifting me clean off the ground, pinning me against the wall as I wrap my legs around his waist.

For a moment, he just looks at me like he's savoring every inch.

My heart stutters. I smile and drop my gaze to his mouth, then pull it into mine. He groans, a deep, guttural sound and presses in closer, kissing me like he's starving. Tongue sliding against mine. Hands gripping stiffer. It's erotic. It's sweaty. It's so good I swear if he reached for the button on my jeans right now, I wouldn't stop him.

He presses me harder into the wall, his hands finding my chest and roaming freely. I let out a moan as his fingers graze over my breasts, then under my shirt. He leans down, pulls one of my breasts free and kisses it, tender at first, then more desirous. His mouth closes over my nipple and the warmth of it, the rhythm of it, has me gasping like I might lose my mind. His mouth is somehow both fierce and sweet, like he knows exactly how to wreck me.

I reach down, rubbing the front of his jeans. He's fully hard now.

He lifts his mouth from my chest, his breathing ragged and cups the back of my neck, pulling me into another intense kiss, then breaks away just enough to whisper in my ear. "AJ, I need you."

I kiss his cheek, his nose, his lips; anywhere I can reach, like I'm trying to pour everything I'm feeling into each touch. Ninety percent of it is pure, unfiltered lust. But the other ten? It's something else. Like the kind of emotion you feel right before making love to someone you trust. Someone who's yours. It catches me off guard for a split second, this zap of something deeper but I don't let it stop me. Not when it feels this good. Not when it feels this right.

Still, before we completely lose control and end up having full-on sex in a hallway behind a bar, we both start to come down from the high. Slowly, we pull back. He tenderly tucks my breast back into my top while I stop rubbing the front of his jeans, my breath still coming in short, shallow gasps. He keeps holding me there, his arms secure as he places kisses along my jaw, my neck, my lips.

"Jonathan," I manage to say between breaths. "That was…"

"I know," he says, shaking his head and smiling down at me, his chest rising and falling like he just ran a mile.

He lowers my legs from around his waist and my feet drop to the floor, still leaning against the wall. I smooth my jeans and adjust my top while he steps slightly to the side, shielding me from anyone who might walk by. He's a gentleman without even trying and a tiger, barbaric and unapologetic, when he kisses me like he means it. How can both versions of him exist in the same body? And how have I been so blind to it all these years? Did I always know this about Jonathan? Or has he just never let me see it?

We finally settle, both of us still catching our breath. He reaches for my hand and laces our fingers together like it's second nature. Like this is who we are now.

"Let's get another drink," he says, flashing a wicked grin, "before I make a mistake and have our first time making love be in a hallway at some club." He winks.

I'm taken back a bit. He doesn't say *sex*. Doesn't even say *fuck*, which, knowing Jonathan, would've been very on brand. No. He says *making love* and in that moment, my heart does a full, uncontrollable somersault. Because I realize I'm falling for him and I'm not scared of it.

24

Jonathan

Riding back on this loud coach bus is driving me absolutely insane and not because of the noise. It's because all I want to do is grab AJ from her seat, pull her onto my lap and kiss those full lips until we forget anyone else exists. But I can't. For a few painfully obvious reasons. One, we're surrounded by coworkers. Sure, they all think it's cute when we sneak a peck, but full-on grinding and groaning make-out mode? Not exactly retreat-appropriate. Two, there's the Manny factor. He knows we're supposed to be pretending and if he saw us going at it like we did back at the club, he'd know something was up. I'm not ready to hurt him, not yet. And then there's Marcus. God, I'd love to let him watch me touch AJ. Just so he knows he lost. Just to flip him a massive, metaphorical middle finger. But he's technically my boss now, so yeah… I have to chill.

AJ is sitting beside me, thankfully Tanya didn't steal her this time. She's tracing her fingers across the palm of my hand, staring at me with those big, sapphire eyes. She bites her bottom lip and smiles and I swear I feel my self-control snap one fraying thread at a time.

I slide my hand onto her thigh, discreet and careful not to draw attention. She shifts, just slightly but enough to let me slip my fingers a little further down her jeans. She giggles and I fucking melt.

The drive back to the main house isn't long, but it feels like an eternity with AJ sitting so close. As soon as we unload, Tanya and Manny are already begging us to hit the resort's karaoke bar with them.

"Come on, Grandpa!" Tanya yells at me.

"Bro, you *have* to sing again," Manny chimes in, already swaying a little.

I shoot AJ a look and like the queen of quick exits she is, she's already pulling off one heel like it's Exhibit A in a courtroom.

"I need to change out of these heels," she says, holding it up. "These things are killing me."

"I'll drive you," I say immediately. No one's going to question me giving my *girlfriend* a lift back to the cabin to change her shoes.

"We'll meet you guys in a few," she adds, wobbling off toward the golf cart like a woman on a mission.

"Okay, fine, but you *better* come," Tanya shouts as she heads toward the bar, already dancing to some imaginary beat.

Manny throws his hands up in a dramatic sigh, then shrugs and slings an arm around Tanya. The two of them stumble off together, already half-singing, half-yelling some throwback anthem. Manny's going to be too drunk to remember we were ever supposed to come back. And that's perfect because we're not coming back.

I glance at AJ and she winks, just a flick of mischief that sends heat shooting through my chest. I'm not even sure golf carts *have* a speed limit, but I slam my foot down like we're in the Indy 500.

She squeals and slides closer to me, wrapping her arms around my torso, gripping the front of my shirt like she can't get close enough. I love her touch. It's not just the way she feels, it's the way she *reaches* for me, like she needs me back just as much.

When we reach the cabin, we both pause, still sitting in the cart. It's not nerves, it's the weight of knowing. Knowing that once we cross that threshold, everything changes. There's no going back from this.

But AJ? She doesn't hesitate long. She hops out first and jogs up the porch steps, glancing back at me with fire in her eyes. She waits by the door, lips parted, heart pounding. I can see it in the way her chest rises and falls.

I join her, key in hand, but I don't open it right away. Instead, I tilt her chin up and press my mouth to hers.

It starts out gentle. Like we're savoring the last calm moment before everything ignites. Her lips are warm and patient, but beneath that patience, there's hunger. It doesn't stay soft for long. She tugs at the waistband of my jeans, finding the button and popping it open with ease. Her hands trail up under my shirt, dragging heat across my stomach and chest. I groan against her mouth, already losing whatever grip on control I thought I had. We're not even inside yet and I'm already undone.

I can't take it any longer. I jam the key into the lock and shove the door open, practically bursting through it like a man starved. I scoop AJ up, her legs wrapping around my waist and we stumble inside; still tangled in kisses, still clawing at each other like we've been waiting years for this moment.

She's tugging at my jeans, I'm juggling her weight and somehow I manage to slam the door shut behind us. I twist the lock because, let's be real, with nosy-ass Manny and stealthy Tanya roaming around, we're not taking any chances.

She drops her purse, I drop the key and we leave everything else behind. I set her down on her feet and yank off my shirt in one motion.

She steps back and lets her heated gaze roam. Her eyes flicker over my chest, my stomach and the look she gives me? Pure want. I've seen that expression on women before but this time it lands different. This time it's AJ. And that changes everything.

She starts walking backward toward the bedroom, laughing under her breath, then crooks a finger at me to follow. I do without a pause.

When I catch up, she unties the strap behind her neck and tugs the halter down, revealing the kind of mouth-watering breasts that belong in naked art museums and daydreams. They're round, perky and were made to fill my hands and my mouth. Not too big, not too small. Just… perfect. Of course they are. She's perfect and I'm about to lose my goddamn mind.

I'm right in front of her now and I drop to my knees. I press my lips to the smooth skin of her flat stomach, trailing soft, open-mouthed kisses upward until I reach her breasts, exactly level with my face from this angle. She lets her head fall back with a moan as I kiss, suck and playfully bite at them, tasting every inch. Her fingers thread through my hair and tug hard, like she can't stand how good it feels. I grip the small of her back and pull her closer, burying my face between her breasts as she gasps again.

"Jonathan," she breathes, her voice strained with need. "Take me to the bed."

There's no world where I'd argue with AJ. Not when she sounds like that. I rise to my feet, sweep her into my arms and carry her to the bed. I lower her down and crawl over her, bracing myself as she unzips my jeans completely and slips her hand inside my boxer briefs. I've been hard since the dance floor but now that I'm in her hands? I swear I get harder. Her eyes flick up to meet mine and when she smiles, it's a look that tells me she likes what she feels. A lot.

I lean down and kiss her again, because at this point I'm officially addicted. Her taste, her mouth, the way she kisses me back like I'm the only man she's ever wanted. I shove off my pants, then my boxers. She grabs my hips and pulls me down until our bodies are flush, chest to chest. I pull the rest of her top over her head and some strands of hair tumble into her face. She giggles, eyes sparkling, breasts bouncing as she laughs and I nearly lose it right then. That sound, that view, it's lethal.

I toss her top to the floor and push the hair from her face, letting my fingers skim her cheek. Her skin's warm, her cheeks flushed and for once, she looks completely at ease. She looks happy. And somehow, so am I. The woman underneath me is sexy as hell and she's mine.

I reach for the button on her jeans, pop it open and take my time sliding them down her legs. What's left is something I'm not forgetting anytime soon: AJ laid out in nothing but a black lace thong, legs shifting around me like she already knows what she's doing to me.

I kiss my way down her body, starting at her neck, then lower to her chest, her stomach. She shifts beneath me, already restless. When I reach her panties, I catch the lace between my teeth and pull. Her breath hitches and when I glance up, her lips are parted in a sound I feel in my spine.

I slide the thong off and toss it aside, then move back over her, pressing my hands to the mattress on either side of her. And I stop, for just a second. Because this view? This woman? It's unreal. Her eyes on mine, the way she breathes like she's bracing for impact.

"You okay with this?" I ask.

She nods without hesitation, then pulls me in by the face and kisses me like she needs it. Like she needs me.

I shift between her thighs, guide myself to her and push in.

She tears her mouth from mine, head tilting back as a sound slips out; something between a gasp and a curse.

"Oh…my…" she breathes, her back arching under me.

I've never felt anything like this. Like she was made for me. Like I was made for her.

I start to thrust, delicate at first. But it's almost impossible to hold back. The buildup, the tension, the way she feels wrapped around me… it's been simmering for days. Years, if I'm being honest with myself. I've always wanted AJ. I just didn't let myself admit it until now. Until I'm buried inside her.

I cradle the back of her head and pull her lips into mine, kissing her through every breathless moan. I speed up, driving deeper inside her as we're both unraveling. The sounds rising from us grow louder, needier, until she gasps and digs her nails into my back. Her thighs tense around me, then relax completely. She just came. I hear it in her voice, feel the wetness in her and I'm not far behind because that's all it takes, pushing me faster into her.

I'm done holding back. I thrust one final time and release. A groan tears from my throat as the sensation shoots through me. I press into her, burying my face in her neck, then collapse on her chest; still inside, still trying to remember how breathing works.

Our bodies rise and fall together, sweaty, hearts hammering in sync.

She runs her fingers down my back and into my hair; her touch is soothing. I hold her like I never want to let go.

"That was…" I exhale, still catching my breath. "Amazing."

"Yes. Yes, it was," she says, her voice airy and wrecked in the best way.

We lie there, wrapped around each other in silence. A few minutes pass, the quietness not awkward, just… full.

"Want to shower?" she asks eventually.

I lift my head to meet her gaze. She looks peaceful and her eyes, damn those eyes, shine like she's never looked at me this way before. I kiss her, meaning to make it quick, but she catches my face in both hands and kisses me again, fuller this time.

"Jonathan…" she starts, pulling back from our kiss, then trails off.

She doesn't need to finish. This wasn't just sex. It wasn't casual and it sure as hell wasn't a mistake. It was more. It *is* more.

"I know," I whisper.

I press a kiss to the tip of her nose, then start to get up and offer her my hand. She takes it and I help her to her feet.

"Let's go shower," I say with a grin, already thinking about how hard it'll be to keep my hands off her once the water's on.

As we walk into the bathroom, I take her all in; completely naked, lit by the white glow of the bathroom light; she looks like a goddess. She walks to the shower and leans in to turn it on, giving me a full view of her ass as she bends. It's like the universe is testing my self-control and failing. I'm hard again just watching her. She turns around, catches the look in my eyes, then glances down and smirks.

"Round two?" she asks, one brow lifting like a challenge.

I think I might actually be in trouble with this woman.

I clap my hands together. "Hell yes."

I immediately lift her and rush into the shower. The hot water hits my back as I carry her in. No preamble this time. I lift her against the wall, her slick skin warm in my hands and slide back inside her in one smooth penetration. She gasps, clutches my shoulders and wraps her legs around me like we never stopped. This time, I last longer. Long enough for her to come; twice. I already know her body well enough to tell. It's like we've been doing this for years.

She kisses along my jaw, bites my earlobe, groans into my neck. Her fingers rake down my back, gripping my ass and pulling me further with every thrust. Her body is coiled around mine, like she never wants to let me go.

And when I finally can't hold back, I let go with a grunt, my forehead pressing against the tiled wall as I spill into her. Just the kind of pleasure that knocks the wind out of you.

She kisses the side of my neck and whispers in my ear, "My sexy man."

The heat that spreads through me has nothing to do with the hot water. It's all her.

I lift my head from the wall and kiss her cheek. I'm still pushed in her, so I give one more deliberate thrust like punctuation. Like I'm telling her without words: *I'm completely yours.*

She pants and grips my arms. We're both demolished in the best way. I lower her legs to the floor and then she surprises me with a hug. Not a flirty squeeze or a post-hookup lean. A real hug. Full-bodied, arms-wrapped, chest-pressed kind of hug. It knocks the air out of me in a sweet, surprising way.

I hug her back, lifting her off the floor for a second and then setting her down again.

She giggles, tilts her head back and asks, "Is this real?" Then she turns and starts washing her body, like we didn't just cross a line we can't uncross.

I'm still standing there, frozen, watching her like I've never seen a naked woman before. She notices.

"Hello?" she says, laughing as she tosses a bar of soap at my chest. "Earth to Jonathan."

I catch it mid-air, grinning. "Sorry. I just… I can't believe this is real either."

I finally start soaping myself down, but I can't stop stealing glances at her. If this is a dream, I'm not waking up. Some moments in life feel too important to let pass. This is one of them.

I step fully under the water, letting the soap and steam rinse away the haze of sex and sweat. Then I do something I can't control even if I wanted to, I reach for her and spin her into me.

She startles and looks up at me with wide, questioning eyes.

"Abigail Jean," I say, my voice rougher than I expect. "I think I'm falling in love with you." My chest is lifting up and down like I've just run a mile. I mean it, every word and it terrifies me in the best way.

She stares at me for a second, blinking through the spray, her lashes wet. Her gaze drops to my mouth, like she's checking to see if I genuinely said that out loud, then her eyes find mine again as her lips part.

"Jonathan," she drawls, water splashing around us, "I'm falling in love with you too."

25

Abby

I must've passed out right after our shower. Between the champagne, the all-night adrenaline rush of being completely turned on, and oh yeah, finally getting that release with Jonathan, I was exhausted. Three times. He shattered me three times, in the best and most surprising possible way.

I wake up to clanking in the kitchen, coffee mugs knocking together, the faucet running, a drawer sliding open. I smile and push my face into the pillow, breathing in the smell of him, that signature Jonathan scent I used to claim I hated.

He's not in bed with me, so I assume he's the one making all the noise. Probably fixing us coffee, because he's considerate like that. Jonathan Slack: unexpectedly kind, infuriatingly sexy, and… so much more than I ever gave him credit for. His words roll around in my head: *I think I'm falling in love with you.*

I grin like an idiot, cheeks flushed even though no one's here to see it. He said my whole name too, *Abigail Jean,* like it meant something. Like I *mean* something. For the first time in a long time, I experience an emotion I didn't realize I was capable of feeling again after what Marcus did to me.

And then, like clockwork, self-doubt creeps in. Would Jonathan lie about loving me? No. Why would he? We'd already had sex twice by then, so it's not like he needed to sweet-talk his way into my pants. They were already on the floor.

Still, a wave of uneasiness washes over me, dragging bliss out to sea and replacing it with dread. Anxiety blooms in my chest, familiar and unwelcome. This is what happens when you get left at the altar and never actually process it, your baggage starts leaking into everything.

Me and Jonathan… a real relationship? Does he even want that? I mean I'm sure he does. He basically said *I love you*, you emotional moron. I shake my head like I can knock the thoughts loose. Nope, still there.

I crawl out of bed and tug the sheet around me, wrapping it like armor. I just need to see his face. That'll tell me everything. I know him better now. I know his expressions, his moods, his energy, like a dog-eared, favorite book. If he's legit, I'll know. And if he's full of shit… well, I'll know that too.

I step into the doorway, just in time to hear his phone ring.

He answers in a low whisper. "Hey, Manny."

I exhale. Okay, it's Manny. Not some secret girlfriend. Crisis averted.

"I can't really talk, bro," Jonathan says, his voice still hushed.

I tiptoe closer, curiosity overriding every polite boundary I've ever had.

"No, I'm not lying. I told you in the text," he says, sounding… frantic?

A chill runs down my spine and my stupid-happy smile

falters.

"Bro, stop it. I told you already. I don't like AJ," he admits.

The words hit me like a punch to the gut. My heart drops straight into my stomach and I go ice-cold. I can hear Manny's voice on the other end; it's indistinct, but Jonathan keeps going.

"I'm just using her to get that promotion from Victoria. She's using me too, for Marcus. I have no feelings for her like that."

My ears start ringing, body goes still and every nerve in me curls into a knot.

"Yeah, I know how it looked last night," he adds casually. "But it was all a show." He laughs, freaking *laughs*. "Bro, you know how good I am at faking it with women. How many times have I lied to them?" And then the final blow: "Yes. I'm sure. I'm not *in love* with AJ." He says it with a weird emphasis, like the phrase itself is a joke.

Silence passes for a few second and then he adds. "Okay. I'll see you at the lake."

He sets his phone down and turns back to the kitchen like nothing happened. Like he didn't just shred up my heart with a fillet knife.

I think I'm shell-shocked. That's what they call it in the military when your body just shuts down and you can't move, right? Because I can't move. I'm frozen; somewhere between wanting to cry, scream, or punch Jonathan Slack right in his infuriatingly perfect face.

I force myself to breathe. In and out, repeating until I avoid a full-on panic attack. Then I bolt into action. Clothes. I need clothes. I'm still naked under this sheet and there's no way in hell I'm letting him see me like that again. Not after hearing what I just heard.

I throw on a lake outfit for later today, swipe on some deodorant, jam a toothbrush in my mouth and thrust my hair into a ponytail like I'm about to run a 5K fueled by heartbreak and spite. Tiptoeing through the cabin, I grab my bag like a thief escaping her own dignity, then fling open the door and slip out. He doesn't call after me. Doesn't even notice I left.

The second the door closes behind me, I start walking with not the slightest idea of where I'm going, but I don't care. As long as it's away. Away from Jonathan *Jerk Face* Slack and his fake declarations of love. Away from his lies and his stupid charming grin and the way he made me *feel* something. How could I be so naïve? So stupid? He never loved me. He doesn't even have a heart. He got what he wanted, sex and that's all I'll ever be to him. A pawn. A game. A distraction on his way to a promotion.

Well, fine. He got his one night and that's all he's getting. The second this retreat ends tomorrow, I'm making it crystal clear: whatever we were pretending to be? We're not anymore. This charade is over.

Maybe I should just come clean. Spill the whole messy truth to everyone: Marcus, Victoria, the team. So what if I lose face with Marcus? So what if I tank the promotion I've been gunning for since last year? So what if I get fired? Okay, yeah. Crap, Abby. Let's not spiral that far. I can't tell the truth.

What I *can* do is avoid Jonathan like the lying, smooth-mouthed traitor he is. I've survived him before, so I can fake it for one more day. Hell, I've faked smiles in worse situations. Like when he stole my campaign idea in '23 and I had to clap for him in front of the entire marketing floor without launching a stapler at his face. Unfortunately for me, that was when I hated him. Back when my heart didn't skip a beat every time he smiled at me or called me AJ like we've been a couple for our whole lives. Back before I thought, clearly *felt* that maybe I loved him. Which, now I know I don't. Because you can't love someone who was just pretending. If it wasn't real to him, then it's not real to me.

I glance up and realize I've wandered so far I don't even recognize where I am. I've crossed the entire resort on autopilot. Oh great. I'm emotionally wrecked *and* directionally challenged.

Off to the side, I spot a cluster of empty picnic tables shaded by trees. No people. No noise. No Jonathan. It's the most optimal spot for me to gather my thoughts.

I beeline over and sink onto the bench like a limp rag filled with stinky chemicals and regret.

My phone suddenly buzzes. It's a text from Liar Slack himself.

Hey! I made you coffee and you're not here...

Another one immediately follows.

You okay?

Sure. I'm *fantastic*, thanks. Just replaying your fake love confession in my head on loop while contemplating throwing steaming coffee in your face.

I don't reply. Instead, I grip my phone so tight I swear I feel it begging for mercy. Then, in a fit of rage and chaos, I do what any self-respecting woman betrayed by a hot coworker would do. I hurl it over my shoulder like a javelin of fury.

"Ouch." I hear a voice cry out.

I freeze, then start to twist around to see who it is. It's not Jonathan thankfully. It's *Marcus.* I literally just hit Marcus with my phone.

He flashes that signature slant-smile as he bends down and

scoops up my phone from the grass. Without a word, he places it on the picnic table, then rubs his arm where it hit.

"I forgot you've got an arm," he says with a chuckle.

"Yeah, well, that's what happens when your grandpa wanted a grandson and raised you on Yankees stats." I grab the phone like it personally annoys me. "Sorry," I add. "Didn't know you were back there."

He waves it off. "It's okay." Then he pauses, his gaze shifting from light to concerned. "You okay?"

My phone buzzes again. It's another text from Jonathan.

I guess I'll see you at the lake. Please call me.

I roll my eyes so hard I'm surprised they don't pop out of my head and land on the picnic table. I slam the phone down on the wooden top like it burned my skin.

"Relationship troubles?" Marcus asks, eyes flicking to the screen.

"Oh, I'm sure you wish," I snap, folding my arms across my chest like a bratty six-year-old whose favorite toy just broke.

He sits down beside me, close enough for warmth but far enough to test the waters. "I *do* wish it."

I blink. My mouth opens, ready with a retort but then the words actually sink in. "Wait. You *wish* it?"

He nods and takes my hands, surprising me into stillness.

"Abby, I messed up. Big time. And I've regretted every single day since I hurt you," he says with an urgency behind it. "But how do you make up for something like that? For breaking someone like you?"

I stare at him, unsure if I died from shock or if I'm just speechless.

"I'm so sorry. I'll always be sorry. That's why I bought the company. To be close to you. To see if I still…" he trails off, like he can't find the right words or maybe he's afraid to say them. "And I do. I still have feelings for you. A lot of them. Probably more than I ever did."

He lets go of my hands, as if even he knows he might've crossed a line.

"I thought you said you didn't know it was my company at first," I say, narrowing my eyes.

He sighs, evidently caught. "I lied. I knew it was your office." He shrugs like it's no big deal, like people throw down giant checks just to flirt. "I even bid way over asking, just to make sure I got it." He smiles, proud of himself.

Meanwhile, I have absolutely no words. Me, the girl who can talk to a tree, a lamp, or a bathroom mirror for three hours straight is without words.

"Why are you telling me this *now*?" I ask, my throat suddenly constricted.

"Because I need you to know how I feel. And I need to know how *you* feel." His voice dips lower. "Abby, please. Just… give me another chance."

And just like that, my eyes burn and the tears come. Tears I've held in for almost four years. I've waited so long, literal *years,* to hear those words. To know he regretted it. That he still thought about me. That I mattered. But now that they're here, laid out like some kind of emotional buffet, all I can think about is insufferable Jonathan Slack.

Why? Jonathan is nobody to me. The worst, phony boyfriend at best. A long-time nemesis. A walking red flag with really good arms and way too much tongue talent for someone who doesn't truly care. He used me. Lied to me. Seduced me like it was all part of some game. And still… my heart is not breaking over Marcus. It's breaking over Jonathan.

I cry harder now, no longer able to tell if I'm mourning what could've been with Marcus, or what should never have happened with Jonathan. Maybe both. Maybe neither. Maybe I'm just pitiful.

Marcus wraps his arms around me and for a second I feel it, that recognizable safety I used to cling to like a lifeline. The kind of safety that made me believe in soulmates once. Marcus used to be mine… until he wasn't. He still smells exactly the same, stupidly expensive cologne mixed with just… him. Known in a way that makes my chest ache.

I pull back slightly and he wipes a tear from my cheek, his fingers stroking my skin with that similar gentle confidence that used to undo me. He cups my face like he's memorizing it, then leans in and kisses me. It's the kiss I've been dreaming about since the day he walked away. It's intimate. The kind of kiss that says, *I still love you.*

Lord help me and my mental spiraling, because I kiss him back. I let myself melt into him, let him pull me in and kiss me deeper, like no time has passed. Like we're still the same people. Except we're not. Because the second his lips touch mine and his hands find my waist, the only thing running through my head is one traitorous, involuntary, unwelcome thought: *He doesn't kiss like Jonathan.*

26

Jonathan

I'm not exactly sure why I get up so early. Probably because I'm still blissed out from one of the best nights of my life. I roll out of bed practically high on endorphins and make a beeline for the main lodge to grab AJ and me, both coffees and croissants. I go completely overboard at the condiment station; one of every jam flavor, three kinds of butter, honey I'm not even sure she likes. But I want it to be a thing. A cute gesture. A "Hey, I care about you so much I'm willing to fight off anyone for the last cherry preserve" kind of thing. Is it too much? Perhaps. I'm still figuring her out. What makes her laugh. How she takes her coffee; it's strong with two creams and two sugars. Whether she's a raspberry jam girl or a ride-or-die grape gal. She's been in my life for years, but this feels new. Like something that was always there, just waiting for the right moment to show up.

When I get back to the cabin, high on caffeine and optimism, I start setting up the breakfast spread. That's when Manny calls, freaking out. He says someone told him they saw AJ and me making out at the dance club and then we never showed

215

up to karaoke. He's certain I'm lying to him, that I've caught feelings. And yeah, he's not wrong. But I can't tell him that. Not yet. So I lie. Just to shut him up.

Once we hang up, I go back to laying out the food, start fluffing the croissants like it's a Michelin-star brunch and peek into the bedroom. It's empty.

I check the bathroom next. Also empty. No spunky, beautiful, golden-haired girl brushing her teeth or stealing my hoodie. I blink. Her phone's gone, too. Which rules out kidnapping… unless someone abducted her and graciously let her grab her iPhone on the way out. Still, it's weird.

I text her and get no response. We're all supposed to meet at the lake today for some relaxed team-building thing; sunscreen, paddle boards, awkward icebreakers, the works. Maybe she went ahead without me. But something feels off. Instead of heading straight there, I decide to walk the retreat and see if I can find her. Something in my gut says I need to.

And boy, do I find the *hell* out of her. There she is, sucking face with none other than Marcus. Mr. Ex-Fiancé. Mr. Steal-Your-Girl. What an absolute asshole. And her? I don't even want to think a bad word about her, but if she could read my mind right now… she'd burst into flames.

But she can't. Because she doesn't even know I'm here. Just standing. Watching her kiss Marcus. Watching her eyes flutter shut like she's enjoying it. His hands are cupped around her face. The exact same spot my hands held last night, not even twelve hours ago.

Damn. AJ gets around, doesn't she? I feel like the world's biggest idiot. I really thought what we had was different. I thought it was maybe real. I don't usually feel used by women, probably because I'm the one who usually does the using but right now? I feel played and I hate it.

The heat bubbling in my chest is nuclear. I want to throw something. Anything. But all that's around me are pinecones and broken bark, like a passive-aggressive nature display. So not too helpful. I consider throwing my phone. Why the hell would I shatter a thousand-dollar device just because AJ decided to tongue-wrestle her ex after riding me into next week? We shared something sexy and passionate last night, multiple times and in the middle of it, right when my heart was hanging out there like a fool on a ledge, I told her I was falling for her. She looked me in the eyes and said it back too. Was she drunk? Was she just acting? Was she thinking about *him* the whole time? What the actual hell is going on?

Before I do anything stupid or fireable, for that matter, I walk away. I leave them there, mid-make-out, like two horny teenagers who don't give a damn who sees them.

I find Manny outside his cabin and within seconds, I convince him to skip the lake and get drunk with me instead. Not exactly a tough sell, this *is* Manny we're talking about but he does ask where AJ is.

"She's busy. Off doing some girl stuff with the other women," I lie, as casually as I can. Because if I told him the truth, that I found her playing tonsil hockey with her ex, he'd just shrug and say, "So? Who cares?" And he'd be right. I shouldn't care. I *don't* care.

I down a shot to prove it. Then another, just for good measure. But the thing about lying to yourself is that it only works until your phone buzzes and you're reminded all over again why you're sitting at a bar guzzling shots.

It's AJ.

Heading to the lake.

I stare at the message for a second too long before slamming my phone face-down on the glossed stained bar. I'm not answering. She doesn't get a reply. Not after sneaking out of our cabin like nothing happened, after telling me she was falling for me and then running straight to her ex to mouth-maul him like *that* was her real happy ending. So yeah, screw her. And screw cherry jam. I hope she hates cherry jam.

Manny orders another round and I slap him on the back. "My man."

He grins. "I got you, bro."

Tanya and Elaine won't stop texting him, asking where we are and when we're showing up to the lake. Manny flashes his screen at me.

Tanya: *AJ is here without Jonathan. Are you guys off getting drunk?*

He laughs. "I think Tanya likes me," he says, smirking.

I shake my head. "Nice. She's not bad. Talker. But cute."

"Yeah… she's no Abby, though," Manny says, like he's fishing for a reaction.

I drop my head and spin my empty shot glass in slow circles. "Man," I mutter. "AJ's just like every other woman out there. She's nothing special."

Manny exhales through his nose. "Damn. I thought you guys were actually becoming friends."

I pause, my throat becoming dry. "We were. Until I saw her making out with Marcus this morning." I slap my palm against the bar. "Now she's just back to being the dumb girl who'll fall for anything. And I don't befriend dumb girls," I add flatly.

Manny blinks, then laughs under his breath. "Okay… whatever you say, man." He claps me on the back again. "Still can't believe she's back with Marcus. Welp, there goes my shot. No man stands a chance against a soulmate ex-fiancé."

I groan and rub the bridge of my nose. He's right. You don't compete with that kind of history. Not when it's written in rings and vows and broken promises.

I signal the bartender for another shot. If I can't have AJ, I can at least drink her out of my system. Even if I know damn well it won't work.

We knock back our third… maybe fourth shot. I've lost count. Manny convinces me to go to the lake and I figure what the hell. Why should I be the one hiding? She's the one who should be ashamed. She's the one who screwed things up.

We head down to the lake and the vibe is exactly what you'd expect: grilling, loud music, red solo cups everywhere, a couple drinking games already in progress. It's fun, chaotic, laid-back in that summer-camp-for-adults kind of way.

Tanya runs up to Manny and practically drags him toward the group. He shoots me a grin over his shoulder like this is the best day of his life. I hang back, scanning the crowd. Looking for *her*. Looking for *them*. And then I see her. She should be wearing a scarlet letter across her chest. Instead, she's wearing a barely-there bikini with some useless little crochet wrap that doesn't cover a damn thing. Her thighs. Her stomach. Her perfect, ridiculous, bouncing breasts. It's the same body I kissed every inch of last night. The same body I held all night, thinking maybe I'd found the person I wanted to share more than just a one-night stand with. Man, what a joke. What a complete, delusional, pathetic joke.

AJ marches over with her arms crossed taut like she's ready for battle. What's her problem? Did *she* catch *me* making out with *my* ex? Oh right, she didn't. Because I'm not the one filled with evil betrayal.

"Hey," she says, lowering her sunglasses just enough for me to see those sharp, furious eyes. She looks pissed.

"What's up?" I ask, doing my best impression of someone who couldn't care less.

"Been drinking?" she asks.

"Yup," I quip back.

She shakes her head like I'm some disappointment of a man. "Cool," she mutters. "Well, enjoy your time." Then she turns and walks away.

She's really trying to ice me out now, after I caught her lip-locked with her ex.

"Wow," I say loudly, making sure she hears it.

She stops and turns around. Her glare hits me before her feet do.

"What is *that* supposed to mean?" she fires back.

I wave a hand dismissively. "Nothing. Guess you don't need me anymore."

She scoffs. "That's rich coming from you, the user."

My eyebrows shoot up. "User? Yeah, okay."

She rolls her eyes, turns again and storms off like I just ruined her day.

User? What the fuck is she talking about? And why is she so furious with me when she's the one playing kissy-face with her ex-fiancé? I shake my head, unsure if I'm too buzzed to keep up... or if she's just flat-out lost her mind.

I wander back over to Tanya and Manny. Manny hands me a beer and I take it without a word. I don't usually drink beer, it tastes like carbonated regret but I want to feel numb, so it'll have to do.

Hours pass at the lake and none of them feel remotely fun. Not for me and from the looks of it, not for AJ either.

Marcus shows up at some point, but they avoid each other like they rehearsed it. I keep my sunglasses on and my gaze trained in her direction because I'm apparently a glutton for punishment. Still, not once do I see her speak to him. Not even a glance. Marcus, on the other hand, watches her constantly. He even tries to slide up next to her when they're grabbing food, but she shifts away like he's contagious. I don't know what to think anymore. Didn't they just share some second-chance-romance kind of kiss? Are they hiding it? Regretting it? Pretending it never happened?

"We're all heading inside for karaoke!" Manny jogs up and tugs my arm.

The sun dips low behind the trees, casting a warm orange glow over the retreat. The main house staff starts rolling out the dinner buffet and hauling in the karaoke setup like it's Coachella for corporate zombies. People from other companies start showing up too, it's apparently a weekend tradition around here, this group sing-off-slash-networking nightmare.

As we walk inside, I catch Marcus leaning in to whisper something in AJ's ear. She doesn't respond, just keeps walking, but it's enough for the heat to flare up in my chest. My fingers curl into fists at my side and I can feel my face flush with a predetermined kind of anger. The kind that comes from humiliation.

I told this woman I was falling for her and the next morning, she's locking lips with the guy who ditched her at the altar. And somehow the group still sees us as a couple. Because after two cringe-worthy performances, Tanya stands on a bench and grins like she's planning our wedding.

"Jonathan and AJ! You're up!" she shouts.

I'm about four drinks past sober when I shoot to my feet, grinning like I've just been handed a mic on *The Voice*. The liquid courage is loud in my veins and yeah, maybe I'm not exactly pitch-perfect in this state, but I've still got enough swagger to charm the cute blonde at the corner table. Maybe she'll end up in my cabin later tonight. Maybe AJ will see it. Maybe she'll care.

AJ's already waving her hand, laughing like she's too polite to say *hell no*. Her cheeks are pink and not from the alcohol. *Perfect.* I already know what song I'm singing. It's newer, it's brutal and it hits every single nerve I want her to feel.

Tanya joins the mission, tugging at AJ's arm like this is some wholesome bonding moment. "Come on, AJ!"

"Come on, AJ," I echo with a smirk.

She glares at me, the same glare she used to throw me across boardroom tables. Cool, we're back to our old ways. She shakes her head at the group, all sugar and diplomacy, like she's not boiling inside.

I lean into the DJ booth and say three words: "Vampire. Olivia Rodrigo."

The DJ gives me a thumbs-up and hits play before AJ can object.

AJ finally walks up beside me, arms crossed, mic dangling in her hand like it personally offended her.

"Okay," she says flatly. "I'm not singing that."

I grin wider. "That's okay. I'll sing for the both of us."

The opening piano hits and Elaine screams from somewhere in the crowd, "I love this song!"

I glance at Manny. His face is frozen somewhere between

confusion and horror. Even he can tell something is off with me and AJ.

I take the first verse like it's my personal battle cry. Mic in one hand, my gaze locked on AJ like I'm about to light the stage on fire. I start with a slow burn, throwing shade in melody—how I'm not about to give her the satisfaction of small talk, how her glittering life is built on fake concern and stepping on anyone in her way. I toss her a petty thumbs-up between lines.

"Look at you—living the dream," I say in rhythm, riding the beat.

She folds her arms tight, eyes narrowing. I keep going, weaving in digs about the parties, the diamonds, and the so-called paradise that was anything but. My voice slices through the room, and a few heads start turning her way. She notices.

I hit the part about loving someone so much you laugh at your own stupidity. Her arms loosen, her face softens for half a breath. Then I crank it back up—how I've made mistakes, but hers made mine look saintly; how she only shows up when the lights are low.

Without warning, I step closer, leaning into the mic like it's a dare. The next line is about being sold for scraps, about someone sinking their teeth in and draining you dry. I let my voice crack in the perfect place, half-scream, half-melody. Then I'm right in front of her, holding the mic toward her mouth like I'm handing over a loaded weapon.

She takes it. Doesn't flinch. Doesn't run. Her voice is serrated enough to cut glass as she fires it straight at me—how every warning about me turned out to be dead-on, how I called people crazy for daring to tell her the truth, and how she hates herself for ever falling for my lies.

Her palm smacks into my chest, a shove timed perfectly to the beat. The crowd erupts. She keeps going, venom laced through every note—singing about how I can sell a lie without blinking, how I make betrayal look effortless, how she should've seen me coming a mile away. Then she rolls her eyes, smirks, and lets out the kind of line that makes the whole place gasp—how older women would've known better.

AJ steps toward me, voice climbing higher, fiercer, laying out every bitter detail in technicolor. I don't even hear the cheering anymore—just her.

When she hits the "vampire" hook, the room freezes. You could hear a pin drop before she turns and struts to the far end of the stage, tossing out another blow: that you can't love anyone without a heart, and she's damn sure I don't have one.

I don't give the crowd a second to breathe. I cross the stage, cutting in with my side—how I tried to save her, how her mind works in ways I'll never understand. I lift a hand like I might stop her, but I don't.

We hit the last chorus together, circling each other like predators—lines about mistakes, late-night shadows, and losing yourself to someone who only ever wanted to break you apart.

By the final hook, we're toe-to-toe. The "bloodsucker" punch lands, and the song crashes to an end.

The room is silent. We're both out of breath, locked in a stare-off neither of us is willing to lose.

She throws her hand back and slaps me across the face. It's not hard, but it's enough to sting and loud enough to echo. The crowd collectively gasps and then the shock drops like a curtain. You could hear a pin hit the hardwood.

Her eyes shine, not with rage but something real, filled with gut-punched hurt. I should know what that feels like.

I hold still and keep my face stoic. I can't let her see what's erupting inside me. The heartbreak. The humiliation. The part of me that still wants to chase after her and beg her to explain why she kissed Marcus.

She shoves her microphone into my chest and storms off the stage.

Somewhere in the back of the room, a single person starts to clap, then it dies immediately.

I glance out at the crowd. All I see are stunned faces and open mouths. Clear confusion. Maybe a little secondhand sorrow, too. I blow out a slow breath, my aching jaw clenches.

Well… that could've gone better.

27

Abby

I slapped Jonathan Slack.

Not in a fun, flirty way. Not even a dramatic soap opera-style slap where my hair blew perfectly in the wind and I walked off in heels like I'd rehearsed it. Nope. I straight-up slapped him, hard enough that my palm still stings and my wrist kind of aches from the follow-through.

I've never slapped anyone in my life. The movies make it seem effortless, like a flick of the wrist and *boom*, instant power and vindication. But no one tells you your hand might throb after. Or that your breathing will turn erratic like your body's trying to launch itself into space.

And I didn't even stick around to see the aftermath. I ran off the stage like I was the one wronged, leaving Jonathan standing there, stunned, with fifty pairs of eyes watching.

Now I'm sitting on a bench outside the main lodge, heart still racing, trying to pull myself together and pretend like I didn't just slap my fake boyfriend in front of the entire company. That's when I hear footsteps stomping in my direction. Of freaking course it's Jonathan.

"What do you want?" I snap without even turning around.

He comes to a stop beside me, hand pressed to his cheek. "What the hell was that?" he demands. "A slap? Really?"

I look up at him, my jaw tense. "Maybe that was a little dramatic," I admit. "But I couldn't stand your smug little smirk for one more second."

He blinks, caught off guard. "Well, you sure took care of that, didn't you?" A heavy silence falls. Then he starts again. "This was your stupid idea," he adds. "All of this. I didn't have to play fake boyfriend. But I did it so you could make Marcus jealous. And it worked. *Clearly*."

"Clearly? What does that mean?" I shoot back, standing up and stepping toward him until we're face to face.

"Oh, you didn't think anyone saw your little make-out session, huh?" His voice is honed. "Well, I did."

My breathing freezes. I didn't know anyone was watching, let alone Jonathan.

"So *that's* why you've been acting like a total jerk tonight?" I ask, my voice still simmering.

He shrugs, like this whole thing doesn't matter, like I didn't just rip myself open and fall into his bed last night. "I don't care," he says. "But it's not a good look, AJ. Sleeping with me and then kissing your ex the next morning?" He flashes a smirk. That same stupid smirk I was trying to slap off earlier. "Didn't take you for a trashy girl but here we are."

I want to slap him harder now or at the very least, kick his kneecap out of spite. But I don't. I clench my fists and hold my ground.

"Did you see the part where I pushed him away from me?" I say through gritted teeth.

Jonathan lifts a brow and for a second, his composure slips.

"I mean, yeah we kissed. I was caught off guard. But then I stopped it," I add, my voice shaking now; not from guilt, but from fury that he won't even give me the benefit of the doubt.

His mouth opens, then shuts again. He rubs his cheek like he suddenly remembers I just smacked him and I notice the mark still there, faint but visible.

"Oh, so you left. Was that to call Manny again? Tell him how much you're faking it with me?" I snap again.

Jonathan blinks. "Huh?"

"I heard your conversation with him," I say, arms crossed now, heart pounding. "I'm nothing to you, right? So all that crap about falling in love with me, that was just for show?"

His face shifts into an empathetic yet confused look. "I didn't know you heard that call," he says slowly. "Is that why you left this morning without saying anything?"

I nod. "Yeah. I ran into Marcus and when he kissed me, I'll admit I kissed him back. But only because my head was spinning. I was confused. I was hurt." I clutch my forehead like I can squeeze out the whiplash of emotions.

Jonathan exhales. "I only said those things to Manny because... he likes you. And I didn't want to tell him how I really felt."

I pause, blinking. "Manny *likes me*?"

"Yes. But so do I," he says, then winces. "Or... did. I don't know anymore."

"According to you last night, you *loved* me," I say, keeping my arms folded, like they might hold me together and stop me from falling apart all over the concrete.

He sits down on the bench, sighs and buries his face in his hands. "I should've never offered to be your fake boyfriend," he stammers out.

The words land like a knife. They cut into me deep and my chest squeezes. God, it actually hurts. Because I wasn't faking any of it. I wasn't confused. I was falling for Jonathan. No. Scratch that. I *fell*.

"You kissed Marcus back," Jonathan continues, the words landing like an accusation he's been holding in for hours. "That means some part of you wanted it. Enjoyed it. That was the whole point of this entire lie, wasn't it?" He runs a hand through his hair, frustrated.

I want to argue, to say he's wrong, but I can't. Because if you'd asked me three days ago, did I want Marcus pining after me, kissing me, begging for another chance? I would've screamed *yes* from every rooftop in Manhattan. But now? Now I've been with Jonathan. Now everything feels upside down. And I don't know what the hell I want anymore.

I don't say a word. Silence settles thick in the air before he speaks again.

Jonathan steps closer, his voice shallow as he takes my arms in his hands, his thumbs stroking tiny, deliberate circles into my skin. "Tell me you want me."

I feel the tears building and then they're spilling down my cheeks. "I…" My voice cracks. "I don't know what I want." The truth tastes bitter in my mouth.

Jonathan looks at me for a long beat. His eyes flick to my lips, then back to my tear-streaked face like he's memorizing it, committing it to some private gallery of *what-could-have-beens*. His chest rises and falls, then he gives my arms one last gentle squeeze.

"That's what I thought," he exasperates out. He drops his hands and lowers his gaze, like even looking at me now hurts. He takes a small step back. "Whatever this is… it's over." He protests and turns, walking back inside the building.

I wipe my eyes and chase after him. "Jonathan!"

I push open the door and immediately freeze. He's standing there in the middle of the room, completely still, facing a wall of stunned faces, our co-workers. Tanya, Elaine, Manny, Victoria, Marcus. All of them wear the same look, pure disbelief. Except Manny and Victoria. They look furious. And Marcus? He's got a little smirk on his face, braced with a touch of sadness, but mostly satisfaction. Like he's just won.

Jonathan glances over his shoulder at me, then down at his hands still holding the microphones from our little karaoke war.

That's when I realize. They heard us. All of it.

Jonathan exhales hard and shakes his head, his disappointment radiating off him in waves. He turns back to the group and says, loud and clear, "I'm sorry, everyone. Abby and I were never a real couple." He pauses, then lets the microphones fall to his sides in defeat.

I start to move toward him, but I'm too late. He's already walking away.

Manny rushes after him, grabbing his arm. They argue in hushed tones, but I can see Manny's expression. He's angry and filled with frustration. His arms flail as he gestures toward me, toward the crowd, toward Jonathan's chest. Then Manny shoves him. Just once, but it's enough to make everyone stop breathing.

"Fuck you," Manny snaps, booming enough for the whole room to hear. He storms off, leaving Jonathan standing there, alone, with his head bowed like the weight of it all just finally crushed him.

I want to go after Jonathan. I want to scream, to cry, to ask him to take it all back. But I don't. Because I know I shouldn't. There's nothing I can say to fix this. I don't even trust that he meant what he said to me. I don't trust that I didn't want Marcus to kiss me. I don't trust relationships at all, to be honest. Not anymore.

So instead, I turn to leave. That's when Marcus grabs my hand, his fingers close around mine like he's been waiting for this moment.

"You okay?" he asks.

I shrug. "Define okay."

He gives me a half-smile. "I don't care that you were faking it with Jonathan."

Of course he doesn't.

"I came here for you before I even knew you were with anyone," he continues. "And I'm still here now."

Of course he is. Marcus always knows what to say, what I want to hear. That's his superpower. He knows me. Maybe even better than Jonathan ever could.

I crack the smallest smile, my face still stiff from everything that just imploded.

"Grab your stuff from the cabin," Marcus says. "Come stay with me."

I raise an eyebrow, unsure.

"Not for that," he adds quickly. "I just… I don't think you should be alone tonight."

He's probably right. Even if everything inside me feels wrong.

I turn to Victoria.

"I'm sorry, Victoria," I say quietly as Marcus lets go of my hand.

Her arms are crossed, her face unreadable. "Just get some

rest, Abigail," she replies. "We'll talk on Tuesday."

Oof. That doesn't feel like a conversation I'll enjoy. She throws Marcus a pointed look before walking off, her heels clicking with purpose.

Marcus exhales beside me. "I never told her about us," he admits. "She's mad at both of us. Don't worry."

Oh, I'm worried. It's comforting, I guess, to know I'm not the only one in the doghouse. But the difference is, Marcus is her boss. He can't be fired. Me? I very much can.

28

Jonathan

I wake up to sunlight slicing through the blinds like it's the happiest damn day in the world. Unfortunately, I know better. All I can think about is last night, my ridiculous, over-the-top karaoke performance where I basically called AJ a bloodsucking vampire in front of everyone. Real classy. Not exactly my proudest moment.

And then there was everything that came after. The blow-up outside. Our confessions. The yelling. The slap. The complete emotional unraveling. We were both pissed, both hurt and still… *still* she couldn't tell me the one thing I needed to hear. She couldn't say she wanted *me*.

Maybe I should have some empathy. I saw it in her face. The confusion, the panic, maybe even the regret. There was turmoil in her eyes when I asked what she wanted. But the thing is, I can't unsee what I saw. I can't erase the image of her kissing Marcus like no time had passed at all. I don't care if it was only a few seconds or if she pushed him away, those few seconds were enough to brand themselves into my memory.

So maybe what I felt wasn't love. Maybe it was just lust.

Intense, messy, all-consuming lust dressed up as something deeper. But either way… she had her shot. She could've chosen me and she didn't. That's all I need to know.

Then, like a flash in the pan, the moment with Manny hits me all over again. Right after AJ and I spilled our mess of a truth in front of the entire group, he came up to me, furious, shaking, on the verge of tears. Not because he was distraught, but because he was disappointed. He was gutted and I deserved every second of it. His voice cracked with frustration and there was this look in his eyes I'll never forget, the look of someone who expected better from me. Someone who thought I was a friend. His feelings were valid. I lied to him. He told me he liked AJ and instead of doing the decent thing and backing off, I went after her in secret. Hid it. Let it snowball into something that blew up in all of our faces.

Bros before… yeah, I broke the damn code. I didn't just break it, I lit it on fire and danced around the ashes. Turns out I'm not just a shitty fake boyfriend. I'm a shitty best friend, too.

I grab my phone from the coffee table, hoping, stupidly that I missed a text. A missed call. Something from AJ. But the screen is blank. Radio silence. Not a single message.

After the whole group witnessed our implosion, I walked the resort for a while like some brooding movie cliché. When I finally came back to the cabin, all her stuff was gone like she'd never been here at all. I don't even know where she could have gone. Tanya's maybe. Or worse, stayed with Marcus.

My stomach flips when I think of her curled up with him in some cozy corner of the resort, letting him play hero. That smirking bastard probably welcomed her with open arms the second I walked away from her.

I hover over Manny's contact in my phone, thumb just barely

grazing the call button. I can't do it. What would I even say? Sorry I betrayed your trust and lied to your face? Sorry I let some chaotic, infuriating, amazing girl turn me into the worst version of myself? If I were him, I'd punch me. If I were AJ... well, I guess she already took care of that.

I throw the blanket over my head like that'll somehow erase everything that happened last night. It doesn't. If anything, the silence just makes the memories louder.

Eventually, I give up and drag myself out of bed. I make a cup of coffee, extra strong and try to focus on something productive. Like packing. We leave this morning. Back to reality. Back to the office where I'll have to see AJ and Manny every day. And now, apparently, Marcus too. My best friend at work won't talk to me. The woman I've fallen for doesn't love me back or doesn't know if she does, which somehow feels worse.

Honestly? That's if I even *have* a job. One look at Victoria's face last night said everything I needed to know. She was livid. The kind of livid that doesn't end with a slap, it ends with a termination email.

I glance down at my phone again. Still no messages. No missed calls. The blankness on the phone is almost mocking now. But I can't just sit in it. So I scroll through my contacts and land on the one name I never thought I'd actually call. I hesitate... then press it.

An hour later, after a long, uncomfortable-but-surprisingly-grounding conversation, I hang up. For the first time since this whole mess exploded, I feel like I made a good decision. Maybe even the right one.

I step into the shower and let the hot water burn away the tension in my shoulders. When I finally get out, I feel a little more like myself. Still a mess, just not totally drowning. I towel off, get dressed and zip up my suitcase. Time to go home.

I head to the main lodge to grab breakfast before we all load onto the bus. The place is buzzing with people trying to soak up one last meal before returning to real life. I just want caffeine, carbs and zero conversation.

From across the room, I spot Tanya and Elaine. Tanya's already strutting over, motioning for Elaine to follow. This should be great.

"Hey," Tanya says, her voice unusually soft, almost… cautious.

"Hey," I reply, not bothering to fake enthusiasm.

"I just wanted to say I'm sorry. About you and Abby." She tucks her hair behind her ear like she's trying to look innocent, which is new.

I pause mid-bite, halfway through a chewy mouthful of bagel and raise an eyebrow. "You're sorry?"

She nods. "You guys were so cute together," she says. "I know it was fake," she adds, complete with dramatic air quotes and an eye roll, "but it didn't feel fake. It felt like you actually liked each other."

Elaine nods along beside her. "For what it's worth, we're here for both of you," she chimes in. "No judgment."

And just like that, the two biggest gossip hounds in the office aren't whispering in a corner. They're being… supportive? Weirdly sincere?

I blink at them. "Thanks," I say, offering a faint smile.

But the smile doesn't last as the front door swings open and in walks AJ and Marcus. She steps through first and he holds the door open behind her, all chivalrous charm and pretentious timing. My stomach knots. Of course they were together. Where else would she have gone?

I stab my fork into my eggs harder than necessary and keep my eyes down.

Tanya gives my shoulder a gentle pat, then walks away with Elaine, leaving me with my breakfast and the bitter taste of watching someone I still care about walk in with someone who isn't me.

AJ doesn't even look at me when she walks in. Doesn't glance, doesn't flinch, just slides into a booth with her back to me like I'm not even here. Marcus sits across from her, leaning in close, whispering something. She nods and he stands, making his way toward the breakfast buffet, right where I'm sitting.

He moves through the line like he owns the place, grabbing eggs, a few strips of bacon, then pouring himself two coffees in to-go cups like he's got somewhere heroic to be. He's just about to turn back to her when he stops short and pivots toward my table.

I shift in my seat and take a slow sip of coffee, preparing for whatever ridiculous, backhanded comment is coming. He steps up beside me, glancing at my plate, then at me. The tension hangs like a fog.

Unexpectedly, he exhales and says, "I want to say I'm sorry."

I raise my eyebrows. That's… not what I envisioned.

"Okay," I say, guarded.

"I had no idea…" He adjusts his posture, like he's trying to square up for something brave. "I didn't know you and Abby weren't really a couple. It just… felt real."

He runs a hand through his exceptionally tousled hair and glances back at her, still sitting with her back to us. "She told me last night that she actually..." He trails off, the words falling apart mid-sentence.

Actually what? Say it, I yell to myself.

He shakes his head. "It doesn't matter," he mumbles. "I just wanted to apologize."

I nod slowly, like that's all I'm capable of. Because I don't know what else to do. And because I don't know what he meant.

Marcus gives me a half-smile, somewhere between arrogant and sincere, then walks back to their table. He slides the coffee across to AJ and she starts picking at her food like she's too polite to say she doesn't want it.

What the hell just happened? Marcus... being a gentleman? Is this some kind of Jedi mind trick? Did I just get diplomatically outmaneuvered by a guy in loafers?

I scratch the back of my neck and rub it. Sleeping on the couch last night did absolutely nothing for my posture or my mood.

Then Manny walks in with Stan, which definitely doesn't help my tenseness. Both glance in my direction before veering silently to the buffet like I'm radioactive. Fair, I suppose. I guess I deserve it.

This bus ride's going to be a blast, I mutter to myself.

But surprisingly... it isn't the nightmare I dread. AJ sits with Marcus, no surprise there and Manny grabs a seat a few rows ahead of me. He keeps turning back like he's trying to decide whether to punch me or just let karma handle it. I shove in my AirPods, shut my eyes and ride out the silence. The two-hour drive passes in a blur. Next thing I know, Tanya's tapping my arm. "We're here," she says.

I blink awake and everyone's already shuffling off. AJ and

Marcus are gone, vanished the second the wheels hit pavement. *Good riddance. Hope they make a happy couple.* The thought carves an unwelcome ache through my gut, like a punch that lands after the fight's already over. I exhale, sluggishly, trying to breathe through the sting.

Most of us headed upstairs to grab our things and check emails; it *is* still Monday, after all. I kill some time clicking through my inbox, waiting for the post-retreat buzz to die down. Once the crowd thins, I make my way toward Victoria's office. Her door's open, but I knock anyway. She swivels in her chair. The moment she sees me, her expression shifts from vaguely content to visibly annoyed.

"Hi, Victoria. Do you have a minute?" I ask.

She lowers her glasses and gives me the kind of once-over usually reserved for gum on a shoe. "For you, Jonathan, I have just *one* minute," she replies, crisp and clipped.

I step in and gently close the door behind me, then take a seat across from her.

"I just wanted to say I'm sorry for how everything played out this weekend," I start. "It was stupid and childish for AJ and me to fake being a couple just to mess with Marcus."

She lets out a sharp chuckle.

I blink. "What?"

She shakes her head, a smirk tugging at her lips. "If my ex-fiancé, the man who left me at the altar, mind you, suddenly bought into the company I worked for? I'd probably do the same thing."

The tension in my shoulders loosens an inch.

"Really? So you're not mad that we lied?" I ask, my voice lined with sheer desperation.

She shakes her head. "Honestly, I'm impressed Abigail had it in her to pull something like that off," she says, almost proud. "I had no idea who Marcus was to her."

"But *you*," she adds, suddenly pointing a finger at me, "you're the one who pissed me off."

I sit up straighter.

"That little performative song of yours," she says, rolling her eyes. "Then Abigail joins in. And then she slaps you! What the hell was that?"

She throws her hands up in exasperation. "*That's* what I'm mad about."

"I know, and I really am sorry for that," I say, pressing my palms together like I'm praying.

Victoria raises an eyebrow. "Why'd you do it?"

"Do what?" I ask, confused.

"Why did you get like that? Was it because you were jealous of Marcus?" she asks, her tone drifting into something close to sarcastic. "Falling for Abigail?"

I don't answer. Not directly at least.

She sighs and leans back in her chair. "You need to figure out what you want," she says.

I drop my eyes to the floor. Her rug is pink and patterned, it's so *very* Victoria and I can't focus on anything but what I'm about to say.

"I know what I want," I say, my voice strained as I swallow. "I'm taking a job in Boston. With Elite Visions."

Victoria doesn't flinch. She just inhales, then lets it out calmly. "I figured you might," she admits.

I blink, sitting up straighter. "Wait, you knew about the job?" I question.

She lifts her glasses to her eyes like she's done with the theatrics. "Who do you think gave you the glowing recommendation? Told them they'd be idiots not to hire you?" she says with a confident little grin.

"Wow. Victoria. I mean… wow," I stutter through.

"You could say thank you," she deadpans.

"Right. Thank you," I say, still stunned. "But… why?" I press.

She adjusts her posture and leans forward, giving me that no-nonsense, cut-to-the-chase stare.

"Because I'm giving the promotion here to Abigail. Always planned to, honestly. She's the right fit. You and I both know it." She gestures with her hand. "And the Boston job? That's a better move for you. Bigger role, better pay. A real leap forward."

I have no words. She's right. The position in Boston isn't the one I initially wanted but it is a more commendable position.

I sit in silence for a few seconds longer, letting it all settle in.

"Is that all?" Victoria asks, already reaching for her next task.

"Thank you, Victoria," I say, offering a small smile.

She gives me a pointed look. "Just remember who your friends are here in New York."

That's about as tender and fuzzy a goodbye as I'll ever get from Victoria and frankly, it's spotless.

I nod, then head back to my office to start packing my desk. I forward all my outstanding client work to Stan, draft a quick all-office email saying goodbye and shut my laptop. No dramatic exit. No speech or farewell cupcakes. Just an idyllic, clean break. Which fits me better anyway. But there's still one person I need to say goodbye to, personally.

29

Abby

I don't even wait for the bus to come to a full stop. The second it slows, I'm up, grabbing my bag and making a break for the parking garage. Most of my coworkers are heading upstairs to check emails or pretend they're being productive. Not me. I can access my inbox from home and right now, I need distance. From the whispers, the side-eyes, the pitying head shakes. And most of all, from Jonathan's stupid face.

I'm sure he went upstairs like the good little overachiever he is, which means I'm safe, at least for now. I wish he'd just disappear so I could have one normal workday without emotional whiplash.

When I screw up, I really do it big time. Faked a relationship with a coworker, but worse, *that* coworker. The one who's made a sport out of infuriating me for years and I fell for him anyway. Stellar decision-making, Abby. Gold star.

It's fine though. Totally fine. The feelings weren't that deep. I can move past them like I move past any other fleeting emotion. That's what I'm telling myself as I yank open my

242

car door and hurl my luggage into the backseat like it's aimed right for Jonathan's evenly distributed jaw muscles.

"Hey."

I hear a voice behind me. I turn around, half-hoping it's Jonathan being dumb enough to chase after me. It's not. It's Marcus.

I shut my back door. "Hey," I mutter, sweeping my hair out of my face as I open the driver's side.

Marcus walks toward me, hands clasped like he's about to confess something. "Is there any way we could have dinner tonight? Just talk?" he asks, his voice carefully walking a tightrope.

I press my fingers to my temple. Everything feels too fast, too much. My brain is still tangled in last night and now this?

Before I can respond, he cuts in. "You have to eat, right? I know you don't have food in your fridge. And, let's be honest, last time you tried to cook, you almost burned our apartment down."

He laughs lightly and despite everything, my frown dissipates.

He *is* right. I nearly took out the roof.

"Your apartment," I correct with a small laugh.

He shrugs. "Technicalities. Point is, you shouldn't be cooking in *anyone's* apartment," he says, grinning.

I glance down at the scuffed black concrete, like it might give me an answer. But there is no answer, no cosmic sign. It's just me, standing here, realizing I can do whatever I want. Maybe being with Marcus is what's meant to be.

I look up and meet his eyes. "Sure. I'd love to have dinner with you," I say, chipper.

His smile stretches wide, it's genuine and bright. He steps

closer and presses a soft kiss to my cheek. It's not sexual or anything like that, it's comforting. Even after everything Marcus did, I still feel safe with him. That's got to count for something.

He pulls back. "I'll pick you up at eight."

I nod. "Okay."

Then I slide into my car and drive off, the air clumps around me with questions I'm not ready to answer.

Part of me wants to call Jonathan and ask if this is okay but the thought vanishes as quickly as it comes. He made it clear to Manny that he doesn't love me and when I confronted him, he threw out some lame excuse about Manny liking me as the reason he said those things. Like that makes it any better. I don't trust a word he says.

He had the chance to fight for me. To say something more, *anything more.* But instead, he just waited and put the decision on me. Like I was supposed to say the exact right thing, even though I had no clue what that was. Moreover when I couldn't? He walked away.

When I get home, I immediately start unpacking. I'm one of *those* people. If I don't do it the second I walk in, the suitcase will sit in the corner for a week, maybe two.

The second I'm inside, the scent of lavender hits me. I've got it scattered all over the living room between candles, oil diffusers, dried bundles. It's calming. The exact opposite of the weekend I just survived.

I grab a water from the fridge, guzzle it like I've been stranded in the desert, then take a deep breath in and out. I could go work out to burn off the anxiety and frustration, but the couch is calling. Specifically, the *Love Island* marathon queued up on my TV. I sink into the cushions and let the

British drama lull me into a nap I didn't know I needed.

Thankfully, my phone rings and wakes me before I sleep straight through my dinner date with Marcus. I grab my phone and see it's Lila. I stare at the screen for a second, not ready to unpack the weekend from hell and send her to voicemail. Then I shoot her a text: *Will call you later*.

She replies with a smiley face and a thumbs-up emoji. Classic Lila, always cheery, always sunshine. I miss her. I can't wait until she comes back next week to pack up her place. I already took the time off to help her move back to California and explore the new chapter of her life. A *real* vacation. One I desperately need. It's crazy to think I already need a vacation to recover from my work retreat vacation.

I decide I've slept enough and roll off the couch straight into the shower. The hot water helps, but the minute I step out, I'm stuck staring into my closet like it holds the answer to a question I haven't figured out how to ask.

Is this a date? Or just catching up? Marcus clearly wants to get back together and a part of me, traitorous as it is, missed him when he kissed me. However, there's the rational voice in my head, screaming over the butterflies: *He left you at the altar, remember?*

Still, I land on a black corset dress that hits just above the knee. Stylish, fun and not too sexy, but not boring either. I keep my makeup natural appearing, with a small, smoky eye that says I tried. Then I straighten my hair. Marcus always said he loved it straight. Normally I let my soft waves do their thing, tamed just enough to look intentional yet tonight I'll wear it the way he likes it. Maybe that says more than I want it to.

As I finish getting ready, nerves flutter through my stomach.

Am I really doing this?

Before I can overthink it to death, my buzzer goes off. It's Marcus.

"I'm here," he says through the speaker.

"Okay, I'll buzz you in," I say, pressing the button.

I hold it down for a second longer than necessary like I'm already regretting this.

He knocks on my door seconds later, holding a bouquet of my favorite flowers, pink tulips.

"Hi," he says with a mushy smile, leaning in to kiss my cheek as I open the door. He hands me the flowers, then steps back to look me over.

"Wow," he says, his face lighting up like he just got everything he wanted for his birthday.

"Thank you," I reply, cheeks already warming. "And thank you for the flowers." I bring them to my nose, inhaling their sweet, herbal scent, before heading to look under the sink for a vase.

I can feel Marcus's eyes on me as I fill it with water.

"You look gorgeous," he says.

I nod, slipping the tulips into the vase and adjusting the stems until they stand just right. "They're beautiful," I say quietly.

"You're beautiful," he replies, stepping closer and taking my hand. He pulls me toward him, his lips brushing against mine in a delicate, lingering kiss.

He still smells like cedar and expensive cologne, it's memories and money wrapped into one. When he pulls back, he's grinning. I can feel the blush rising in my cheeks.

It's a nice kiss sure, yet doesn't spark anything. Not like *him*... like Jonathan.

"Let's go to dinner," Marcus says, still holding my hand.

I smile and let him lead me out the door as we head downstairs. Parked out front is his car. It's the same sleek Jaguar; two-door, convertible coupe but this one's newer, glossier and in a different color than the one from years ago.

"New car?" I ask, raising a brow.

He nods proudly. "Yeah. Just got it a few months ago. Do you like it?"

I give it a once-over, impressed. "Like it?" I laugh. "It's stunning."

I reach for the door handle and before I can touch the shiny exterior, Marcus steps in to open it for me. He's still the gentleman. Still the charmer.

It's nice not feeling tense around him. With Jonathan, my shoulders were always tight and pressure built behind my molars like I was waiting for the next fight or flirt or jab. That edge isn't here now. It's replaced by something unsettling deep in my stomach, like the world's tilted slightly off-axis.

The drive is smooth. We talk easily about his family, my family. I tell him about Lila.

"I'm heading to California next week," I say. "Spending a week with her to help her move in."

He grins. "That's convenient timing. I have business out there. I could fly you out with me. On the jet. We could go together."

My eyebrows lift. "You mean… me and you *and* Lila?"

He hesitates, then smiles again. "Well… yeah."

"That's sweet of you," I say, carefully. "But I haven't told Lila about any of this." I pause, swallowing hard. "Not Jonathan. Not… you."

He glances at me, then nods slowly. "I get it," he says. "Not sure how the best friend's gonna feel about me being back in your life."

Back in my life? The way he says it, it feels like it's already decided. Like it's fact. Is it?

"I mean… yes. I guess," I admit, unsure if I even believe myself.

"Well, she'll just have to get over it," he says with a shrug. "She's moving on with her life. Starting fresh in California. And you have to do what's best for you."

The arrogance in his tone catches me off guard. I shoot him a look. "Lila was there for me when you left me," I snap. "And getting back together with the guy who broke my heart, is that *really* what's best for me?"

Nothing but silence. Not his… mine. A prickling, stifling quiet that clings to the air inside his glossy, overconfident car.

He clears his throat. "I'm sorry. That was out of line. Lila's a great friend. I just…" He pauses, choosing his words. "I don't want outside voices influencing your decision."

"Outside voices?" I repeat.

"You know," he says, glancing at me. "Lila. Or…" He trails off.

I stare at him, but he won't finish the sentence. Instead, he pulls up to the valet outside the restaurant.

"Or Jonathan," he finally says, just before stepping out and handing the valet a folded fifty-dollar bill.

A second valet opens my door. As I slide out, the weight of Marcus's words press on my sternum and now I'm finding it difficult to take in a solid breath.

He straightens his blazer, his eyes scanning me. It's a look I know too well, part admiration, part possession. He's being sincere, sure, with a hidden edge. That confident, commanding energy that used to feel magnetic now just feels a little suffocating.

I forgot this side of Marcus. He's equal parts charming and polished and cocky and controlling. A little too sure of himself.

I walk up beside him and he grabs my hand as we head into *The Shell*, a well-known hotspot for rich pasta, louder-than-necessary servers and violin-backed ambiance. It's the kind of place people pick for proposals or milestone anniversaries. Definitely not "just catching up." That uneasy feeling in my stomach returns like a rolling wave.

We're seated right away and handed drink menus. Marcus doesn't even glance at his before ordering a bottle of Cabernet Sauvignon, no doubt one with a price tag so high it could pay my rent for one month. I glance around, letting the smells and sounds soak in. The room is filled with well-dressed people bathed in the scent of garlic and roasted tomatoes, while Italian waiters bark toward the kitchen in dramatic flair. A pianist plays something romantic in the background.

It's all... too much. I shift in my seat and catch Marcus watching me, his half-smile tight. He can sense I'm off.

"You okay?" he asks.

I don't answer right away. His earlier words are still bouncing around in my head: *You have to do what's best for you.* But if this is what's best for me... why does it feel like I can't breathe? I reach for the gold heart necklace at my throat, spinning it between my fingers. My grandmother gave it to me before she passed. It's the one thing that always centers me.

"You're fidgeting," Marcus notes.

I try to speak, but the words catch in my throat. When I

finally get something out, it's too jumbled to hear.

"What was that?" he asks, leaning in.

"It's because I can't do this, Marcus." The words come out clearer than I expected.

The waiter, who'd just walked up to take our order, stops mid-step, eyes darting like he just stepped into a minefield.

"I'll come back," he quips, then disappears with the urgency of someone fleeing a kitchen fire.

Marcus lowers the menu and leans across the table, reaching for my hand.

"I said I was sorry for what I said," he begins, his voice genuine. "And I meant it."

I shake my head and pull my hand away. "I know. But this… doesn't feel right."

He sits back, his jaw stiffening just a fraction. "What's the issue?" he asks. The words are calm, but they carry that familiar *Marcus* edge.

My pulse climbs. "The issue," I say, heat rising in my chest, "is that you jilted me. You left me at the altar. You made *me* the jilted bride. Who the hell does that?"

I stand, hands thrown in the air, barely noticing the heads starting to turn around the restaurant.

"Abby, please sit down," Marcus says quickly, trying to shush me like I'm a child mid-tantrum.

I laugh; a bitter, breathless kind of laugh. "No. You don't get to ask me to lower my voice. You don't get to sweep it under the rug like you forgot to RSVP to a dinner party." I pause, breath catching. "Why did you leave me?"

He stands, reaching for my arm, but I jerk it away.

"I don't know!" he says, his tone cracking. "I wasn't sure. But I'm sure now. Abby, please," he demands again, more desperate now.

"You know now? After you humiliated me, vanished for years and only showed interest because you thought I was with Jonathan?" I throw at him.

Marcus runs a hand through his hair and glances around the restaurant, clearly mortified. He lets out a short, incredulous laugh.

"So what, now I'm the villain and Jonathan's the hero? Abby, you can't seriously believe he's better than me. Look what he did to you." He gestures toward me with a self-righteous toss of his hand. "Now sit down." He drops into his seat like he expects obedience.

I lean forward, meeting his eyes without flinching. "Jonathan may not be perfect," I say, "but at least he had the *balls* to end things to my face," I yell. Then I straighten, grab my purse and turn on my heel. "Goodbye, Marcus."

I don't look back, but I hear him huff; still parked in his seat, still stuck in his own ego. What I do hear is a faintly, scattered applause rising behind me. A grin spreads across my face, not because of the clapping, but because I feel it. I feel the weight I've been carrying for years shedding away. I finally said everything I needed to say. I finally got my closure.

Now… there's *someone else* I need closure from.

30

Jonathan

Who would've thought I'd be this nervous to have a conversation? Especially one I know needs to happen. But here I am, shirt clinging to my chest, palms slightly sweaty, hands cramping from how many times I've fidgeted; standing in front of a door, about to knock.

It might get slammed in my face. Honestly, I wouldn't be shocked. If it does, I'll just turn around, head home and finish packing I guess.

The second I walked out of Victoria's office earlier, I called my new manager in Boston. They asked if I could fly out tomorrow to finalize paperwork and meet the team I'll be overseeing. I said *yes*. No sense dragging things out. I already forwarded all my outstanding work to Stan and he texted back: *Got it. I'll handle everything.* Thankfully, there wasn't much to send over to him. I wrapped two major projects last week and the third one in the pipeline? Practically finished. I'll keep my apartment in Manhattan for now, maybe sublet it eventually. Real estate's always a good asset to have in your portfolio. I've decided to rent in Boston for the next six months, explore the city, figure out where I actually want to live, then make a move on buying something.

Look at me, investments in both New York and Boston. Really out here turning over a new leaf and making a clean exit with zero drama. Well, except for this part. The part I'm currently standing in front of. I take in a deep breath that I may pass out from, then let it go as I knock on the door in front of me. It takes a minute, but then the door swings open and there he is. Manny. Arms crossed and a no-bullshit look on his face.

"Hey, man," I say. "Can I come in?"

He rolls his eyes and then steps aside so I can walk in.

"Thanks," I say with my head down like a puppy who was just scolded for chewing on shoes.

Manny stands there and huffs. "What do you want?" he asks, his lip set in a serious, stern line.

"I want to let you know how sorry I am for hiding the truth about Abby," I admit, not losing eye contact so he knows I'm sincere.

Manny looks dumbfounded. Maybe even a little disappointed.

"Abby? No more AJ?" he asks, referring to the fact I'm not calling her *AJ* anymore.

I shake my head. "Nope. She's just Abby now to me. Well, she's nothing more to me anymore, I guess," I add.

Manny shakes his head. "Damn, man. You're either an asshole or just stupid," he says with a chuckle.

"What do you mean?" I ask. "I mean, I know I'm an asshole for how I treated you…" I start to say.

"No, bro. You're a stupid asshole for letting go of Abby," he says as he walks toward his kitchen.

I let his words sink in as he picks up a bottle of bourbon and gestures to me. I shake my head *yes*. He pours two glasses, one for me and one for him, then slides mine over. I take a sip, letting the burn drag me back to a time when things made more sense.

"It's nice to have a drink with you," I say.

He nods his glass toward me. I nod mine back.

"So why am I a stupid asshole?" I ask, taking another sip.

Manny walks toward the edge of the counter and sits on one of the bar stools.

"Abby is an amazing girl and you guys had something real," he says. "Plus, you admitted you liked her, man." He hits my arm. "I can't remember the last time I ever heard you say you like someone," he adds with a smirk.

I take the seat next to him and rest the glass against my temple.

"I know. But I gave her a chance. I asked her what she wanted and she didn't say *me*," I reply, dragging out a sigh.

"But she didn't say that tool Marcus either," Manny adds and raises his glass.

"Why are you saying this to me?" I question with a lifted eyebrow. "You should be happy I'm not going after her."

Manny takes a sip, then downs the rest of the amber liquid. He wipes his mouth with the back of his hand.

"I should be," he says and pauses. "But I want to see you happy. And if Abby's the girl who does that, then my little crush doesn't mean anything." He pats me on the back.

"Well, thanks, man," I say.

"Plus, I think Tanya has a thing for me." He laughs. "She's wild but in a fun way. I may ask her out," he says with a wide smile.

"Wow," I say back. "Look at you."

"And look at you. Sitting here like a beat-up dog and not running back to Abby," he says as he pushes me.

I stand up from the seat. "She doesn't want me," I snap. "Trust me." I shake my head and look around his freshly organized apartment. "Even if she did… how could I trust she wouldn't run back to Marcus?" I say rhetorically.

Manny shrugs. "I guess you can never know anything for sure," he says. "That's love though, bro. You've got to take chances, or you sit back and let others have what you want." He turns to face me directly. "You're just going to let Marcus take what you want?"

I stare at him and don't say a word.

"The Jonathan Slack I know never walks away from a challenge," he jokes, yet truth-bombing me at the same time.

I chuckle. "Yeah. Maybe love changed me."

"Into being a pussy?" he says with a hard laugh.

"Haha. Funny," I laugh back. I gesture my glass toward him. "Just get me another drink, will you?" I demand with a grin.

Manny takes the glass from my hand and heads back to the counter, where the open bourbon bottle glints under the white kitchen light. The apartment smells of citrus cleaner and whatever candle he has burning on the windowsill, woodsy I'm guessing.

He pours more bourbon into my glass. "So, are you going to tell her about Boston?" he asks with a smirk.

"How did you know?" I raise my head, surprised.

He laughs.

"Tanya?" I ask, already knowing the answer. "Man, nothing gets past that woman," I add with a laugh.

"Yeah, she overheard your conversation with Victoria,"

Manny admits.

"You mean eavesdropped," I quip.

Manny chuckles and takes a sip of his drink. "True."

"I was coming here to apologize *and* to tell you about the job," I say quickly.

"I know," Manny says. "I'm happy for you, bro, but…" He shrugs, tossing his shoulders upward. "I think you're running away from your feelings."

I run a hand through my hair, letting my fingers stay there for a second. "It's a great career move," I say back.

Manny nods like he gets it, even if he doesn't agree. "Well, cheers to you," he says, lifting his glass toward mine.

I smile and raise mine to meet it. "Thanks, man," I say with a wink.

After I leave Manny's apartment, I can't help but think about what he said. *Running away from my feelings.* I'm not running away. I gave AJ the chance to tell me she wanted me and she didn't say a word. And if I'm being honest with myself, I was already waiting for something to push me to take this job in Boston. The whole debacle with our fake relationship just set it in motion. It was inevitable, me taking this job.

At least, that's what I'm telling myself as I pack the rest of my suitcase for my flight tomorrow. I wonder if AJ will even reach out to say goodbye. I hate to admit this, but part of me hopes she will.

31

Abby

The day is here. No more stalling. No more hypotheticals or daydreaming or rerunning our last conversation like a scratched-up record in my head. I'm going back to work. Back to my office. Back to Jonathan. Back to the man I walked away from without saying the one thing I should've said: *I choose you.*

That night outside the karaoke bar, it already feels like a lifetime ago, he stood in front of me, bare, vulnerable, hopeful even and asked me what I wanted. And what did I do? I froze. I stood there like a deer caught in the headlights of my own emotional traffic jam, paralyzed and unsure what I wanted. I'm not unsure anymore. I know exactly what I want. *I want him.*

I tried to go to his apartment last night after storming out on Marcus mid-dinner, an exit that felt dramatically overdue, if not slightly theatrical but Jonathan wasn't home. I thought about texting. Calling and even leaving a voice memo like one of those tearful podcast confessions. But no. This conversation deserves more than that. He deserves more than that. He deserves to see my face. To hear the words directly from my mouth. To know, without a doubt, that I'm sorry for everything. The games. The chaos. The stupid Marcus moment. All of it. I want to apologize for the mess I made over that wild, emotionally unstable, career-jeopardizing weekend. And if he's willing to forgive me… if there's even a sliver of hope… maybe we can start over. Actually start something real.

I know I'm taking a risk. He might shut me down. Walk away. Still, I'm doing this anyway. Because for the first time in a long time, I'm clear-headed. Leaving Marcus last night was the best decision I've made in months, most likely years. That relationship was always about comfort and control. It was never about connection.

Jonathan though? That kiss. That stupid fake dating pact. The shared cabin. The arguments. The whispered confession in the woods. That *was* connection. Messy, complicated and a real connection. Even if it started with a fake label, there was nothing fake about what I felt.

I want to kiss Jonathan again. I want him to hold me like he did that night in the woods. His hands firm at my waist, his lips sturdy like he knew what he wanted. Like I was what he wanted. I really hope I didn't ruin everything.

The moment I step into my tiny office, a place that usually brings me a small jolt of peace with its warm lighting and worn-in office chair, I feel my stomach twist. I sit down at my desk, trying to will myself into productivity. My inbox is overflowing, the red badge practically screaming at me and I haven't even opened a single email when my office phone rings. It's Victoria.

"Good morning, Abigail. Can you come into my office?" she

says, in that ambiguous tone that's not quite kind, not quite rude, just unsettling enough to make me nervous.

Every ounce of blood drains from my body. Her voice is calm. Gravely calm. The kind of calm that says, *I'm going to destroy your soul with grace and precision.*

"Yes, ma'am," I manage to say, my voice catching halfway between terrified intern and regretful felon.

I shoot up so fast I nearly trip over my own feet. My chair rolls backward and hits the bookshelf with a light thud. I smooth down my khaki pants and tug my blouse into place, praying there aren't any coffee splatters on it. I swipe under my eyes, hoping my eyeliner hasn't smudged into a gothic novella subplot.

I walk down the short hallway toward her office like I'm on my way to a sentencing hearing. The second I step inside, her bubblegum-pink rug glares up at me like a warning sign against my beige-on-beige outfit. I swear it's mocking me. The scent in her office changes daily, some kind of psychological warfare and today, it's a fresh and clean citrus smell. She must be trying to fake me out. Bright scents before the carnage.

She gestures to the seat across from her desk. "Have a seat."

I do, carefully, knees stiff, back straight like I'm taking a polygraph. She takes off her glasses with a dramatic movement. That's not good. Nothing good ever happens when Victoria removes her glasses.

"Alice," she calls over her shoulder to her assistant outside the door. Her voice crisp, yet too relaxed. "Can you close the door, please?"

Alice pokes her head in, eyes scanning the obvious tension. When she sees me, she gives a tiny, pitying smile. The kind people give when they drive by a car accident and aren't sure if anyone made it out.

This is it. I'm getting fired. The door clicks shut behind me and my throat suddenly feels like it's filled with dry cotton.

Victoria studies me in a way that makes me feel like I'm under a microscope. Her eyes sweep up and down, pausing at my face like she's trying to read every flicker of emotion that might give me away. Then, finally, she takes an unhurried, controlled breath; in through her nose, out through her mouth.

"I had no idea Marcus was your ex-fiancé," she says at last, her tone softer than I've ever heard it. "You know, the one who left you at the altar." She doesn't say it with malice. Just a long-buried, also humiliating fact.

I nod once, small and tight. There's no use denying it. The whole thing's out now, anyway.

"I feel like a bad boss," she continues. "But more than that, a bad friend, for not knowing who he was to you."

I blink. Victoria… expressing genuine emotion? Empathy? She even sounds like she means it. This is starting off weirdly wholesome. Maybe she lit that eucalyptus candle I bought her for Boss's Day last year.

"I'm sorry," she adds quietly.

She says it so directly, stripped of any performative flair and somehow that's what makes it hit hardest. Everything crashes down at once, thickening my throat until I have to force myself to swallow.

"Victoria… thank you. But I should've told you the moment I saw Marcus. So I'm sorry too." I meet her gaze and own it. I've made enough mistakes lately, I can at least take responsibility for this one.

She gives an approving nod. "Well, I appreciate that, Abigail.

And that kind of ownership? That's exactly why..." She pauses. "...I'm giving you the promotion to Vice President of Marketing when Allen officially steps down at the end of this month."

My brain stutters. *What?* There's a two-second delay between her words and the explosion of realization that hits me like a bottle of champagne to the face. My chest fills so fast I swear I could levitate. My cheeks go hot, a blush rising so fast I can't stop it and before I can rein myself in I squeal, full cheerleader mode unlocked.

"Thank you so, so much, Victoria! I promise I won't let you down."

Her lips twitch into a proud smile as she slides her glasses back onto her face with a practiced little flourish, the moment sealed like a ceremonial stamp.

"I know you won't," she says with a smile. Then she starts again, just as I'm trying to settle the excitement bubbling up in my chest. "I have to say, Abigail, I'm impressed you faked a relationship just to get back at Marcus."

I blink, caught off guard by the bluntness and the grin tugging at the corners of her mouth.

"I wouldn't have pegged you for being so... ballsy," she continues with a chuckle. "But I get it. And honestly? I respect it."

I let out a laugh, partly from amusement, partly from relief that she's not scolding me for my walk-the-line, workplace violation.

I reach up and smooth the collar of my blouse, trying to play it cool.

"Well," I say with a sheepish smile, "it was kind of a spur-of-the-moment decision... me and Jonathan."

His name still stings in the center of my chest like I haven't spent the last twenty-four hours trying to will it away. I shift in my seat.

"Have you told him yet?" I ask, gently. "About who you're picking for the promotion?"

She nods once, businesslike. "I did."

I feel a knot tighten in my stomach. "What did he say?"

Victoria leans forward on her elbows and reaches for the glass bowl of candy perched on her desk like it's her crystal ball. She selects a peppermint, unwraps it slowly, then pops it into her mouth like punctuation.

"He took it fine," she says between a thoughtful suck on the mint.

That seems… not right. Not *Jonathan*.

"That's because," she adds, eyes flicking up to meet mine, "he resigned. Took another job in Boston."

I blink. "Boston?" My voice cracks on the word. "Wait. When?"

She shrugs, still infuriatingly composed, like she didn't just lob a whole emotional grenade into the room.

"I probably shouldn't say more if he didn't tell you himself," she says, leaning back in her chair. "But he won't be working here anymore. Effective today, actually."

And just like that, the room feels like it's tilting sideways. He's gone? He didn't even tell me?

I open my mouth, close it again. There's a buzzing in my ears that wasn't there a second ago. I pause, trying to swallow the lump in my throat before it gives me away. Then I clear my throat and nod once.

"Okay," I manage. "Thank you again for the promotion." My voice is surprisingly even, despite the fact that my brain feels like it's spinning inside a snow globe someone just shook too hard. I rise from the seat, my legs carrying me toward the door, even though my thoughts are still stuck back at *Jonathan took another job in Boston.* Just as I reach for the handle, Victoria calls out behind me.

"Abigail," she blurts.

I turn, forcing calm onto my features.

Already reclined in her chair, arms crossed over her stylish, tailored blouse, she gives me the kind of look only a woman who's seen her fair share of life and heartbreak can deliver.

"He's leaving this afternoon," she says. "One o'clock. JFK." She lets the moment hang. Then, with a glint in her eye, adds, "If you've got any more of that *ballsy* energy left and wanted to catch him before he leaves."

A slow smile pulls at my lips, but I can't tell if it's gratitude or panic. Maybe both.

I nod. "Thank you," I say.

Then I walk out like a zombie with a mission. A very confused, wildly spiraling zombie.

Back in my office, I stare at my computer screen like it might give me answers. It doesn't. He's really… *leaving.* I drag my fingers through my hair, the promotion forgotten, the world still spinning. I try to force myself into productivity, working through a few emails like a robot.

The clock becomes my worst enemy: 9:20 a.m. 9:45. 10:10. Every few minutes, my eyes dart back to the time like it's some kind of emotional countdown clock.

What are you doing? I ask myself. He made his decision. He left. He didn't tell you. He's probably on his way to the airport now.

I close my eyes. This isn't some rom-com where the girl

runs to the airport in a grand gesture and magically gets waved through TSA without a ticket because of love. *No.* This is real life. In real life, you can't get to your fake-boyfriend-turned-real-love before his flight unless you *are* the TSA. Or the President.

Still, I could… call him or text him. Something. Anything.

A knock at my open doorway jolts me out of the doom-scroll in my head. Manny steps in, Tanya hovering just behind him like a human exclamation point.

"Hey," he says.

"Hi!" Tanya wiggles her fingers in a little wave.

Their timing is perfect; the vortex in my brain loosens a notch.

"Hey, guys," I manage, even forcing a smile.

Manny moves closer, worry lines pinched between his brows. "Congrats on the promotion," he says.

I glance at Tanya. She lifts both hands in mock surrender. "I can't help it if I eavesdrop," she giggles.

"Thank you," I say, then notice Manny still rubbing his palms together like he's trying to warm them over a campfire. He clearly has more to say.

"What's going on, Manny?" I ask with a lifted eyebrow.

He exhales, eyes turning to the hallway then back to me. "I was told not to say anything," he admits. "But I want to."

"Then just tell me," I quip.

He hesitates, dragging a hand through his hair.

"Manny," I press.

He finally blurts it out. "Jonathan's leaving today. He's moving to Boston and I think… I think he still loves you."

I blink, trying to process words that hit like fireworks and ice water all at once. "You do?" My voice comes out small but hopeful.

Tanya bounces on her toes, nodding hard. "Yes, Abby," she squeals.

My heart slams against my ribs. Hope flares and then sinks. "He didn't tell me anything," I whisper. "No text, no call."

Manny rolls his eyes. "You know Jonathan. He was hurt, bad. Crawling back isn't his style."

"I know I hurt him," I say, then the old bruise rises in my chest. "He hurt me too."

Understanding dawns on Manny's face. He looks skyward, exasperated. "That's because I had a crush on you. He was hiding his feelings so I wouldn't feel like trash." He throws his hands up, as if this should have been obvious.

I press my fingers to my temples, brain officially overcooked. Heat rushes to my cheeks; equal parts relief, embarrassment and a spark of something fierce. Jonathan was telling the truth *and* still loves me. He's on a one p.m. flight. And I've got exactly one chance to fix this.

I stand, chair scudding back against the carpet. "I need to get to JFK," I say, heart already racing ahead of me.

Manny's practically vibrating with anticipation, slapping the desk like we just won the World Series. "YES. GET IT, ABBY!"

"Yay!" Tanya hollers, clapping her hands like a delighted Disney sidekick.

I bolt out of my office and rush toward Victoria's. She's mid-spin in her pink velvet chair when I burst in.

"I'm heading to JFK!" I shout.

She lets out a laugh, eyes lighting up. "Smart girl," she says and waves me off like she's releasing a dove into the wild.

"I'll take you!" Manny calls, already jingling his keys.

We race to the elevator, Tanya trailing behind yelling, "Text me updates!" as the doors shut.

Manny's car is, how do I put this? Nimble. Like, if a Hot Wheels car had a baby with a jet engine. It's red, low to the ground and has racing stripes splashed across the sides. He speeds like he's in a Fast & Furious reboot that no one asked for. I'm clinging to the dashboard and my seat belt like they're life preservers on the Titanic. We're weaving through traffic, zipping past yellow cabs, hot dog vendors and wide-eyed tourists who clearly didn't read the part of their travel brochure that warned *New Yorkers don't stop, they swerve.* It doesn't take long before we're at the airport. He tears past a mounted police officer, an actual man on a horse and barrels down the terminal road, screeching to a dramatic halt at the *Departures* entrance.

"Go!" he shouts to me, motioning frantically with one hand while keeping the other on the wheel like a getaway driver. "Run!"

I throw the door open, slam it behind me and sprint into the turmoil-filled building that is also popularly known as JFK. The sliding glass doors part and I'm hit with a wave of noise, motion and very confused travelers trying to juggle coffee, carry-ons and emotional baggage, probably literal and figurative.

I dial Jonathan's number as I weave through the crowd. There's no answer. I call again. Still nothing.

I pivot around, my eyes darting through the sea of travelers, desperate to find him. No familiar tall frame. No tousled sandy-brown hair. No jawline carved by the gods. But then I see him. The build seems to match. The posture in the way he stands like he's pretending not to be annoyed by the wheel on his suitcase wobbling slightly is on point. My heart lurches before my brain can catch up. I don't overanalyze. I just move.

"Jonathan!" I yell, grabbing the man's arm and spinning him toward me like we're in a soap opera airport scene.

Except it's not Jonathan. It's a stranger. A terrified stranger with wide-eyes, thinning hair and clearly convinced he's about to be mugged in Terminal B.

"Oh my God. I'm so sorry!" I gasp, releasing him instantly.

He clutches his arm, shuffles backward and disappears into the crowd, probably rethinking his entire travel itinerary. Not only have I failed to find Jonathan, I'm now terrorizing innocent men in public spaces. Cool, Abby. *Really cool.*

Just as I start to think this was all a colossal mistake, me running through JFK like a deranged heroine with frizzy hair and zero dignity, I hear my name.

"AJ?" the voice asks.

I spin around so fast I nearly roll an ankle.

There he is. Jonathan Slack. All six feet of him. Sexy stubble, travel bag slung over his shoulder, blue eyes locking onto mine like I'm the only person in the room, even when we're in a literal airport surrounded by thousands.

"Jonathan," I breathe, this time saying it to the *actual* Jonathan.

The confusion in his eyes hardens into caution. He steps closer, brows drawn. "What are you doing here?"

"I heard you're moving to Boston," I say, still panting, hands uselessly smoothing my wind-blown shirt like that'll help this moment make any more sense.

He nods, standing tall. "Yeah. I took a job there. A really good one," he remarks, collected. His pride is undeniable and deserved. But it stings like lemon juice in a paper cut.

"Please don't go," I blurt out.

His face tightens. "AJ…" he starts, there's an edge in his tone, one that means his walls are back up.

"I need to board my flight," he adds and steps past me like he's about to walk out of my life forever.

I don't think. I reach and grab his arm; not hard, just enough to make him pause.

"Jonathan, your phone call with Manny. That morning. I thought you meant it… when you said you didn't love me," I admit.

His jaw tightens. I see it, the hurt he still carries. I rush to explain.

"That's why I didn't stop Marcus. Not right away. I froze. I thought you never cared about me. But the second I realized how wrong I was, I pulled away. Then you asked me what I wanted and I froze again." I swallow hard, my voice cracking as I say, "I was an idiot. Please forgive me."

He doesn't move. Just stands there, eyes on the floor, my hand still resting on his sleeve and then, too quietly, he says, "I can't trust that you won't do something like that again."

The words slice through me as he gently removes my hand from his arm without ever looking up.

My heart sinks and for a moment, all I can do is stare at him, wishing I could rewind time and do everything differently.

"Jonathan…" My voice trembles. "I love you."

His back is still half-turned when I say it. I watch his shoulders stiffen like the words hit him anyway.

"I really do," I continue, stepping closer, heart pounding like it's trying to launch itself out of my chest. "It's stupid and quick and naïve of me, maybe. But I do. I love you, Jonathan."

He slowly turns around and our eyes finally meet. For a

split second I see it; that tiny, shining ember of hope in his eyes that makes my breath stutter.

But just as fast, it disappears.

He exhales, the kind of sigh that carries disappointment, exhaustion and something dangerously close to heartbreak. "Prove it," he quips, then turns and walks away.

I stand there as the crowd swallows him up, one step at a time. Each footfall feels like it's stomping on whatever chance we had left. I should move. I should say something else. I should run to him. Because if I don't do something right now, he's gone. Not for the weekend. Not for a business trip. For good.

I take in a deep breath, adjust my wrinkled blouse and decide; no more overthinking. No more freezing. No more silence. I know exactly what I have to do.

32

Jonathan

rove it. I can't believe those were the last words to come out of my mouth. What am I? Sixteen years old, storming off after drama club rehearsal?

I shake my head, like maybe the motion will dislodge the weight of embarrassment pressing down on me. My suitcase bumps along behind me, wheels catching on the floor like even it doesn't want to go. The damn thing is resisting the airport tiles like it knows I'm making a mistake. I can still feel her behind me, the ghost of her presence tugging at my spine. AJ, standing there, stunned. Probably still staring.

I should turn around. I should look at her. Say the thing I actually want to say… that I love her too. That I'm sorry. That we can figure this out. But instead, I keep walking toward the gate. Toward my plane. Toward the shiny new future I've mapped out in Boston. It's uncomplicated and full of unfamiliar faces who don't know anything about fake dating or falling for someone when you're supposed to be keeping things strictly professional. This is what's best for me. That's what my head is telling me. Screaming, evidently.

Still, I pause. I glance back and tell myself it's just one last look. Just a final glimpse at the girl who ruined me, good and bad, in a matter of days. The girl who kissed me like she meant it and then left me standing in the wreckage of my own resolve.

But she's not there. The space she occupied only moments ago is empty. Gone. No more AJ looking at me like I'm the last thing she wants to lose. No more wide eyes or apology trembling on her lips. She left. I mean *duh*. Because I told her to *prove it*. Instead of grabbing her ridiculous little cheeks and kissing the hell out of her like I wanted to, I tossed out a one-liner, wannabe mic drop and walked away like a jackass.

I close my eyes for a second, exhale slow and run a hand through my hair. *I'm a fucking idiot.*

My internal rant doesn't get far before I hear music playing behind me. It's faint at first, just a few notes that float through the airport like background noise until I register the melody. It's familiar, *way too* familiar.

I whip around so fast I nearly give myself whiplash. The terminal is buzzing with people dragging suitcases, announcements echoing through overhead speakers, families arguing over boarding groups but all of that fades as I scan for the source.

And then I see her. AJ is in the elevated customer service booth perched above the Delta ticketing counters, a glass-walled cubicle typically used for announcements and airline supervisor calls. She's holding her phone up to the small PA microphone, feeding the music straight into the terminal speakers. She looks… calm yet determined. A little deranged in the most AJ kind of way.

The song she's feeding through the sound system? "Hopelessly Devoted to You" by Olivia Newton-John.

My mouth drops open as the intro plays, soft and theatrical, reverberating through the high ceilings of JFK. It's the exact song I told her, only half-seriously I might add, was the type of dramatic declaration I dreamed someone would make if they were ever hopelessly in love with me. Clearly, she took that very literally.

I take a few steps closer to the booth, my feet moving before my brain catches up. I can't even pretend to act cool, I'm too busy staring at her like I've never seen anything like this in my life.

Then she starts singing. The first words are about her having pure heartbreak.

The mic trembles slightly in her hand, but her voice is not half bad, actually. Not great either. Let's just say it's passionate and loud. Mostly off-key in that one spot.

I chuckle, stunned, as people stop to stare. Phones come out. A little girl claps. One TSA agent looks like she's about to blow a whistle, then hesitates, probably wondering if this counts as a threat or just the most chaotic declaration of love she's seen on a Tuesday morning.

AJ powers through the second verse with eyes locked on me. Not blinking. Not backing down. She's singing about knowing she's not the only one who's been through this, about how there's no getting over *me*.

A janitor leans on his mop like this is better than any reality show. A woman in a pantsuit whispers, "Is this real?" to her husband, who replies with an impressed, "I hope so."

I just stand there, heart slamming in my chest, trying to figure out how this became my life. How this woman, this fiery, infuriating, completely unpredictable woman, somehow crawled under my skin and lodged herself there so permanently that my only reaction to this entire insane spectacle is... awe. She's singing a *Grease* ballad to me from a restricted airport tower and all I can think is how cute she is.

Airport staff are scrambling below the tower like ants in a panic. One security guard gestures frantically to another, who's jabbing buttons on a walkie-talkie. None of them can get to her though. The narrow staircase to the glass observation booth, usually reserved for flight coordinators, is sealed. She's locked herself in. Of course she has.

AJ stands tall behind the wide glass panel, one arm holding the mic, the other clutching her phone like it's her lifeline and just when I think it couldn't get any more absurd, she continues to sing.

Her voice wavers slightly, but not from fear—from conviction—as she declares she's the *fool* who's still here, waiting for me, because there's nothing else she can do.

She lifts her finger dramatically and points it straight at me through the window. Like she's casting a spell or delivering a final mic drop. Passengers around me gasp and giggle and start to cheer and somehow, despite the fact that she's standing in an off-limits airport control booth serenading me with Olivia Newton-John, I've never loved her more.

I shake my head and drag a hand over my face, caught somewhere between secondhand embarrassment and total admiration. A few people around me are already looking, connecting the dots. Yeah, I'm the guy she's singing to. Heat rushes up my neck and settles in my cheeks. *Great.* I'm actually blushing. My palms are sweating now, but not out of anxiety, out of joy. That ridiculous, overwhelming kind of joy you feel when someone does something so unexpected, so unhinged and so exquisitely *them* that your heart can't help but swell.

AJ is up there, clearly having lost her mind, singing completely off-key by the way but doing it for me. *Me*, of all people.

And… here comes the chorus.

She's singing about how there's nowhere left to hide, how her love's been pushed aside, and how she's out of her head and completely, *hopelessly devoted* to me.

She belts it out and despite the microphone crackling under her enthusiasm, I hear it, her smile. That sexy, crooked little grin bleeding through the words. Damn, I missed that stupid smile.

I walk closer until I'm practically touching the tower, just in time for her to hit one final, dramatic line—a breathless promise that she's hopelessly devoted to me.

She lets the last word hang in the air, out of breath and flushed, her chest rising and falling. Then she glances down and yells to airport security, "Okay. I'm coming down!"

The music shuts off and her phone disappears into her back pocket. She turns, climbs carefully down the narrow stairs and unlocks the door.

Airport security is there, looking like they're ready to detain someone twice her size and ten times more dangerous. One cop grabs her arm gently but firmly. She holds up her hands and says, "I'm fine, I'm fine," still catching her breath.

I jog forward. "Where are you taking her?" I ask, stepping between them.

The officer eyes me. "Why? Is she with you?"

I don't even hesitate. I nod. "Yeah. She's with me."

He lets go and that's when I do the one thing you're absolutely not supposed to do when you're surrounded by police and security guards seconds from tackling you into oblivion. I walk straight up to her, cup her face in both hands and kiss her. So hard. So passionately. Like I've been waiting my entire life for this exact moment.

She kisses me back with enough force it knocks me a tad off balance. Then she wraps her arms around my neck, laughing into my mouth and I lift her off the ground. She squeals, kissing me again as the crowd around us erupts into applause and cheers. A few people whistle. It's insane. It's completely absurd. And it's the best moment of my entire life.

"All right, all right. You're both coming with us," the cop barks, grabbing both of our arms now, less gentle than before.

We break apart, still breathless from the kiss and follow him as the sound of the cheering crowd fades behind us. The deeper we go into the back corridors of the airport, the more it feels like stepping into another world, one most travelers never see. I've flown plenty of times in my life, but I've never had the privilege of being escorted through the restricted doors by someone with a badge and a bad attitude.

AJ walks beside me, her elbow brushing mine and glances up with a grin. I can't help but wink at her. She's radiant even under fluorescent lighting.

"Jonathan," she whispers. "I'm so sorry."

"I know, me too," I say, looking at her, keeping my voice low.

"No talking," the officer snaps without turning around. We both bite back a laugh like two misbehaving kids sent to the principal's office.

He leads us into a windowless room with two empty metal chairs and a table straight out of a police procedural. The walls are an uninspired white, the lighting overhead is dimmed in a creepy, hazy way like it's trying to set a tone. The area smells faintly of industrial cleaner, pungent but not quite unpleasant.

I take a seat in one of the frigid chairs and AJ sinks into the other beside me. The officer huffs, the corners of his dark mustache twitching with exasperation. It's the kind of mustache that's probably meant to command respect but mostly makes him look like a Monopoly Man impersonator who swapped the monocle for a walkie-talkie.

"Stay here," he grumbles as he steps out of the room, shutting the door behind him with a dull thud.

AJ and I exchange a look. For a beat, we're silent. Then, like she's been waiting all this time for permission, she suddenly climbs onto my lap, nearly knocking the wind out of me. Her laugh bubbles out, wild and carefree. She plants kisses along my cheek, my jaw, my temple, still giggling.

I wrap my arms around her waist, grounding her to me like I never want to let her go again. Which, let's be honest, I don't. Not now. Not ever.

I find her lips and this time, the kiss deepens. No audience. No noises. Just us. Despite being in the most sterile, uncomfortable room imaginable, it somehow feels like the most intimate moment I've ever experienced. I've never wanted a woman more than I do in this moment. Her legs tangled with mine, her breath brushing my face, her laugh still hanging in the air; it's almost too much. I pull back just enough to look her in the eyes, my heart practically begging me to say what I've been holding in.

"I love you too, AJ," I tell her softly, a smile tugging at my mouth. "Of course I love you."

Her face lights up as she throws her arms around my neck, squeezing like she's trying to fuse us together. I'd let her melt into me right here in this freezing interrogation room if it meant we never had to be apart again.

The moment is short-lived as the door swings open and a tall man walks in, filling the doorway like an ominous shadow. He's all angles: broad shoulders, square jaw, dress shirt with the tie yanked loose and sleeves rolled up like he's halfway through a long, exhausting day of dealing with stupid people. He clears his throat.

AJ quickly lifts herself off my lap and slides back into her chair, straightening her blouse with a small, guilty smile. I sit up too, though I don't bother pretending I'm sorry.

The man steps forward and introduces himself in a tone that's both bored and vaguely threatening. "I'm Special Agent Thomas. FBI liaison to TSA."

FBI? Wow. AJ really messed up this time.

I sit up straighter, hands out slightly like I'm ready to plead our case. "Listen, this is all a big misunderstanding."

He nods slowly, like he's humoring a toddler. "Sure." Then he looks directly at AJ, arching a single unimpressed eyebrow. "If I had a dime for every person who illegally locks themselves in a restricted control tower and sings Olivia Newton-John into the public address system..."

He shrugs, impossibly pleased with himself. "I'd have ten cents."

I snort.

AJ, to her credit, swallows hard and somehow holds eye contact. "I'm sorry," she says, her voice quieter but clear. "I couldn't let him get on that plane."

Agent Thomas tilts his head, intrigued. "Why?" he asks. "What's on the airplane?"

That's when I can't help myself; I lean forward, arms on the table and laugh. "Wait, wait. Are you seriously trying to suggest she's some kind of terrorist?" I gesture toward AJ, who's looking adorably rumpled with her smudged eyeliner and shirt wrinkled from climbing a literal tower.

AJ smirks at that, then tries to pull herself together as the agent continues to size her up like she might suddenly pull a bomb out of her purse and blow up his afternoon paperwork.

"I suppose not," he says after a beat. "But what the hell were you thinking?"

AJ draws in a breath, squares her shoulders and scoots her chair closer to the table. Her voice is balanced now.

"Mr. Thomas, sir," AJ begins and I can already hear the nerves and sincerity mixed in her voice. "This man right here was about to leave for Boston and I'm madly in love with him. He needed to know how much I loved him." As she says it, she grabs my hand under the table and holds it tight, her fingers warm, trembling.

Agent Thomas blinks once. "So, you thought locking yourself in an airport tower and singing into a microphone was the best way to show your love for him?" His tone suggests he's not expecting an actual answer. But this is AJ. Of course she answers anyway.

"Yes," she says without hesitation. "He loves that song. And it's exactly how I feel about him."

I can't help it, I chuckle and squeeze her hand back, even as I shoot her a *you're completely insane but I'm obsessed with you* look. She meets it with that crinkled-nose smile I haven't been able to stop thinking about for days.

Agent Thomas exhales a long, theatrical sigh and I brace for it. The reprimand. The get-your-affairs-in-order lecture. I even release AJ's hand like it might soften the fallout. Whatever happens next, I'm already thinking about bail money, lawyers, a fake medical excuse. Maybe we claim she has low blood sugar, like if she doesn't get a snack every two hours, she loses it and hijacks public announcement systems. Yeah. That might fly.

But instead of yelling, he says, "That's... that's the sweetest thing I've ever heard."

My jaw drops. Literally unhinges.

He leans forward, lowering his voice like we're sharing a secret across a café table and places a giant hand over AJ's. "They say true love is dead. But what you did and why you did it..." His voice softens into theatrical awe. "Just wow."

Ohhhh. I get it now. Special Agent *Tower-of-Muscle* Thomas is gay. And apparently a sucker for a romantic gesture. This man, who looks like he wrestles bears on his lunch break, just turned into the president of our love story fan club. Who would've thought?

AJ's smile is bright enough to light the whole sterile room. "Thank you for understanding."

Agent Thomas shifts his focus to me. "Did it work?" He gestures between AJ and me.

"Did *what* work?" I blurt out, for a second I honestly don't follow.

He sighs, impatient. "Are you staying here instead of flying to Boston?"

Oh, that. I nod. "Yes, sir. It worked." I slide my fingers through AJ's again. She beams, now holding one of my hands and one of his, a bizarre but oddly sweet little chain.

Agent Thomas releases her hand and claps once, loud and delighted. "Yay!" He catches himself, lowers his voice and grins. "All right, all right. Let's keep it down." He lowers into his chair and steeples his fingers. "Here's the deal. We'll say you tried a new CBD gummy, lost your head for a second and that's why you commandeered the PA system. No need to arrest you."

"Arrest me?" AJ's eyes go wide. "Oh my God."

The agent shakes his head. "You're not being arrested. We can make this disappear."

Beads of sweat break out along AJ's hairline. I'm not exactly dry either. Time to wrap this up before we test the agent's goodwill.

I stand and extend my hand. "Agent Thomas, thank you. This will never happen again."

He rises, shakes my hand firmly. "Good. Toss the gummies when you get home and we'll call it a day."

AJ stands too. She shakes Agent Thomas's hand and says softly, "I'm sorry again."

He leans in with a conspiratorial grin. "You go, girl."

AJ giggles and somehow that small sound feels like the full-circle moment we didn't know we needed.

The agent escorts us out of the holding room while a few nearby cops glance our way, clearly still unsure if we're romantic lunatics or actual threats to national security. Probably a bit of both. We pass through a side exit where I spot my suitcase, very obviously the victim of a thorough TSA search; zippers unzipped, contents askew, one sock dangling out like a white flag of defeat. I grab the handle and pull it upright, then reach for AJ's hand without even thinking. She laces her fingers through mine like it's second nature and we step into the sunlight outside the terminal.

The air is cooler than I expect. A little breeze kicks up, brushing against us as we head toward the Uber stand. I order a car through the attendant, then we sit together on a bench, quiet for the first time in what feels like hours. Not an awkward silence, just the kind that follows mass mayhem, like the world finally took a deep breath for us.

She leans her head against my shoulder and exhales slowly. I do the same. I can feel the tension melting off both our bodies, seeping into the bench and the concrete beneath us. I slide my hand into hers again, anchoring us in the peace of this moment. For once, nothing needs to be said.

Then, like a movie we forgot had one last scene, Manny appears, sprinting toward us, breathless and grinning. "Yes! You found him!" he shouts like he just won a game show.

We stand up, laughing, as Manny throws his arms around both of us in a dramatic, full-bodied bear hug.

"You did it," he says to AJ, practically bouncing on his toes. "I got my car," he adds, nodding toward the parking lot like he's about to whisk us away in the Batmobile.

"Perfect," I say, smiling as I glance toward the Uber attendant.

I walk over, nod politely and slip the guy a twenty. "Thanks, man. We're good."

No more disruptions. Just a long car ride ahead with the girl I almost left behind and no airport detainment required.

The late afternoon sun casts a warm haze over the pavement, the kind of golden light that makes everything feel cinematic. Just as we reach the passenger door, I stop walking.

She turns to me, curious, lips slightly parted like she knows what's coming.

I don't say a word, I just cradle her face in both hands and kiss her like I've been waiting forever to do it properly. Her lips are warm and the second she breathes into my mouth, I feel her drop into me like she never wants to let go again.

I was a fool before. I let fear drive too many decisions. But not now. Not anymore. Because in this moment, with AJ in my arms, New York fading behind us and a future I never expected unfolding ahead, I can honestly say that Jonathan Slack is a changed man. A stupidly happy, hopelessly in love, completely reformed fool of a man.

And he wouldn't change a damn thing.

33

Epilogue

Abby

Today's meeting is going to be a chaotic one. Tanya, who now works directly under me as my assistant in the VP of Marketing role, is off on her honeymoon and I've got Elaine stepping in to cover for her. We always knew Tanya would be out this week. After all, she and Manny threw a shotgun wedding last weekend that none of us saw coming. I still can't believe they actually got married. It happened so fast and yet they're disgustingly, ridiculously, make-you-roll-your-eyes happy. And honestly? I love it for them.

What we didn't expect was for *Kylie freaking Jenner* to request an emergency meeting with our team to pitch her company's next marketing campaign. Kylie Cosmetics. Emergency. Meeting. When we talk "big fish" in the industry, that company isn't a fish... it's a whale. A glam, filtered, contour-perfect whale. Apparently there's been some drama with her current marketing team. I don't know the full details and frankly? I don't care. All I know is that she's going to be sitting in our conference room in less than an hour and I am freaking the heck out. Also, I am one hundred percent going to be starstruck. No shame. I'm a Kardashian stan. I mean, what self-respecting reality TV lover *isn't*?

I gather all my materials, smooth down my blazer and head for the conference room. Elaine's already in there and to my surprise, she's setting up the most aesthetically pleasing tray of pastries and coffee I've ever seen in this office.

"Nice touch, girly," I say as I step inside.

She turns around, beaming with pride. "Thanks! I heard Ms. Jenner likes raspberry-filled croissants from Becca's, so I ran down and bought the whole tray this morning." She giggles as she lines up the pastries like a little pastry stylist.

I laugh, giving her a thumbs-up. "I still can't believe Tanya and Manny got married," I say, shaking my head.

Elaine squeals, like this is the highlight of her week. "I know! Look, she sent me this."

She holds out her phone and I lean in. On screen is a picture of the Bahamas, all blue skies and sunshine. Tanya and Manny are wrapped in each other's arms, tanned, barefoot and glowing with post-wedding bliss.

"Aww," I say, grinning. "They look so happy."

Elaine gives me a quick hug, then goes back to fussing over the pastry layout like it's the Met Gala of croissants. Even though I'm technically half the office's boss now, nothing has really changed between me and the team. If anything, things feel better, more collaborative, more fun, less... chaotic. Maybe because people are no longer whispering about whether I'm qualified to lead. A year in the VP of Marketing role and I think I've proven myself a few dozen times over.

The office has been booming since I took over. We've

landed several new high-profile clients, ones that have not only exceeded our five-year revenue projections but made us one of the fastest-rising agencies in the city. Every time we hit another milestone, Marcus congratulates me via email with a champagne emoji or tells me in person at our quarterly meetings. He's... fine. Polite. Handsome as ever, but weirdly non-threatening. We exchange a few pleasantries, talk numbers and then he's off to whatever rich-man thing he does next. I hear he's dating another model, naturally.

I don't lose sleep over Marcus anymore. My job is incredible and I finally feel like I was made for this position. Just last month, we wrapped a campaign for Selena Gomez's mental health platform and the team was so impressed they signed on for three more projects down the pipeline.

Which, yes, I managed to do *without* mentioning that Selena once got suspiciously cozy on the dance floor with my now real-life, no-longer-fake boyfriend, Jonathan Slack. Not that I'm jealous. I mean, come on. If given the chance, I'd probably shake it with Selena Gomez too.

That night, after the meeting, I came home and casually dropped it into conversation over takeout. "So, ran into your ex-dance partner today," I teased as I popped open a container of pad Thai. Jonathan, unfazed as ever, just grinned and said, "She was a good dancer."

I smacked his arm, maybe a little harder than necessary and he laughed, yanked me into his arms and proceeded to plant kisses all over my face like I was the prize in a kissing booth.

"But nothing compared to you, babe," he murmured against my cheek, lips soft, eyes so annoyingly full of love it made my knees weak.

Do you know what it feels like to be in a relationship with

your best friend? Because I do.

Jonathan Slack, my former nemesis, my favorite person to argue with, my fake boyfriend turned very real boyfriend, is now also my best friend. Sometimes I wake up in the middle of the night, heart pounding from a dream where we never got together and I reach across the bed just to make sure he's there. And he is. Sleeping soundly, snoring softly, one arm thrown dramatically over his head like he's posing for a Renaissance painting. That's when it hits me all over again… this is real. The last year with him has been real. He's not a bit I made up for emotional survival. He's mine and I'm his.

He's no longer my work nemesis. Mostly because we don't work together anymore. I would never hold him back from an incredible opportunity and I didn't. After the great airport serenade incident of last year and two full days of doing nothing but "debriefing" in his bed, Jonathan still took the job in Boston. But we made it work. Somehow, seamlessly.

He works from home three days a week, tapping away at his laptop with his glasses on and my pink coffee mug in hand. The other two days, he heads into Boston for meetings or client events. His new firm works almost exclusively with sports figures. Just last month, he met Shaquille O'Neal and came home with wide eyes and a fresh existential crisis about his own height. "I've never felt shorter," he said, dramatically flopping onto the couch. "I felt like a toddler next to him."

He doesn't mind the travel. Actually, I think he enjoys it. It gives him his own space, a little independence and when I can, I go with him and turn his work trips into mini getaways. We've found the coziest hotel in Beacon Hill that does the fluffiest Belgian waffles and knows us by name now. I pack my laptop and we work side by side, stealing kisses between client calls and campaign drafts. We've figured out our rhythm. And it's good. *Really good.*

Victoria lets me work remotely when needed. She's been incredibly supportive, possibly because our agency has never been more successful and she's well aware of the numbers I've helped bring in. The other day, while we were chatting about Tanya and Manny's whirlwind honeymoon, Victoria sipped her oat milk latte and casually said, "I expect an invite to your wedding, by the way." I laughed it off at the time because Jonathan and I are *not* talking about marriage. Not seriously. Not *yet.*

Sure, Jonathan talks about the future all the time. He's a planner, a big-picture guy. And yeah, sometimes I catch him staring at me with that look, the one that makes my heart trip over itself a little. But getting engaged? Getting married? That still feels far off.

Or maybe… not that far. The truth is, as much as I try to play it cool, the idea of marrying him, of waking up next to him for the rest of my life; fills me with a warmth I can't explain. I didn't think it was possible to love him more than I already do, but somehow, every day proves me wrong and if this is what the rest of our life looks like? Sign me up.

* * *

Jonathan

Today's the big day. I'm going to propose to AJ. No one knows it but me. Though soon, everyone will know. Most importantly, AJ will know.

I've been carrying this secret like a live wire buzzing in my chest, barely able to sit still. But from the moment she hijacked the airport PA system and belted out that tragically off-tune version of "Hopelessly Devoted to You," I knew I was going to marry this woman. I would have married her right then and there, in front of TSA agents, a stunned crowd of travelers and one emotionally shaken FBI agent. I would've dropped to one knee if I'd had a ring in my pocket and a plan that didn't involve potential arrest.

But I waited. A whole year. Not because I had doubts. Not because she needed convincing. Just because I wanted it to feel right. I wanted the date to mean something. Technically, today marks one year since we stood in front of the entire company and pretended to be madly in love. The fake dating weekend at Cedar Lakes. The retreat that started it all. The moment our enemies-to-lovers pipeline launched itself off a cliff, caught fire and crash-landed directly into my heart. So, maybe we weren't together-together that day but it's when everything changed and *hell yes*, it counts.

I've got everything laid out seamlessly. Like *chef's kiss* levels of thought-through.

First, dinner at her favorite French restaurant, the one with the candlelit windows and the raspberry crème brûlée she dreams about. Then, I'm taking her to a Broadway show. Not just any show; *Just In Time* starring her all-time favorite, Jonathan Groff. Front-row seats. Nearly close enough for her to see the sweat on his forehead and cry about it for the next week. The woman clearly has a thing for *Jonathans*.

She doesn't know about the show yet. She thinks we're just doing dinner and heading home. She'll probably assume that's the end of the night. But it won't even be halftime. Because after that, I'm taking her to The Plaza. I booked one of their best suites, which I may or may not have bribed someone to get on short notice. Then, my masterpiece, the rooftop. I managed to rent out a private terrace with the skyline glittering behind it, candles everywhere, all fire-code approved and one lone violinist waiting in the corner to play the song that ignited it all: "Hopelessly Devoted to You."

Right there, surrounded by everything that makes this life with her feel surreal, I'll drop to one knee and ask the funniest, kindest, most stunning woman I've ever met to marry me. I'll probably cry. No, let's be honest, I'll sob like a baby. But it'll be worth it. Because if she says yes… then I get to be the luckiest man alive, forever.

AJ has changed so many things about me I didn't even realize were changeable. I'm softer now. Braver. Willing to be a little ridiculous if it means making her laugh. I used to roll my eyes at grand romantic gestures and now I'm the guy who replays our chaotic airport reunion on YouTube like it's the season finale of my favorite show.

Tonight, when I pop open that ring box, she'll see it, the custom three-carat oval diamond with a pavé diamond-encrusted gold band. Classic but bold. Sparkly but elegant. Very her. I sleuthed my way into her Pinterest board, purely for research purposes. I also may have measured her finger while she was sleeping using a piece of string and an app. Creepy? Maybe a little. Worth it? Absolutely. Because this night will be perfect. It has to be.

Me? Jonathan Slack; once her nemesis, then her fake boyfriend and now the idiot who's head over heels, is about to propose to Abigail Jean Madison. When she says yes, because she *will* say yes, we'll get our happily ever after. Just like we both always wanted.

And if she starts serenading me again? God help us all.

About the Author

Ashley Lynn East writes witty, heartfelt, and slightly unhinged stories about complicated women, messy love, and the entertaining disasters that come with both. When she's not plotting fictional drama, she's chasing her adorable son and ever-enthusiastic miniature schnauzer, or daydreaming about her next book. The Nemesis Pact is her debut novel—and she hopes it makes you laugh, swoon, and maybe scream into a pillow. In a good way.

Follow her on Instagram and TikTok *@ashleylynneasta uthor* for bookish updates and behind-the-scenes fun.

You can connect with me on:

🌐 https://www.ashleylynneastauthor.com

Subscribe to my newsletter:

✉ https://form.jotform.com/251875760699173